TALES OF WONDER

WELCOME PAGE

ONLY IN FANTASY CAN EVERYTHING COME TO LIFE!

ENCHANTED TALES

RIVITING EXCITEMENT

ANTICIPATION · ADVENTURE

TALES OF WONDER

GRAHAM FAMILY ADVENTURE

ISBN 978-1 -9 59071-1 2-9 (paperhack)
ISBN 978-1-959071-13-6 (digital)

Chapter image by freepik.com

CONTENTS

TABLE OF CONTENTS

Chapters which can be read separately as short stories
2, 7, 9, 22, 25, 37

Chapters for Blue's story only
11, 13, 15, 17, 19, 21, 23, 26, 28, 29, 30, 34, 35

Chapters Hero's Story
1, 2, 3, 4, 5, 6, 7, 8, 9, 10, 12, 14, 16, 18, 20, 22, 24, 25, 27, 31, 32, 33, 36, 37

CHAPTER 1

The Young Warrior

"What's that noise?" ten-year-old Jesse Mason woke up wondering. Pulling the covers over his head. There was someone or something in his room. "Are you sure he is the one?" a voice whispered. "Yes, it has to be him. Look at these readings. It is him!" Another voice whispered, "Do you see The Stone?" The beings continued to bicker;

"No, just the warrior, who is not of age yet. It is pointing to the bed but the signal is very weak."

"The Stone of Wonder is not here, but the child must have come in contact with it to have these types of readings on the meter."

"Let's take the child, we have waited to long for such a one to be born. We cannot let him come of age and connect with the Stone."

"He's already been in contact with The Stone according to the meter and he is registering a trace amount of the Stone's Cosmic energy."

"Should we take the boy with us?"

Jesse's eyes widened as he heard this. He reached over quietly to his night stand and slid his heavy Mag flashlight off and under the covers. "No! If we take him off planet

The Stone will become dormant and we will never find it. Then we will have to wait for another chosen one. It must be nearby. We need to wait and watch till The Stone becomes active again, this delay could make, (you know who) very mad." The being sternly said.

The other suggest "Put a tracker in the child. Then we will know where he is at all times." Then one held up an instrument and pulled the covers back from over Jesse's head to insert the tracking device.

Jesse jumped up, shocked when he saw two creatures from outer space, he begun slinging his arm around accidentally bashing one of them in its eye! It roared out in pain, shouting "You little human! You smashed my eye!" The startled alien dropped his instruments on the floor. The device which held people in suspended animation broke. "Everything should be in a frozen status, how is the child still awake and not effected by our technology?" one of the Aliens asked.

As soon as the Aliens weren't looking Jesse promptly slid off the side of the bed and went underneath. The aliens assumed Jesse was in a frozen state. They didn't know it was because of the close contact with The Stone that Jesse wasn't affected by their device. They pulled off the covers, "Where is, that blasted child?" one said. "He is here! The door is still closed. Search the room." The other shouted.

The beings looked at each other then looked down, peeking under the bed, they could see Jesse. One alien reached under trying to grab him. Jesse reached over and hit the aliens hand with the flashlight causing him to shout

out loud and quickly holding tight to his hand. The other one, still holding his swollen eye, became furious grinding his jagged teeth, he said "You will pay for that child!" Jesse was not scared as most seven-yearolds would be. Still under the bed, he scooted back against the wall shouting "Leave me alone, I'm not scared of you!"

"HMM, Not scared of me you say!? That gives me an idea!" the alien thought to himself.

"That's right crocodile face, stick your head back down here and see what happens!" Jesse shouted. "Come out from under the bed child. We are not going to hurt you….. Much!" The Alien slyly remarked to his partner as they smiled at each other. They pointed the little device towards the bed and it started rising up. Jesse stood up really quick and hit a home run on the alien's foot! You could hear it crack. The alien rolled across the floor in growling in pain, holding tight to his foot and his busted eye. He dropped the device causing the bed to fall back to the floor and Jesse quickly got back under it.

The Alien sighed in pain as he once again stood looking down at the bed, growling with anger. "So, you really must be the chosen one! The great and mighty Wonder warrior, huh, little one? Brave you may be Wonder child, too brave in fact! Now with this device, I will make you know fear, little demon human of a child! You will live in fear of confrontations, every time you stand up for a fight it will overtake you and you will never know the reason why. Just look at you, all already to fight with your little light. I see you like lights, I have my own light, just look here and watch my light. Watch, that's right, just watch. I'm going to teach you a lesson child, listen closely to my voice."

Jesse was mesmerized and unable to turn away. With the aliens face behind the light he was in a trance, as a strange new feeling, a new fear started to overcome his every thought. As the light started flashing Jesse became more and more petrified. His head was swirling and flashing, he couldn't move. He tried but he couldn't look away from the strange light. Jesse's body was frozen, only inside his head there was a battle brewing, the wheels grinding. "This device, this light, is used to install emotions, for you brave one it will be fear, placed within your little human mind. I have placed a block on your memories and when you seek these memories, they will evade you and your mind will become blank!" The aliens both growled and laughed saying, "Fear will rule you, young warrior!"

All of the sudden Jesse's mom was heard coming down the hall. The alien looked toward the door, growled, then back towards the bed saying, "Once we locate The Stone we will no longer need you. Then I will come back while you sleep and pluck out your eye, boy! We will see how tough you are then warrior child." They picked up their instruments off the floor and suddenly disappeared.

Jesse sat on his bed terrified, as his parents came rushing in "Are you okay son, did you have another bad dream?" Jesse told his parents about what happened as the memory of the event becomes less clear, "I hit one of them with the flashlight

Dad, I think! He was going to get me!" "Calm down Jesse it was just a dream son." Mom said, as she comforted seven-year-old Jesse. "But he said they would be back to put a thing in me!" he replied in terror. "A thing in you, ah baby, nobody is going to put anything in you sweety, come son you can sleep with us tonight." She assured him. As his dad started to walk out, looking down at the floor, he saw the flashlight picked it up and noticed a strange liquid on it. He quickly wrapped it in a plastic bag and took it into work with him at the FBI. Jesse's dad (also known as Agent Mason) belongs to a top-secret government agency that is known only to a select few! These secret agents work under top secret clearance and you will find each agent carries a badge, their Shield, if you will, a shield which is given no name!

The agency believes Jesse is some sort of Mutant, but they have never seen or come in contact with this kind of energy readings before. All they can is do monitor this force, which they probably will for the rest of Jesse's life. For they have no clue to the origin of his power except from ancient Mythology! This is the perfect agency for a father to be in, when he had proof aliens were in his son's room. The great news for Jesse's dad is this agency knows about many other realms, aliens and the Eternity stones, already known throughout the galaxy. But this story is about a certain powerful stone which no one is even aware exist except these aliens and the Wizard world. It is by no means one of the Eternity stones, as it is something much more, something different, ancient and very powerful.

After that Jesse's dad knew it was an actual visit and knew he had to protect his son. Deciding to keep the event secret from his family, he told them he had a new job in NY. Then packed up his family and moved to the bustling city where there are so many types of frequencies, like TV signals, radios, cell phones that would mask the frequency that Jesse's body is unwittingly giving off. Making him invisible to the aliens who seek him.

CHAPTER 2

War of the Wizards!

It was the year 1829, the streets of New Orleans were abuzz with chatter and soirees, the horizon like a sea of colorful masks, Mardi gras lurked a sinister force. The evil voodoo Master Kumba King, who eagerly awaited the annual secret gathering, when all the great wizards assembled. Among them he knew his old friend Lord Asher would come. In the Wizards temple is the precious Ring of Wonder, whose wisdom and spellbinding powers Kumba desires above all else.

The two are no strangers to each other, having met 10 years earlier when Kumba was a humble slave for Mrs. Marie Laveau. Then a gangster in the city streets, Kumba is an infamous warlock and black magic witch. Donning a black suit adorned with silver, a silver-studded top hat and gold-capped incisors which glistened when he smiled. He conjures evil creatures that no one dared to speak of. Unfortunately, not yet the master that Kumba is, Lord Asher is vulnerable to Kumba's dark magic.

In the Grand Temple, a wizard society session was unfolding. Only one of these wizards is deemed worthy by The Ring, Lord Asher. While he never completed the trials needed to reach the status of Emissary the Stone seemed to

have its heart set only on him, and with a simple chant, he can summon The Stone's magical powers.

Out on the streets of Louisiana Kumba's wicked army, all of them Cutthroats and zombies, searched far and wide for the ring as the wicked sorcerer's crow energy blanketed the whole town. Feeling this strong energy, The Stone glowed blue then yellow in its case, then a flash of blinding light illuminated from its core.

The wizards' eyes grew in surprise. Yellow was the color of a warning; a flash meant a battle cry. The Stone has awakened! Has the day finally come for the wizard's guild's formidable training to be put to the test? The odds of survival are low, and deaths high. Everyone had only one thing in mind: stay alive until morning.

Dread filled the hall. From a seat at the table, one wizard hollers, "Does anyone have an idea what The Stone is trying to warn us of?" Another says that his spies tell him of the arrival of the voodoo master "Kumba!" The wizard's gasped in chorus. "Do you think he's coming for the ring?" another asks. "What else could it be? Kumba knew the wizard's order would be meeting tonight. He knows the ring is here!"

Overcome with fear, a man of the order proposed, "Kumba is only after the ring."

One word to his minions and we will all be dead! Maybe we should just give it to him."

"Then what? Watch as the man makes zombies of us all?!" another wizard remarks. Kumba knows about the ring, and he wants everyone to know, he comes to get it," Lord

Asher whispers to a friend as they move with haste toward the temple "He will do anything to seize The Ring."

At the temple, the men are at their wits' end. The door creaked and opened. "Look! It's Lord Asher!" they shouted. Wasting no time, the wise wizard spoke at once. "Kumba is coming for the ring! We cannot allow him to possess it. For if he does, it could alter or change the whole world as we know it. Quick! Prop the timbers against the door!" A man from the temple yelled "Get your wands and charms and prepare for a fight!" "If what you say is true, the ring can't stay here. We must not allow it to fall into Kumba's hands," a wizard chimed in. One of the men doubts this possibility "What are the odds of Kumba controlling the ring with magic? The Stone is much too wise. It won't work for him. It never has!"

"Kumba would not make such an attempt with a temple full of wizards to collect a ring he has no use for, unless he has found a way - Some spell or another with which to control its power," Lord Asher spoke with gravity, "Are you willing to risk the whole city in the hope that he might not be able to use its power?" "But, Kumba has block off the streets. How can we move it out of the city?" one asked.

"The catacombs," another suggested. Hidden deep within the temple's underbelly, the catacombs are tunnels built by the ancestors for this very occasion. One tunnel leads to the stables where horses are being made ready for an escape.

Kumba can be heard just outside the temple's mighty doors, demanding the ancient stone of Wonder. Quickly the men cast their votes, and it was decided that Lord Asher, accompanied by two other wizards, will take the ring to safety.

The three sped off into the catacombs as the temple shook. Boom! A battering ram swung heavily against the temple's huge doors, as Lord Asher bolted down the catacombs' lower exit. From a hidden passage beneath the stables, the three wizards made their way to the horses, and with bated breath, they waited to make their escape.

The distant beat of the battering ram reverberated off the walls. Cracks crept through the thick wooden doors, growing bigger and bigger with each pounding. "Heaven help us," a wizard mutter. Mustering all their might, the wizards readied for the onslaught of villains. They pointed their wands at the door and with their combined magic kept it from splintering into pieces. Their goal: to hold off the enemy for as long as possible so Lord Asher can slip out of the city.

"Put your backs to it, men!" Kumba cried out. The door was harder to break down than expected. Kumba knew that more than just thick wood and metal, it was the wizards' magic holding it together. He heaved a deep breath and cast a spell to counter the wizards. The battering ram smashed against the door, as they splintered, then with one mighty blow, the doors made a loud crack. Most of the wizards headed for the catacombs, only a few remained to fight, knowing they would surely perish.

All at once the doors gave way, and zombies poured through the opening. The wizards braced themselves, turning a table over towards the door, where they had some cover, as Kumba's army drew their weapons. Swords clanked as black lightning struck against the temple walls. Wizard magic struck Kumba from all sides, yet one after another the wizards fell. Some were consumed by Kumba's black fire. Their agonized screams echoed through the great hall. Kumba's cackle resounded in the air "None here are a match for my magic!"

The remaining wizards were talking, "I don't understand, I have been shooting death spells, but with no effect." "Of course not, their Zombies" another replied. "That type of spell will not work on what is already dead."

The last of the wizards decided to make a break out of the back. Kumba spotted the wizards, blasting them to the floor, with a wave of his hand. Kumba walked up to the wizards and said "I have no interest in killing you, just give me the ring!" "Not on your life!" one said. Kumba blasted the wizard into a blaze of fire. Screams poured out from the wizard. "One dead, who's next?"

As the battle ensued, Lord Asher and the two wizards mounted their horses and rode off to town, only to find the streets barricaded and laden with traps. Kumba found the ring's glass case empty. He trod carefully searching for the ring among the debris. He grew impatient and barked at his minions, "Bring me the next wizard, we will ask again."

One of the men dragged a wounded wizard across the floor, his face bloodied and swollen, his robe scorched. Kumba stretched out a hand and grabbed the wizard by the throat.

"Look around, wizard. Everyone's dead. Don't be a hero.

Tell me what I need to know, and I will set you free." The wizard kept silent as he wriggled in the air. Kumba hit him with a piercing blast. "Where is The Ring of Wonder? Speak now and I may set you free, or you can die with your friends!" he demanded. "Your choice."

Kumba blasted the wizard once more, and the wizard let out a harrowing scream. Kumba released his grip, throwing the wizard on the floor. Unable to take the pain any longer, the tortured wizard mumbled, "It was Lord Asher. He has taken the ring." "Taken it?

Where has he taken it?" Kumba growled.

With a wry grin and tired blackened eyes, the wounded wizard gazed at Kumba and said "Far away from your grasp, you monster! You will never have control of its power, none of us can, but the chosen! I told you all I know! Now let me go!" "Hmmm… Let you go?" Kumba replied, then ordered his men to find Lord Asher in an instant. Turning his attention back to the wizard, he swished his black lightning and handed him a death blow. He stood over the lifeless wizards, mocking them with his evil laugh "I said I will set you free. I never said I will let you live." Kumba walked out of the temple, surrounded by his army of villains. One of them pointed to the direction of Lord Asher in the distant horizon. "After him!" Kumba commanded.

Lord Asher and his comrades turned a corner only to find one of many traps set by Kumba's men. Kumba had anticipated every possible escape route, and now the three wizards, slowed down by the barricades, were completely trapped in the city. A magical blast flashed across the sky. The crowd cheered believing the light to be fireworks.

From two streets away Kumba and his men marched forward. There is no mistaking it, such magical light can only come from a wizard.

"Lord Asher, hurry! Move the ring to safety. We will create a diversion," one of the two brave wizards said. Lord Asher slipped stealthily into the crowd, with his friends while excruciating screams heard in the distance. Kumba's men were everywhere, and after a brief battle with Zombies, they defeated the poor wizards Lord Asher found a dark one-way alley where no cutthroats and zombies could be seen. He ducked in an inconspicuous spot where he waited for an opportunity to flee.

"Quiet!" Kumba commanded as he scouted the alley, sensing every small movement. Lord Asher was nowhere in sight. A rat made a noise from one of the bins and was quickly turned to ash by Kumba's blast. The evil wizard grew impatient and surrounded the area with a mighty fire shield, stunning a few pigeons that flew nearby. "You cannot run away from me, Asher!" he yelled. "I sealed every inch of this alley. There is no escape! Give me the ring now, and I will spare you some mercy. Refuse, and I will kill you where you stand!"

"Never!" Asher replied, buried beneath the trash. Kumba grew even more furious. "Search every inch of that garbage and kill anything that moves!" he told his men as they surrounded the trash bin. "You like to hide like a rat, eh?

Then, I'll give you something to be afraid of," he mumbled. The evil wizard transformed into a terrifying thirty-foot monster of a snake and slithered over where Asher was hiding. He slithered with caution, ready to take on any of Asher's attacks.

"You are no Wonder," he hissed. "You never received The Stone's protection. Now, it's time for you to die, my friend!" "You are no friend of mine!" Asher retorted. "Gotcha!" Kumba smirked, moving fast as lightning to where Asher was hiding. From beneath him, the ground suddenly rumbled and shook, as if an earthquake was about to unfold. A giant blast exploded, throwing trash everywhere and revealed a massive bluish - green gorilla startling Kumba and his men. It was Lord Asher! Towering high, the giant 10-foot ape roared and gripped the snake tightly by its neck. The massive snake turned pale as the gorilla pounded him relentlessly against a brick wall.

Crashing hard into a building and falling out into the busy streets, leaving a gaping hole. The crowd panicked and ran off in different directions, away from the battling wizards. The gorilla soared up high stomping on Kumba's serpentine body. Things were looking up for Lord Asher until Kumba began swelling to three times the gorilla's size!

He cackled, unperturbed by Lord Asher's fierce pounding blows. His head grew monstrous, with frightening eyes and two sharp golden fangs protruding out of him.

He wrapped his body around the giant ape, who squirmed in agony. Then in a puff of smoke (poof)! The ape disappeared!

A small mouse leaped out of the snake's tight grip. Light and quick on its feet it sprang on top of the snake's head and darted into the streets. Kumba's men ceaselessly fired at the agile creature and missed every opportunity. "You cannot get away from me!" Kumba hissed, as he chased after the mouse turning buildings into piles of rubble as the giant snake stormed past. He slung his enormous tail at the great wizard landing hard upon the little mouse. Lord Asher sapped and wounded, turned back into his old self. "You're done for, Asher. Hand the ring over!" Kumba demanded.

With little energy remaining, Lord Asher threw a fireball at the dark wizard, but missed destroying the roof of a nearby building. Kumba laughed. "You truly are worthless!" "And you are a traitorous snake! You will never get the ring!" said Lord Asher. This sent Kumba into a rage. "Then, death it is," he opened his mouth, orange flames glowed from behind Kumba's enormous fangs as he blew the intense flames delivering his final blow.

Lord Asher held up the ring and turned Kumba's flames upward into the sky.

The ring began to glow, brighter and brighter by the second. Kumba squinted, blinded by the piercing blue light. Lightning poured from the sky, striking from every direction, intensely zapping Kumba's men. Overcome with fear the rest fled, as an incredible force lifted Kumba's giant snake body above the ground. Summoning The Stone's magical power Lord Asher cast a spell upon the evil wizard, "A snake you are and a snake you will remain! Trapped in limbo! Far, far away!

Until a new Wonder is chosen, so shall your fate remain?"

Kumba attempted to counteract the spell, but the ring was far too powerful. Unable to move or speak, he felt a consuming sense of dread - perhaps for the first time in his existence. "I tried to warn you, Kumba. You cannot defeat The Stone. The Stone will never choose you," Lord Asher muttered. Kumba became smaller as the snake spun in a whirlwind. Another flash of lightning shone in the sky. Now reduced to the size of an average snake he was sucked n tail first, disappearing into the magical stone.

Lord Asher smiled as he tossed the ring up in the air. It shot off into the night sky with the speed of a comet, leaving behind a rainbow-like mist. Blue flames surrounded Asher's body before he vanished up into a cloud of mist.

CHAPTER 3

Twisting Reality:

(Present day)

"So, you are having nightmares again?" Jesse's psychiatrist asked. Anxiously he replied, "Oh yes they have started back and are getting more realistic." "Really? Well let's talk about when the dreams first to start again," he responded to the nervous answer. "As you already know doc, I was seven and we just visited my grandma's store, I was overwhelmed by a bright light and passed out for a whole day. Then the dreams came. Snakes, dragons, bugs, but after we moved to New York the dreams stopped. Now they are back."

"Unbelievable, from what I can tell, you are suffering from several phobias. Herpetophobia – reptiles, Ophiophobia – snakes, Astraphobia – aliens, and fear of the dark. Any one of these alone would be terrifying." he explained. "I guess so doc, it's difficult to go near any reptiles, lizards or anything which resembles one. Plus, every time I do, I just kind of freeze up, frightened, so you tell me?" Jesse sarcastically rebuttals.

"Well, your fear started with an unusual visit you say? Tell me about it?" doc continued. "It had to be a dream?" "I don't remember much about it and the harder I try to remember, the harder it is and then my mind goes blank. They seem

more than just dreams doc and every time I close my eyes, I have one.

Maybe we need to up my medication?" Jesse expresses with concern. The doctor quickly replied "Take this prescription home, it should stop the nightmares. Come back a week from Friday."

Jesse arrived home, ate some lunch and sat down to watch some TV and relax. As he was about to take a nap he was awakened by gunfire and explosions. It was suddenly dark outside and there were creatures flying everywhere. Strange looking creatures, very frightening in appearance. He looked up and saw a cluster of these being looking straight at him. He closed the curtain fast and wondered what to do. Fear once again overtook him like it has done all his life. Then suddenly like a bomb going off, glass shattering as they came busting through the windows, flying creatures, very demonic looking.

They charged for Jesse as they could sense his energy, the power within him was similar to the energy device these demons were after. They were all over Jesse, pulling him towards the door, grabbing his arms and flying off. Jesse was fighting to break free, with little success, they flew off as Jesse dangled in the air he noticed a bird signal up in the night sky and the city seemed at war. Accept it was no longer New York but a city much more Then as quick as all the commotion started it ended, Jesse was back sitting in the chair, the sun was back out, the windows were not broken and it appeared that everything which seemed so genuine, didn't actually happen, none of this was real. Jesse took a deep breath, still shaking, murmured "Wow! That was one heck of a dream." Taking a couple of the pills, the doctor had just prescribed. He once again sat down but as he started to close his eyes. BAM, another explosion roared!

Jesse looked out the window, the sky had a big hole in it, where spaceships were flying in and explosions seemed everywhere. Then he could see Loki, the god of mischief, flying past with a dragon close behind him, battling alongside the aliens as they came pouring out of the sky. "What the heck is happening to me?" Jesse expressed exhaustion. Dad opened the door and shouted, "Come Jesse we must go now!"

"What's going on Dad, it looks like my comic books out there and the sky is full of aliens?"

"Hurry Jesse, they will come for you!" "Why would they come for me?"

"Never mind, I will explain later!" Dad shouted. Down the staircase they ran, explosions everywhere, the building rumbled as it was hit over and over again. "Hurry son this way!" They climbed into the vehicle and sped off down the streets. Buildings were being turned over, the skies full of spaceships and flying creatures everywhere.

"Where are we going dad?" Jesse pleaded.

"We need to get your mother and sister and get out of New York."

Suddenly a large explosion hit them and they went flying in the air, rolling head over heel till the vehicle finally stopped. As Jesse climbed out, he could see his dad laying still, most likely dead. More ships zoomed by. Jesse ran into a building which was full of people wailing and scared, almost as bad as the fear Jesse was battling within, because of the alien's device which had installed great fear in him.

Then just as quick as it started. Jesse found himself back in the chair, just as he was earlier, before when he first turned on the TV. He jumped up and looked out the window, everything was peaceful and quiet. Jesse was in shock thinking, "What the crap is happening to me?" but no sooner than he caught his breath, Dad came bursting in the door and asked "are you alright son?" Jesse's heart stopped, Oh not again, he thought! Jesse ran up and hugged him, especially after watching him die and said, "No dad, I am not alright, I'm going crazy. I don't know what to think." Trying to console him he said, "Calm down son, I have to tell you something, it is going to be hard to hear. All you just experienced Jesse, is in fact happening, it is a real occurrence! I have also witnessed it. You are not crazy."

"What do you mean it is all real? No, none of this can be real, my dreams cannot be real events, not possible and they are too strange and horrible sometimes. That is why I have to go see the doctor, right!?

"Son, you know that experience you thought was a dream, which you had when you were a kid, with those aliens in your bedroom?"

"Yes, sort of." Jesse said in confusion.

"I took that flashlight to the lab, it had alien blood on it, so you were really visited and that event we just experienced was real."

"You just now telling me this!?"

"Listen son, when I had the alien blood confirmed, the agency wanted to know why they were after you and from your blood work, they think you may have a mutant gene, maybe with some abilities, but we still don't know what or why. Your psychiatrist works for us also. He knows you are not crazy, but he wasn't allowed to tell you. I am sorry you had to go through all this."

"You told me it was all a dream, I finally started to believe you!" "Would you rather have me say to a seven-year-old child, that those bogymen aliens were real and they are coming to get you? Would that have made you sleep better?"

"I suppose not, but if it was all real, then, ahhhh Crap! I am seventeen now, I should have been told!"

"I was going to tell you when you turned eighteen. Just thought I had more time. Look son let's not mention any of this to your mother or sister, okay? Don't want to frighten them."

"I am frightened enough for us all DAD! Why am I so scared all the time?"

"I think it best if we leave New York and move out to the country. Something powerful is brewing, it is causing different realms and universes to collide. This is what you have been experiencing. Nobody, but those who work with me and apparently you son, can remember what happened!"

"Why do I remember it dad? Next you will say the aliens are after me and we need to leave?"

"Well yes son, but how would you know that?" "Never mind dad, just heard it in one of my dreams."

"There is something about you that these aliens want. The agency still doesn't know what it is but they know all about aliens, Asgard and many of the different realms and are working on finding out what it is they are after. When they examined the alien blood the agency began watching you son and has been ever sense. To be honest I like the idea that you were being watched. Now let's go. We must find your mother and sister and move away from here."

CHAPTER 4

A Novel Beginning

As the Mason family headed up the driveway to Grandpa's farm jolly little Berry said, "I have a riddle." "You do? What is it?" Mom replied. "What is it that cannot hear or see but can smell even without a nose?" she giggled. "That's a tough one, little sis," Jesse replied, "Wait, what's that awful smell?!" "Roll the windows down!" Mom cried out. "Who farted? Berry, was that you? It's Berry!" Jesse insisted. Berry argued "no it wasn't me, Mom. It was Jesse!" "How funny", Jesse remarked, "You may have learned that one from me, but we all know it's you who let out that toot! Was that the answer to your riddle?" The whole car erupted in laughter as Mom pulled up in front of a lovely country house hugged by trees and vibrant flowers. Cows grazed here and there, basking in the warmth of the noon sun. "Well, this is it kids, our new home," Mom said as she alighted from the vehicle. The kids' eyes grew large, their voices lifting in excitement "Wow! This is awesome! Grandpa's house is so big!"

An old man came out of the house. "Well, come on in!" Grandpa waved, "Dinner's waiting. I've got fried chicken, mashed potatoes, fresh corn on the cob, and Grandma's special blueberry pie." His face beamed, happy to have found company once again since his wife of forty years had passed away several years before. He lived alone in the family farm, which has been in the family for several generations. The fresh country breeze kept the family company as they spent the rest of the day remembering the old days and looking forward to new ones.

The first light of day brought with it an unusual story.

"Good morning, Jesse! How was your sleep last night?" Mom asked while setting the plates, "Jesse, you look tired. Did you sleep okay?" Rubbing his eyes "I heard music and voices all night.

They were coming from outside." "You mean birds and crickets?

They do make a wonderful symphony," Mom suggested.

"Maybe, but it didn't sound like birds and crickets, but more like people."

"Jesse, dear, it must be a dream." "I'm sure your right, Mom." "Beatrice come down, breakfast is ready!"

"I'm coming ma, please call me Berry!" "Barry is a boy's name dear."

"That's with a B-A-R and I am B-E-R, Berry like a fruit!"

"OK, Berry like a fruit!" Mom said shaking her head. Grandpa came out of the kitchen with a tray in hand, "The blueberry tarts are ready!" "Yum," Berry said with wide eyes, stuffing a tart in her mouth. "It's so good, Grandpa!" her face smudged with blue pulp. Mom looked over and laughed, "Maybe we should call you Blueberry instead?" Berry just smiled and grabbed another tart. "When you two are finished eating, we are going for a walk to town and visit your aunt in her store." Mom told the kids. "Dad has to take the car to work and check in with his office." Jesse's nose scrunched a little "Walk to town? Aren't we a long way from town?" Grandpa laughed "Three miles, my boy. I have walked from here to town and back since I was little. Easy-peasy.

Walking is good for you."

In town, the Mason family walked into Aunt Jane's Emporium. From across the street, three young men - Harry, Kurly, and Moe - all Saint Louis Cardinals fans donning red and white, took an interest in Jesse's Yankees hat which was the colors of their rival gang in the adjacent town. The boys shouted at Jesse "You aren't from around here huh" but Jesse just brushed it off and continued into the store. As they walked in they were startled by a loud voice from the shop staff, "Don't move!" Though clueless, Jesse stood still as a girl, seventeen, same age as he was, slowly walked up to him. With great care she clasped her hands together around the butterfly an inch away from his face, touching part of his nose. Their cheeks both turned pink from embarrassment. "Sorry," the girl said, keeping the butterfly safe inside her palms before releasing it out the front door. "I didn't want it to get hurt. Are you new in town?" she asked. "We're looking for my sister, Jane," Mom replied.

"Oh, so you are Ms. Jane's family. She told me so much about you. My name is Emma. I'll go get her. She's in the back."

Jesse browsed through the shop's concessions, as he did many times when he was younger, odd things which the family had acquired when they opened the shop some seventy years ago. "Oh my," Aunt Jane hollered as she rushed to give her sister a hug, "is this Jesse and Berry? Look at how you two have grown!" The two sisters wasted no time and proceeded to a table nearby to catch up.

Emma leaned over the counter, her hands cupping her chin. From her post she observed Jesse and thought how cute he was. "See anything you like?" she inquired as she began to walk up behind him pressing her hand lightly on his arm. A bit panicked, he picked up a strange box from one of the shelves, a bright blue glow escaping from within its narrow lid. The sliver of light did not escape Berry's keen eyes. "What's in the box, auntie?" she asked. "OH, just some old costume jewelry," Aunt Jane commented, preoccupied with their sisterly chat. Curious, Berry took the box from her brother's hand and opened it at once.

From the pile, Berry tried on a beautiful golden necklace. Jesse reached over to examine the ring, its blue shine glowing like a star all at once. Berry clutched the ring, "Let me have a look." The ring began to dim down, then glowed once more when she held it close to Jesse. "Wow! How strange," she mused. Though almost inaudible, there seemed to be a buzz coming from it. She held it close to her ear, and her eyes grew wide in bewilderment. "Okay. Uh-huh," she nodded. "Alright. If you say so." Jesse and Emma looked at each other in confusion. Berry then handed the ring to Jesse and explained "The ring says it belongs to you." What a strange thing to say, he thought. "The ring told you what?" Jesse laughed.

"If you don't believe me, ask it yourself." Jesse rolled his eyes, thinking it was one of his sister's pranks. He took the ring and slipped it onto his middle finger. It hung loose around his bones. Just as he started to take it off, the ring shimmered in a strong blue hue, before turning bright yellow.

It shrunk! Harder and harder Jesse pulled. Each time the ring clung tighter to his flesh. "It won't come off" he whined. Aunt Jane and Mom took Jesse to the sink and lathered his finger with soap. "It should come off. I don't know why it won't," Mom said.

"It's not supposed to!" Berry interjected, "It told me it is looking for a warrior, and it has chosen Jesse." "What do you mean? That it's some kind of a magic ring?"

Jesse said, unsure whether to believe her sister or not. "Don't worry, Jesse. You can have the ring. It should stay in the family anyway," Aunt Jane assured him. "Now, Berry, how about you pick some jewelry which you like from that box too? My treat." Berry was elated. She tried every piece she could get her hands on. "You don't have to give Jesse that ring," Mom told Aunt just costume jewelry. I never figured it was worth too much. Mom wouldn't have let us kids play with it, if it was worth a fortune," Aunt Jane explained.

Well, I guess I can't take it off without cutting off my finger, so thank you, Aunt Jane," Jesse joked. Outside Aunt Jane's Emporium a brilliant engulfed the shop. Three strange rainbow rays of light shot out across the sky in all directions, precisely when Jesse first slipped the ring on his finger.

Dark clouds gathered over a busy highway and a bright flash of lightening cracked through the sky, Kumba has awakened from his curse. Materializing back to reality, he found himself standing at the edge of a road. A semi-truck zoomed past, knocking the hat off his head. Such strange horseless carriages, he thought to himself, wondering if they were powered by magic. He shut his eyes and heaved a long deep breath, feeling the electrifying energy from The Stone as he did close to a century ago. At last, the time he has been waiting for has finally arrived.

He was thrilled to know The Stone had chosen its next warrior. A black limousine caught Kumba's eye. He stepped on the street, held his hand up, and cast a spell. The car screeched an inch away from the evil wizard. A heavyset chauffeur stepped out "What's wrong with you? Are you crazy? You can't just stand in the middle of the street like that!

And just how did you stop my car?" The driver yelled at Kumba, very angrily. Kumba studied the car from front to back, running his fingers along its shiny chrome plates and black paint. "How does this carriage work?" he asked. "Keep your hands off the car, mister. I just waxed it!" the driver shouted.

Kumba laughed. "Move this carriage, I need you to take me somewhere!"

The driver walked up to him and pointed a finger to Kumba's face. "Not for hire, Bud. Now, get out of the way before I move you myself," he threatened. Kumba burst into an evil cackle and raised a hand at the chauffeur. With his dark magic he twisted the man's body, making him wail in pain. He raised the man off the ground then tossed him in front of a passing semi-truck. Crash! Thud! Thump! Mortified screams reverberated on the streets. The horrified truck driver climbed out and rushed to the man, "Hey, man. Are you okay?"

Kumba walked up to the truck driver, who was still trying to wake up the disfigured man. Kumba held a charm over the man's body and blew into the air. Red mist rained down over the man making him bellow and swell up like a balloon. The dead man's body began to shiver and shake into a fit and rose from the ground. The truck driver was shaken, not believing what he was seeing. "This can't be. The man was surly dead already!" he stuttered. "Would you like to join him?" Kumba asked. Frightened, the truck driver ran quickly back to his truck and fled. Without uttering a word the undead man returned to the car and opened the door for Kumba. His eyes were cold and unflinching. He took his place in the driver's seat, motionless, awaiting Kumba's orders. "Now, what should I call you?" Kumba mused. The driver shivered making a low incoherent sound, the way dulled Zombies do. "Ah, Shiver it is!" Kumba said, holding up an amulet with stars etched on it and a jewel like no other. When opened the pocket watch size amulet, would point Kumba towards the stone, pointing southerly. "South it is then." The limousine traveled for hours finally coming into the sleepy small town, stopping near the emporium. Curious Harry, Kurly, and Moe were rapping on the sidewalk. "Check out this ride!

Sick!" Harry enthused.

Kumba's window rolled down. "You three casting spells? Are you wizards?" he asked. The men looked amused at Kumba's Cajun French accent and his 1820s garb. "Sure. You can call us the Wizards of rap." Moe replied, drawing cheers from his companions. "You fellas been to a costume party or something?" Moe asked. Kumba looked perplexed, asking, "You three noticed any strange lights 'round here?" "Sure did," Harry told him, "it came from that way," pointing to Aunt Jane's Emporium. All three walked around the car, admiring it.

Shiver, remained still as a rock. Kurly pointed at the tire marks across his shirt. "Dude, you got a little something on your shirt." Shiver grunted. "Whoa!" the three said in chorus. Kurly began poking Shiver's cheek. "Get a load of this, fellas. His skin is ice- cold. Reminds me of your ex," he said to Harry. "What happened to you dude?" Harry asked. Shiver grunted, his breath icy and menacing as death itself, called out "Shee-vaa!"

They began to feel shivers down their spines. "Stop poking him, Kurly!" Moe quipped. "What? Are you scared?" Kurly teased. "I'm just saying, something is really wrong with this dude, man." Moe answered, visibly worried.

Kumba wasted no time as he walked over to and entered the emporium "Anyone here noticed unusual lights coming from your shop?" "When we found Jesse's ring, yes," Berry responded. Kumba's eyes widened, "Oh, a ring you say? My, my. May I have a look at this ring?" Jesse raised up his hand. It sent Kumba into a frenzy. He quickly grabbed Jesse's hand and took a long look. He shut his eyes, sensing its immense magic and stood quivering as if in some kind of trance. It creeped Jesse out and he pulled his hand back, snapping Kumba back into reality. That is a beautiful ring. Is it for sale by any chance?" he asked. "No, it isn't," Aunt Jane

intervened before anyone else could answer. "It belongs to Jesse now." "So, The Stone has indeed chosen its warrior," Kumba muttered under his breath.

"What did you say?" she asked as Kumba pretended to scout the shop for antique books. He drew one off the shelf and onto the cashier. "That's a very rare book," Aunt Jane remarked. Very expensive!" "Okay. Hold it for me, I will definitely be back for it later," Kumba said before turning to Jesse, "It would be better for all concerned if you just gave me the ring now!" Aunt Jane found the man incredibly bizarre, "Is that some kind of threat?" Kumba laughed maniacally. "Get out of my store!" Aunt Jane commanded, "We will not be selling anything to you - whatever it is!" "I see," Kumba looked undisturbed. "But remember: I did warn you." He took his top hat off and bowed to the ladies. He pulled the door open then paused to take one final look at Jesse's ring. He stared deep into Jesse's eyes and leaned over to whisper, "You might be the chosen Wonder, but know this, I killed the last Wonder, boy!" Jesse stepped back and gave the man a strange look. He did not understand what this man was saying. Before he could speak, Kumba exited the shop, wearing a creepy grin and laughing ceaselessly.

"What a strange man," Mom commented. "I would watch out for him, Jesse. He seems awfully intent on acquiring that ring, for some reason." While most of the family were looking out the window, Berry picked up the book which Kumba wanted "Destiny's Stone, a diary of Asher. Berry soon understood the importance of this book that it was about the ring which Jesse now holds.

Strange Man Mom shared with her family. Aunt Jane agreed with her sister, "You meet all kinds around here, but I can tell you, that man scares me. I don't like him one bit." Trying to make light of the situation, Aunt Jane suggested a visit to the carnival. "Emma, why don't you take tomorrow off and show Jesse and Berry around town? Maybe go to the carnival and have some fun." Everyone agreed, and for a moment, the tension in the shop was replaced with excitement.

Kumba walked back to the limousine, where the three young men remained surveying Shiver. "How would you three like to make some cash?" he offered. The men looked at each other, eagerly awaiting Kumba's next words. "All you need to do is keep an eye on that boy in the emporium and I'll give you a bonus, if you can get me the ring he wears." "You mean that Yankee's fan?" one asked. "Not sure what a Yankee is, but watch that boy, and I'll make it worth your while," Kumba told them. "We'll be happy to, can we mess with him or do we just watch?" Moe asked. Kumba cackled, "Do whatever you wish, but he must not be harmed. I have been waiting longer than you three can fathom. I'm the only one who can do as I please with the chosen Warrior."

As they left from the emporium, Jesse noticed the three gangsters surveilling them. They pointed to their Cardinals jerseys and then towards Jesse's Yankees hat. Moe ran a finger along his neck, as if slitting his throat. "Let's get that ring now and get our money!" Harry suggested. "No, not with all these witnesses. We will wait until he is alone," said Moe.

When Jesse arrived home, he went straight to his room. The peculiar events of the last two days ran through his head. A sense of overwhelming confusion gripped him as he lay in bed. A talking ring…I don't think so, he thought to himself while staring at the ring. Suddenly, the ring loosened a little. He immediately took it off and tossed it in his bedside night stand. A small voice could be heard from inside, "Jesse… Jesse." Though frightened, Jesse slowly opened it, then shut it quickly upon hearing the soft voice speaking to him. "This is not real. Tell me this is not real," he repeated, trying to convince himself. The Stone responded, "Whether you wear me or not, you are now the chosen Wonder." "This is all just too much. Think, Jesse. Think," he whispered to himself.

There was no mistaking it. That voice could only be coming from the ring, "There is no time to waste. Kumba is coming much earlier than I expected. He knows you are the chosen one, it is you and only you, who can stop him." Dread, filled every nerve in Jesse's body. Only yesterday, he was a boy, having a lovely conversation with a cute girl in the shop and now he is told he is a warrior in a battle between good and evil. The night turned darker, vaguer, and filled with uncertainty for the new Wonder.

CHAPTER 5

Carnival of Enchantment!

The next morning, Jesse sat on his bed looking at the drawer where he had placed the ring and asked, "What sort of ring are you?" "One you must not ignore," The Stone replied. Jesse's mother walked by "Who are you talking to, son?" she questioned. "Just myself Mom."

The Stone spoke again, "you must wear me now, young warrior!" Mom was puzzled, "What did you say, Jesse?" "Nothing, mom," Jesse hollered before whispering to the ring, "Quit speaking, would you?" "Put me on and I will," said the voice. Mom walked on into the room to check on Jesse. In a panic, he put on the ring and said, "Nothing Mom, I'm good. Just thinking out loud what I'm going to do at the carnival." Which put her at ease. Jesse tried to remove the ring again, but it clung tightly onto his finger. "Fine, I'm wearing you, but no talking!" he commanded.

And for once, The Stone kept silent.

Mom dropped Jesse and Berry off at Aunt Jane's, where Emma was waiting. She seemed to have noticed the chemistry between the teens. "So, I'll take Berry around to the rides and exhibits for a couple of hours, so you and Emma could spend time together," she shared, snickering. This pleased Emma, but left Jesse self conscious. "Aunt Jane" he said, gesturing her to hush.

The carnival was abuzz with eager crowds and brimming with life. Colorful flags waved in the wind, and lights hung from every corner. "Where should we go first?" Emma asked the siblings. "Can we go to the reptile exhibit, please?" Berry begged. The two walked behind Berry, holding hands. Berry suddenly turned around and began singing, "Jesse and Emma sitting in a tree, k-i-s-s-i-n-g! First come love, then comes marriage, then comes Emma with a baby carriage." "Berry, shut up!" Jesse told her, his eyes wide with embarrassment. Berry and Emma simply laughed.

"Look at these big snakes," Berry pointed to two massive brown pythons as she pressed her palms against the glass enclosure. The snakes raised their bodies up high and hissed as Jesse passed them by. "That's strange," he said. Emma nodded. "I wonder if that has something to do with what the ring warned Jesse about," Berry pondered aloud. "Jesse, can you also make this spider move?" she asked while watching a tarantula resting still in its enclosure. "Good idea, Berry!" Emma agreed.

Though he meant it as a joke, Jesse inched further toward the enclosure. The tarantula started moving too, its tiny eyes locked in on Jesse. "Huh," he said, amazed and perplexed at the same time. He moved back and forth, and with each movement the spider followed. It then jumped a foot off the ground close to Jesse's face, hitting the window. "Whoaaa!" Berry and Emma said in unison.

"That must be because of Jesse's new ring," Berry proposed. "What do you mean?" Emma asked. Jesse looked at this sister and motioned her to keep quiet. He did not want to give Emma the impression that he was weird. "Okay, okay," Berry nodded while zipping her lips. "Would you like to ride the Ferris wheel Berry?" Emma asked. "Oh, yes!" Berry squealed. From the top of the Ferris wheel the view spanned miles and miles. As the ride approached the top the two teens smiled as their eyes met. Jesse drew himself closer to Emma posing to kiss. Berry giggled, sandwiched between the two who seemed to have forgotten about her. Just then, the ring began to glow to a bright yellow light, surprising Emma. "How is the ring doing that?" she asked. Jesse's heart throbbed a little. He looked around, and from up above he could see the three Cardinals fans not far away inside the carnival grounds. Maybe the ring is warning me, he thought. Little did he know how right he was? They rode many rides and soon saw their mother coming to collect Berry.

"Having fun, Berry?" Mom inquired. "Yes, would you like to go on some rides with me?" "Sure, baby. Let's go and leave those two to enjoy themselves." "Oh, they are. They almost kissed!" She shared as she tittered along with her Mom. "Berry!" Jesse exclaimed, his cheeks turning red once more. "You kids have fun," Mom shouted. "We'll meet you at the entrance, say, in four hours." Then they went their separate ways.

"Look!" Emma motioned to a fortune teller's tent. "Let's go in?" She said; Jesse worried about what he may hear. He

wasn't much of a believer in the mystic arts, but a talking ring changed everything. "Are you sure?" he stressed. "Of course," Emma said, pulling him into the tent. A woman in her forties, draped in a long brocade dress and beaded jewelry, sat at a round table. Madame Romano, she calls herself. She took Emma's hand and studied the lines traversing her palm. "I see a blossoming romance in your future," she tells her, "It is not without obstacles, but nothing you cannot tackle. This is good." Jesse sighed in relief. It's not like this or any psychic could actually see the future, a part of him thought.

Jesse spread his palm on the table, a little excited. Madame Romano gazed at his life line long and hard, the look on her face becoming serious. She reached out for Jesse's other hand as if verifying her earlier reading. Jesse became nervous. "Something wrong?" Emma asked. The fortune teller replied, "Let's try the tarot cards and see what they say." She asked Jesse to cut the deck, then she picked three cards and laid them affront. "What do they say?" Emma asked. "The first card or middle card represents one who seeks an answer to the nature of any problem," Madame Romano explained, "The two other cards work in conjunction and are the key cards. They describe the nature of the situation."

She turned over the first one. The Fool, it read. "Oh, great. So I am officially the fool?" Jesse stated. Madame Romano shook her head, "Not necessarily. It means different things - matters of the cosmos, ideas that transcend this Earthly realm. The Fool could mean emptiness or purity." Emma smiled at Jesse and tightened her grip on his hand.

The second card revealed Death. Jesse's hand turned cold and clammy.

"Now, this one mean redemption through a major change, a new life." she continued.

Jesse heaved another sigh of relief. She turned over the last card: The Devil. "Oh my." Her face spelled concern. "What is it? "Jesse asked. "The Devil could mean negative forces holding you back," she told him, then immediately took the cards and put them to the side.

She uncovered a crystal ball and said, "Let's look in here," clearing her throat, "Maybe we can get a better reading." Emma was immensely entertained not noticing Jesse's nervousness. "What could possibly come next?" he muttered as he took a deep breath. A dark cloud formed inside the sphere, and from it a silver mist. From the mist something else was beginning to take shape. "It looks like a smudge. Maybe you can see it better if we wipe it off," Jesse said, touching the ball to clean the debris. Suddenly, the ball zapped Jesse's hand with a shock, as it glowed as bright as a search light's beam, and Kumba's face appeared! The fortune teller threw a linen over the ball, scrambling to cover it up.

"What is this I'm seeing? There is evil afoot!" the fortune teller cried out, moving as far away as she could from the table. The crystal ball's light grew more intense as it shimmered through the cloth. The ground started shaking. Madame Romano lifted the cloth a little for a peek. Then a red mist of clouds appeared from out of the crystal, the air swirling hard inside the tent. It knocked everything to the floor, and before they could move, a giant snake's head peaked out of the fog and leaned over towards Jesse and Emma as she clung to his arm.

Madame Romano stood in shock trying to move the crystal ball to a box. The ghostly image reared its head and let out a horrifying hiss at her, blowing her hair with the strength of a hurricane before disappearing back into the crystal. Still unable to move, she looked deep into Jesse's eyes in horror, "I have never seen anything like this before." With hands trembling, she escorted Jesse and Emma out of the tent as she insisted "The reading is over - no charge! Please, just leave! Get out!" Sticking her head out the tent one last time, she said, "Beware, both of you. Danger follows you. That boy has a destiny, of which there will be no hiding from!" She then sat back down, trembling, her tent in shambles.

"What did we just see, Jesse?" Emma asked, her voice quivering rambles on; "It must be a circus trick, right? With cameras or something. Do you think any of that was real?" "No, I don't think so." Jesse replied calmly, although deep inside his heart was pounding. "That would be silly. Something like that couldn't actually happen." he assured her.

As they kept walking, they found a high striker. "Ring the bell and win a prize!" a staff member shouted. "Come on!" Emma nudged Jesse, "Let's try to win us a keepsake." Jesse smiled. "How could I refuse?" The three gangsters suddenly burst in front. "Hey, here's our Yankee's fan," Moe announced as they walked nearer the couple. "I don't want any trouble!" Jesse said. "Are we here for trouble, brothers?"

Moe asked with a devilish grin. "No, we don't want trouble," Kurly and Harry replied. "Maybe a little fun would be nice," Moe uttered as Jesse and Emma walked past.

They trailed the two to the hammer swing, watching as Jesse picked up the massive hammer to strike. "Just ignore them," Emma whispered. Jesse reared back and swung the hammer as hard as he could. A light flashed at Wimp. The gangsters laughed. "Wow- a wimp. We expected nothing less," Moe laughed mockingly. "Try again," the stone spoke. Jesse took the hammer as the stone glowed. Wham, the bell rang loud as Jesse's swing of the hammer, put an obvious dent in the bell. The three gangsters just watched in disbelief.

Jesse tugged Emma's hand. "Come on, Emma." The three continued to follow them. Emma egged him to proceed to the Tunnel of Love. "Look, Jesse. I could be tempted to kiss you there." Jesse blushed, "Best offer I have had in a long time. Shall we?" The two took their seats in a big white swan-shaped boat. "Is that the ring Jane gave you?" Emma asked, staring down Jesse's ring, now beaming yellow. Jesse knew it was a warning that something twisted was about to happen. It glowed brighter and brighter as the ride continued. He looked around for signs of danger, and at the tunnel entrance he could see Kumba wearing a devilish grin.

He took off his top hat and waved a hand toward the heart- shaped tunnel, as if inviting them in. "Do you see that man, Emma?" Jesse asked. "See who?" she replied. "The strange man who came into Aunt Jane's store." Emma was puzzled, "I don't see anyone!"

What would That man be doing here, Jesse wondered as their boat floated toward the evil wizard. The tunnel seemed to be melting with blood running down the sides of the entrance. Slowly, it began to transform into a giant snake's head, its fangs bearing down. Jesse was overcome with worry, "Maybe we shouldn't go in there!" "It's too late to get off now," Emma stated, "or are you just trying to avoid kissing me?" Jesse clasped Emma's hand.

The ring glowed, and at last Emma could see what Jesse saw. "I see him now, that's the man from the shop! Where did he come from? He wasn't there a minute ago!" she cried out. "I'm not sure, what I do know is that this cannot be just our imagination," Jesse answered, trying to calm Emma down as they passed through the opening of the ride and traveling between the snake's fangs.

A sinister laugh echoed through the tunnel. Emma's hands turned cold. "Is it me or is the ground moving?" she asked. The floor shook casting ripples in the water, and ghostly figures came out of the waters and a foggy mist rose all around. Evil laughter continued to echo off the walls. Snakes came up and crawled over into their seats. Their boat was shapeshifting into a trap, their seats becoming smooth and damp like a wet tongue.

"This must be what the cards spoke of," Jesse mumbled to himself. The ring was right! He could not escape this dark magic. "Jesse!" Emma screamed. They held on tightly to each other, filled with dread as thunder roared inside the ride, it was pitch black between the occasional eyes shining out from the dark, seemingly watching them. Suddenly, a voice emanated from the ring. "Hold me up high," it said. "Who said that?" Emma asked. "It's the ring," Jesse told her, "I'll explain later."

The boat was turning into snake's jaws, then started closing in around them. With all their might, they pushed their arms against the top and sides to keep it from locking them in.

"Hold me high, Jesse!" said The Stone once again. He held the ring up, and it began to glow ever so brightly that it blinded them, then darkness. A gentle lullaby sounded as they passed through a thick, red mist, making them sleepy.

Jesse tried to fight it off, but Emma was falling under his spell. "Open your eyes, Emma!" he yelled, shaking her "He's putting us in some kind of trance. Fight it, Emma! Emma!" Emma awoke, startled "What? Who is?" Before Jesse could speak, the ring glistened with a dim yellow light as they continued. Then everything turned pitch black, their skin crawled from the sounds coming from the ride. Louder and more evil, the sounds grew. Holding each other tight, waiting for the impending violence. Then suddenly a loud roar thundered into life, Jesse put his arms around Emma to protect her. The ride grinned forward and as they waited for the inevitable attack, suddenly an abrupt stop and then a bright flash of light shone in front of them, they closed their eyes and became silent. The two covered their eyes with their arms, as the light became brighter. Then all of a sudden, a voice rang out, not knowing what to expect, Jesse and Emma held tight, waiting for what may come next, then all of a sudden.

"Please exit the ride. We have others waiting," the ride attendant signaled in a deadpan tone.

Emma and Jesse opened their eyes to daylight, stepped out of the once again normal looking boat, which has now returned to its original swan shape. Both shaken and confused. "What was that?!" They yelled in unison. "Was it some kind of optical illusion?" Jesse fretted. But even then, he was certain it was not. As they walked away, a woman's voice could be heard screaming, "A snake! There's a snake in this boat!" The two looked at each other in bewilderment. "You said you could explain this, so start," Emma demanded. They sat down at a table, each with a glass of Cola in hand. Jesse started to narrate the events that followed after they found the ring at the emporium.

"I swear, Emma. I didn't know it would come to this," he said apologetically. She glanced at Jesse's ring and shook her head. "What kind of ring are you?" she asked. The Stone spoke, "That would take a while to explain." Emma jumped from her seat shouting "So your ring really does speak?" "Yeah," he said with a wry smile. "I don't know what to believe anymore. If you had told me all of this before, you bet I would not be going on a date with you," she remarked,

"So…this is a date? "Jesse quizzed, "What do you think, Ring Man?" "So, you're maybe my girlfriend?"

Emma smiled. She placed her arms around Jesse's neck and planted a kiss on his lips. "Does that answer your question?" she said. Jesse smiled wide and nodded his head. After bringing Emma back to the emporium, Jesse decided to walk home to calm his nerves. Halfway home, he heard a car approaching and a voice shouting from behind, "Jesse, my man! Come over here, we want to talk to you." Jesse turned around to see the three gangsters, then walked faster. "Just give us the ring, and we'll be on our way," Moe hollered. His heart pounded a little as the car sped to catch up to him. Jesse turning ran through the woods without looking back. The three pulled over, jumped out of the car, and quickly started giving chase. Kurly stopped, shouting in between breaths, "Just give us that stupid ring, nobody wants to hurt you!"

Jesse hid behind a tree where he had a good view of the three in pursuit. Before long they grew tired of the search and met in a dark spot in the forest surrounded by very large trees. Moe turned around and was startled by a shrieking squirrel. They laughed. "Darn squirrel," Moe mumbled. Moe looked at the squirrel saying, "Are you growling at me? Hey fellas dig this weird squirrel." The other two laughed at Moe and then Moe shouts, "Yea, well maybe you fellas should look up? You've got some squirrels fussing at you too." "Really," Harry said, "Are you afraid of some squirrels?"

Kurly chuckled at the idea. But when he turned and looked, he could see his brother in crime were both staring up pointing for him to look. He could see other squirrels, hundreds of them, coming like an army descending through the trees above quickly heading towards them.

Squirrels jumped on one of the three, nipping and

clawing the gangster's head. The others took off running frantically looking back at the hundreds of squirrels which were chasing them through the woods. Trees were swaying and shaking all around them, like a heavy wind in a storm. They quickly jumped into their car and rolled the windows up as the squirrels covered the car. One remarked "What did we just see fellas and since when do squirrels attack people?" "What in the world is this?" Harry asked, obviously frightened. "This is some weird voodoo shiz, man," Moe told his companions, "He's not paying us enough for this crap."

Soon, Jesse found himself all alone in the woods with hundreds of squirrels just sitting still watching him from the trees. He quietly and slowly made his way back to the road expecting to see those young men still there waiting for him. He stood at the edge of the forest, looking both ways down the road to make sure the guys were gone, then proceeding on home. He looked back and seen many woodland animals standing close by the edge of the woods just watching as he passed. "Unsure of what just happened, Jesse waved to the squirrels saying, "Thank you squirrels for rescuing me, I think?" Jesse heard about a hundred squeaky little voices say, "Your welcome." Hearing that Jesse quickly headed towards home figuring he understood nothing about the world he was thrust into. Maybe he imagined it all, he was so very tired.

On the way the ring instructed Jesse to walk to a spot where old Indian ruins stood just outside of town near the park. "This place holds mystical powers that draw warriors like you," the Stone said. He sat down on a fallen log listening to the creatures of the forest. The magical stone changed colors and begun to speak, "You have been chosen Jesse." "Chosen for what?" he asked with wide eyes. "How do you work, are you magic? Do I make a wish or what?" "Not exactly," The Stone stated, "You were chosen as the warrior of Wonder." Jesse replied, "And why would I wish to become a warrior of wonder?" "Not for you, but for the innocents of this world, in their time of need."

The Stone explained, "I have been waiting for almost a century for a worthy human. And you are that human, Jesse. But first, you must pass the test of wonder!" "What test? And who or what are you?" Jesse insisted. "I am a sentient, conscious being. Created with the knowledge of the Multirealms. Which you are now part of, whether you like it or not. I am The Stone which you wear upon your finger. I chose to be the bringer of light and protector of the realms from darkness. Which bring many evils, all threatening to destroy this realm and many others realms.

It is not easy to explain or to understand for a human, but trust me Jesse, this is your destiny." Jesse was starting to believe he had little choice, once hearing the ring's words.

"Let's say I believe you. What do you want from me and what must I do?"

"You must pass the warriors test, and if you're successful, you will become the Emissary and hold great power. Is this something you wish?"

"Do I have a choice?"

"Of course," The Stone told him. "If you choose to, then

you will be tested to become the new Wonder! If you choose not to help, then I will become dormant once more and have to wait for another to be chosen, which will not be for exactly forty seven years, three months, five days, and two hours from now. Unless Kumba finds you and collects me before that time. So be warned, the evil Kumba has escaped and will not wait till then." Jesse heaved a deep sigh, "Great. So, it seems there is really no other way then. But one thing I don't understand is, why me? I'm just a kid. I'm not anybody special."

"You are the chosen one, Jesse. For me to awaken one must be and have a pure and selfless heart. I awoke on that day, ten years ago, when you were but a child and at that exact time you picked me off the floor it started.

Which gave you as little seven-year-old Jesse, your Dream of Wonder!"

Slowly he trod the path to the house, his chest heavy with burden from this newfound task. He stood at the edge of the woods, in awe of the animals that saved him. The three gangsters were nowhere in sight. On his way home, he tried to make sense of what had happened. He understood so little about the world he was thrust into. Was he only imagining things? His body felt weary, his thoughts racing. Upon arrival, Jesse proceeded straight to his room and turned on his gamming unit. He needed to take his mind off the day's events, and a game seemed to be an ideal breather. The ring loosened. He took it off and placed it back into the drawer and turned on his gaming unit. Grandpa knocked on the door. "Just checking on my favorite guy in the house." "But I am the only other guy in the house." Jesse smiled. "I'm playing a game called World of Warcraft," he explained, as Grandpa sat next to him. "That's me, the big rhino-looking guy with the huge battle ax." "Wow, this game looks fantastic," Grandpa remarked. "You must be a pretty tough character in that game, huh?" "Oh, yeah. I kick butt," Jesse replied. "Put me on!" a voice resonated inside Jesse's drawer. Grandpa curled his eyebrows, trying to locate the sound. "What was that?" "Oh, nothing, Grandpa. It's just the game."

Jesse closed the drawer tightly. "Put me on," The Stone spoke once more. Grandpa leaned over the drawers. "It sounds like it's coming from behind the night stand. Are you sure it's coming from the game?" "Of course," Jesse told him as he swiftly took the ring out and placed it back on his finger. He whispered, "I'll put you on, so please, no more talking in front of Grandpa, or anyone, for that matter." "Okay," The Stone responded. "I heard it again. Where's that darn noise coming from?" Grandpa asked as he made a quick sweep of the room. "They're probably just bugs or something," Jesse suggested.

Grandpa shrugged his shoulders.

"Anyway, I came by to see if you wanted to go fishing," he said, pulling out two fishing poles from the closet. "That sounds great, Grandpa. Let's do it later, if you don't mind." Jesse grabbed and held his arm, trying to usher him out of the room. "It's late. Maybe you should get some rest Grandpa."

After returning home from the carnival, Mom went to Jesse's room and found him lying restless on his bed. "How did your day go, hon? Are you okay?" "Yes, mom. I'm just tired," Jesse told her, not wanting to worry her over the day's strange events. The night breeze provided some comfort as he turned over to sleep. "Alright. I'll leave you to it then. Get some rest, and I'll see you in the morning," she replied.

"Mom?" Jesse mumbled as Mom was shutting the door. "Yes, dear?" Jesse needed to affirm what the ring had told him. "Do you think, – do you think I have what it takes to do something great for this world, even if I'm just a kid?" Mom walked back to his bed and plopped herself on the mattress. "Jesse. All humans have it in them to be great and do something with their life. It doesn't matter if you're young or old. What matters is that you are brave enough to do what is right, even if it's hard or seems impossible," she explained, placing her hand on Jesse. "Thanks, mom," Jesse said. She nodded "its late son, time for bed."

"Alright, mom, can you please ask the neighbors if they could turn down the music? It's quite loud," he pleaded, as he turned over to sleep. Mom looked puzzled as she peeped out of the window. "What music? I don't hear anything. And it's more than a mile to any neighbor." Unknown to Jesse, only he could hear these strange sounds. To everyone else, there was just the symphony of crickets and bugs in the countryside, plus occasional croaking of frogs. "You must be so tired. Well, goodnight. Get a good night's sleep. Tomorrow I'm sure you'll wake up energized and ready to do something great for the world," Mom cheered, as she walked out the door.

CHAPTER 6

They Came by the Thousands

The dawn was breaking as Jesse laid in bed. From his room he can still hear noises coming from outside. He rose to shut his bedroom window, yet the faint chorus of tiny voices remained. "The ring, the ring! It has chosen. I must spread the web, for the King is mad and he is coming," the voice sang. Jesse looked around. It was early and quiet, and nobody was up yet. Above his head he could see a spider spinning its web. Must be this ring messing with my head, he thought, while holding out his fingers to glance at the ring. "Are you ready for your first test?" The Stone spoke, startling him a little. The long night sleep and his mom's words made the burden lighter. "Ready as I can possibly be," Jesse answered with a smile.

"Good. Your first mission is very easy. You must simply make a family of bluebirds, fly away and leave the park."

Jesse thought it an easy feat. "So, all I have to do is shoo away some birds?"

"Yes. It's as simple as that," The Stone continued. "Then, I am ready for training, sounds easy enough."

"Oh, you think so?" The Stone chuckled. Even Merlin

took a month to complete his training." "What? You tested Merlin?" Jesse asked in disbelief. "Of course. His warrior reality test was a minnow in a big pond," The Stone chuckled again, "He spent a week in the belly of a big fish before he got out of it. It was hilarious!"

"Do you want me to take this test or are you trying to talk me out of it?" Jesse said, a bit annoyed. "Not at all. I just want you to be prepared." The Stone added, "Your first mission will come tonight, as you sleep. You will become a squirrel."

"A squirrel? Why a squirrel?"

"Warriors of the Wonder Stone can become many things once they train. In this case, it's a squirrel. Would you rather be a minnow like Merlin?"

"Okay, okay," Jesse agreed.

The day passed by slowly. Jesse was antsy to get to training. It can be fun to be a squirrel in my dreams, he thought. He came up with all sorts of ways to scare away the blue- colored family of birds, even going on his computer to research about them.

One website read:

Bluebirds are territorial creatures. They would aggressively defend their nests, and for this reason, they tend to attack squirrels. Squirrels are known to love bird egg.

"Is that why you wanted me to be a squirrel," Jesse muttered under his breath. The Stone laughed, "Not to worry, it should be very simple?" Night came, it was time for Jesse's training.

He fell asleep quickly, unaware when Berry clambered up

into his bed to snuggle. The little girl frequently suffered nightmares, and each time she would climb onto her brother's bed and sleep next to him.

A bright flash filled the room, and Jesse was thrust into a completely new world. He found himself sitting high up on a tree branch. Overlooking the park, he could see a family of bluebirds from afar. He looked down on his hands to find tiny paws, and examined the claws protruding from each finger. He looked over his shoulder and saw a tail attached to his behind. He wiggled it, feeling the wind brush against the tip. "I am officially a squirrel.

This is so weird and so awesome!" he exclaimed.

"I know this is all very exciting, but may I remind you that you have a mission?" The Stone said. "Right!" Jesse nodded as he scurried down the tree to locate the bluebirds he saw in the park. He ran up to them to scare them away, but they ignored him. Stealthily, he sprinted behind them, then swatted his tail against a small fat bird in the group. "Fly away! Shoo!" he commanded in his squirrel voice. The young bird squawked, "Watch it!" Jesse tried again, only to get pecked by the birds, which were becoming agitated. He could understand what the birds were saying, but to the birds he talked gibberish.

"This is harder than I thought," he pondered.

Trying one last time, racing toward them and bumping one bird with all his might. This angered the fat male bird. It hopped on to Jesse's squirrel back and dug tight with its claws. "Ouch!" Jesse yelled, feeling a sharp prick on his flesh.

Jesse ran fast, thinking it would fly off. But the bluebird held tightly onto his back.

Down and around benches and into the water fountain they went. The birds' claws sinking deeper with each step. Jesse dashed up a tree, making the little bird lose its balance, falling off to the ground. Giggling it said, "What a ride! Hey, squirrel! Come back down here and let's play some more!"

This absolutely frustrated Jesse. The birds fussed, as if making a mockery of Jesse's attempts. "I guess a little squirrel does not scare anything," he said, downhearted.

The birds' collective chatter growing fainter as he drifted into space. Everything turned into a blur. Jesse awoke to rays of sunlight peeking through his windows.

Shoulders heavy, he sat up in bed, disappointed that he failed his first mission. He played with the ring on his finger and spoke to it, "I guess I'm not your warrior, I couldn't even scare a bird." The Stone remained silent. Jesse found his sister happily stuffing breakfast into her mouth in the kitchen. "Someone seems happy," he commented, "No nightmares last night?"

"No, I had a wonderful dream! I was a blue bird and I found some friends, and then I got to ride on a squirrel's back, like a cowgirl! He took me all over the park. It was so fun!" she expressed. Why would his sister dream his same dream? "Ride on a squirrel's back, you say?" Jesse probed. "Yes! I was a little bluebird, and there's this squirrel who was trying to shoo me away or something," Berry replied. Mom interjected, "Well, I'm glad you didn't have one of those nightmares again." "No, I had one, then I went to Jesse's room and slept on his bed. Then, I had that good dream," Berry continued "Jesse knows.

He was in the same dream, right Jesse?"

Both Mom and Grandpa looked at Jesse, somewhat baffled. Jesse's eyes grew big. "Don't look at me," he said, shrugging his shoulders, "I don't know what dream she's talking about." All the while he wondered why Berry was in his dream and how she knew he was the squirrel. They all laughed, causing Berry to get defensive.

"I will prove it isn't a dream. Here are some jokes I heard from the red birds:

"Which side of the tree are all the leaves on? The Outside." She said while laughing, "Or where do you find a frog with no legs?" Mom giggled and ask, "Well where you find a frog with no legs?"

"Exactly where you left him!" "Ha-ha," Grandpa laughed. "What did the bee say to the flower?" "I don't know," mom said, "What did the bee say?" "Hello Honey."

Here is one grandpa will like, what is the best way to communicate with a fish?" Grandpa looked puzzled and shrugged his shoulders. "Drop it a line."

Grandpa liked that one. Jesse looked at his ring and asked quietly, "Was she awake in my dream?" The Stone said nothing.

"So, I failed the mission and that's it, huh? That's fine, I didn't want to be no hero anyway!" Still the ring was silent. Jesse excused himself and proceeded to the front porch.

Stroking the ring, he asked softly about Berry's knowledge of the dream, "Was she awake in my dream? Why was she there?" The ring was eerily silent."

"You don't want to talk? Is it because I failed the mission?" Still the Stone remained silent. In the afternoon Grandpa enlisted the family's help to clear out weeds in the yard. A year of living on his own at old age proved to be daunting with bushes and weeds burgeoning faster than he could cope. Berry dug into the soil with her small rake. A grasshopper landed on its handle. She caught it with her gloved hands and turned to Grandpa, "Grandpa Look! It's a big grasshopper!"

"It sure is a big one, sweetheart." Grandpa remarked, "Put it in a jar, and I will use it for fishing later. Maybe Henry will like it as bait." "Who's Henry?" Berry asked. "He's a large bass in our pond."

Another grasshopper landed near Grandpa. He lifted his boot and squashed it. Berry looked quite mortified. "Grandpa!

"Grasshoppers are pests, Berry. They would eat the garden up and kill all the plants."

Soon, more and more grasshoppers fell into the garden. Berry picked them up and threw them into the jar as fast as she could, while Grandpa stomped and swatted those near him. Jesse turned his sights to the big trees of the forest. "Grandpa, look," he pointed to what seemed like large heavy rain clouds. "Rain's coming." Berry shouted. "That's not rain! Those are locusts!" Grandpa exclaimed, as a thick swarm of bugs flew nearer. Quickly, they all ran inside the house. Grandpa called Forest Service. "Apparently, they are all over

town," he shared as he hung up the phone. "Forest Service says they are covering a five-mile area." "My goodness!" Mom uttered. From a distance, Berry spotted a black car parked across the farm. Squinting her large, brown eyes, she pointed to a man with a top hat.

"Isn't that the scary man who threatened Jesse at the emporium?"

They stepped closer to the screen door and saw the man waving his hands. "What on earth is he doing here?" Mom said. "I don't know, but I don't like this at all," Grandpa responded. Jesse rushed to his room and spoke to the ring, "There is a bug invasion, and that man is out there again. Are you still not going to say anything?" At last, The Stone spoke, "Yes, that's a plague spell he is using." "What can I do?" Jesse inquired. "Hold me by the window," The Stone commanded, "quickly!"

Out of the forest, thousands of birds flew down covering the farm. With the speed of lightning, they pecked and swallowed every grasshopper that came their way. Jesse watched in awe as the few locusts that remained scrambled away from the farm. Jesse searched for Kumba, but he was gone. "He will be back, for sure," The Stone said, "But don't worry. Next time, we will be ready." "Next time? So, you mean, expect more attacks?

"Kumba is not going to stop until he possesses the ring. We must train."

"But I failed my training!" Jesse retorted. "Jesse, that's why it's called training. Once you pass the test, you will acquire your Dimensional Protection Barrier - your DP. You will then be protected and have the ability to communicate with any creature, big or small, and all who stay near you will be able to do the same," The Stone explained. "I'm listening," Jesse kept silent.

"Kumba should not be this powerful and he should not have found you this fast, he has with him some other form of magic.

This gives us little time for training and until you are ready, you are an easy target for Kumba. If you want to be stronger and ready for him you must not give up. You have to continue training - for you and for everyone around you."

Jesse glanced outside before turning his gaze back to the ring, "So, if I acquire this DP, I will be, like, a superhero? And the people around me will be able to protect themselves too?" "Exactly. Now, is that something you can do?" The Stone asked.

"Well, it seems I have little to say about it."

"Good, your new test will begin when you fall asleep tonight." "You seem anxious to catch this Kumba yourself," Jessie pried. "Kumba hunted down and killed the last Wonder, Lord Asher. He was a selfless and a powerful wizard. We were together for almost eight years. He was a dear friend." The Stone explained. "Forgive me for asking: You said Asher was powerful. How come he was not able to defeat this Kumba guy?" Jesse asked.

"He was not able to complete his final test and did not receive his dimensional power. Kumba is far stronger than any wizard without this protection."

"Great. So, you are training me to defeat a hundred-year-old evil sorcerer who killed a wizard who is better trained and stronger than I am?" Jesse remarking worried. "Only a Wonder can defeat Kumba. I have faith in you, Jesse and so does everyone else," The Stone assured him, "For your next test you must learn to stay alive as a centipede in case you ever wish to change into one." "A centipede? Why would I turn into a centipede when I can turn into a beast like King Kong?" Jesse told the ring. The Stone replied sarcastically, "Okay, then. How about a fly? Would you rather be that? Or maybe a maggot?"

"Okay, okay. A centipede is fine. Geez."

"Remember, Jesse, this might be a simple test, but it is a little harder than the last."

At bedtime, the ring showed Jesse a preview of what the test will be. Inside the now crystal-clear stone he saw a vibrant, three dimensional cartoon world filled with critters and foliage of all sizes and colors. "Ready?" The Stone quizzed. Jesse nodded his head.

He closed his eyes and drifted off to sleep. He blinked and saw a world drawn with lines and strange colorful shapes. He felt the earth beneath his belly, raw and moist, from the last rain.

CHAPTER 7

Living life as a Willy

"Is it really necessary to title my missions?" Jesse asked. "Pay attention," The Stone answered. It then began to narrate a story about Willy, the silly centipede. Willy was a hardworking centipede that for a long time, has been saving up his money to buy new shoes. He always looks for a bargain and spends his money wisely. But no matter how thrifty he always seems to choose the wrong pair. Because of this Willy began to doubt himself. He developed a habit of asking his friends, "Is this a good idea?" when he has a decision to make since buying shoes is very important to a centipede.

"Okay, hold on a minute," Jesse interrupted the ring. "Do we really have to go through this bug's whole history for me to buy some shoes?"

"I am afraid so. In any realm you are in, there is cartoony sweetness, but there is also evil. You are in Willy's body and in his realm, you must adapt to its reality."

"Okay then, if you say so, I'll try."

Examining his new body, with all his feet he headed off to complete his mission. On his way to town Jesse ran into Willy's good friend, a ladybug named Jean Ann who was enjoying morning tea with a few friends. She beckoned him to come over. "Hello Willy, where are you off to today?" she said. "Morning, ladies. I am on my way to buy some new pairs of shoes. I was wondering if you know of a good place where I can get a bargain." He asked.

Jesse found himself with a bag of coins strapped onto his back and speaking very strange. "I have the perfect spot! Jean Ann exclaimed as she showed him her new shoes. "I only paid one coin for each of these." "That is quite a bargain," Willy told her. He asked if she bought them from Peter's shoe store. This store has been around for a long time, and has a nice collection and great service. "They do have good shoes there, but they always cost one and a half coins for each shoe, even when there is a sale," Jean Ann replied. "You should go to Bargain Ben's. He sells his shoes at a much cheaper price, but he has a no return policy.

Now, Jesse had a decision to make. Which store should he go to? He decided to try Bargain Ben's. It sounded like the best place to save some money. He arrived there and saw plenty of shoes on sale. Willy looked around for good boots like Jean Ann had said, they were at one coin a piece. He calculated how much it would cost. He has two hundred legs, so that means he needs 200 coins. Wow, Jesse thought, these are really good boots, but if I buy them, I won't have any money left!

Bargain Ben's did not have 200 boots of the same color, but Jesse did not mind. His boots had nothing to do with him accomplishing his mission after all, so he chose different colored discount shoes. He went on his merry way, sporting an assortment of rainbow colors on his feet. He happily strutted them in full confidence that he had completed his mission. Or so he thought.

On his way home Willy passed by Jean-Ann's friend Kevin, who was surprised to see so many different colored shoes. He did not want to hurt Hugo's feelings, so he gently told him, "I like your boots, but perhaps they would look better if you would wear pairs with the same colors. Maybe two red shoes in front, then blue on the next pair?"

Jesse agreed and switched his boots. Kevin decided to walk with Willy, talking constantly as they moved. Jesse was growing impatient with the banter. I just want to get this over with, he thought. He scuttled faster, but Kevin was agile and kept the pace. On their way they passed Jean Ann and Elisabeth, who also began talking and following him. The nonstop talk made Jesse edgy. He hurried down the sidewalk, not paying attention to where he was going. He turned a corner, glanced back at his friends, then turned back around. He was horrified to see a huge shoe, up in the air, over his body, closing in till all went dark.

Willy was a green pile of gue!

CHAPTER 8

The Agony of Defeat

In an instant, Jesse woke up, feeling dull pain all over his body. He looked down at his feet, then touched his face and chest to check if he was still alive.

"Man, that hurt!" he moaned in disappointed, "I failed another mission! Why can't I get anything right?" He gazed at the ring, awaiting its explanation. Instead, the ring started to laugh, much to Jesse's embarrassment.

"Did you see that goo all over the sidewalk? Hilarious!"

"Stop it." Jesse shouted, but the ring continued snickering. Irritated, Jesse took the ring off and stuck it in his pocket. Still, laughter could be heard echoing from his pocket. After the laughter stopped, The Stone spoke "Jesse, you failed in your mission to protect Willy. A Wonder must protect all creatures.

Tell me, what did you learn from this test?" Jesse pondered. "Maybe I need to be more aware of my surroundings?"

"Yes, that's good. But what else?"

"How about the fact that a centipede's feet stink! Or that each of its feet has a different shoe size! Do you know how long it took me to get the right shoe size for each of those feet?

I mean, come on. What does a centipede even need shoes for? And did you see the way those birds were looking at me - like a buffet. And why did I have to experience pooping as a centipede?

That felt very strange and weird."

The ring stayed silent, as Jesse rambles on, compelling him to re-examine his brief life as a centipede. Finally, The Stone suggest, "Perhaps, the answer is in the question. Or could it be that the question is the answer?"

Berry had stayed in her room last night as Jesse once again was tested. That morning when Berry woke up, she was complaining and pouting at the breakfast table of not having any of the dreams she wanted. She leaned over and asked Jesse's ring to let her come back to the real dream world. "I couldn't get back to my dream, maybe I can only dream of my friends while in your bed, Jesse?" Berry said depressed. She continued telling her mother of her nightmares and asked if she could please sleep in Jesse's room the next time she has awful dreams?

"Okay sweetie, sure you can sleep with your brother, when you have those bad dreams," Mom announced. "Oh, thank you mom." "Your surly welcome."

Berry leaned towards Jesse, whispering towards the ring in Jesse's pocket "Okay, okay!" Berry told the ring, "Thanks"

and went about her eating. "What did the ring tell you Berry?" Jesse asked.

"The ring told me that I have all the information I need to stay in the dream world. Just have to be near you and I can go to other worlds again." "I don't understand how you know this stuff, when the ring hasn't even told me?"

Berry looked down whispering under her breath, "I have my ways." "Well, I am not sure that is a good idea Berry," Jesse explains, "These are not exactly dreams in the normal sense." Berry shouted, "Mom, Jesse said I couldn't sleep in his room, when I have nightmares and you just said I could?" "I didn't mean it like that sis!"

"Well, I am going to tell Mom how mean you are to me! Imagine forcing a little girl to cry alone in bed over a bad dream or you could allow me to go with you on your adventure?" "Sense when did you get so devious little sister? Fine! I guess I don't have much of a choice." Berry walked out the door, skipping with excitement, even though she knew it was a dream, she knew they were dreams like no others she had ever had.

After a day of chores, playing video games, speaking with Emma on the phone and getting ready for another night of training Jesse decided to shut his window to keep the noise down. Then he had a long conversation with the Wonder Stone.

The Stone speaks with Jesse, "Look into your mind, look deep and see the warrior body I have chosen for you to become?" "That's just great," Jesse mumbled, "You made me to be a squirrel, then a Centipede, so don't get mad, if I am a little skeptical and nervous about your choices for me as a warrior, in which I have yet to become."

"No, you will not have to be a squirrel anymore."

"Thank heaven, okay then, can I be about nine feet tall with a big club? NO, wait, an ax, yea a battle ax, that's a cool weapon. Maybe like in the game I play, Warcraft that would be so cool."

"Maybe someday," The Stone spoke, "but not yet, behold," as a picture form on the wall. Jesse, looking confused and says, "Wait, I don't see him, is he behind those bluebirds? Surly not a bluebird?" "Alas, this is your chosen warrior body!"

"Really, that is the warrior? You're going to put me into a bluebird's body?" Jesse turned his head, staring strangely at the idea of being a bluebird. "Wait," Jesse asked, "Is that the same Blue bird family I had in my first test?" "Laughing" The Stone said "That wasn't actually your first test. It was more of a test for the Bluebirds. But I rather enjoyed the whole show." "Are you laughing at me?" Jesse asked. "Sorry" The Stone spoke, "It's just, I haven't had such a good laugh for almost a century." "I see." Jesse told the ring. "So, for a non-human being, you seem to have quite the comical personality?"

"Oh, come on, you must admit that squirrel ride was hilarious."

"Just fabulous, my powers comes with a comedian? A dimensional practical joker is my tutor and he says no worries. When I enter these realms can I actually die in that reality too?"

"No!" The Stone said, "Not in the bird realm, you should just wake up as in the Centipede test. So, you should be fine, at least I have not witnessed any one dying in a test. Of course, there was that one time." "Wait, what one time?" Jesse shouted nervously, "So I could actually die?"

"Well, he didn't as you say die, just became a little deformed, sort of."

Jesse looked at the ground and told the ring, "I do not think I am ready for this. Are you still laughing at me?"

"Maybe a little. Not to worry, new Warrior of Wonder, even Merlin had the same concerns. He was one of my best Wonder warriors, second only to King Solomon, himself."

"So, you also knew King Solomon, I bet you have some stories to tell, what about before Solomon?"

"There was no me before then. I was created by the astral beings who once ruled this realm, before King Solomon. From his request to be a wiser king, my power was created in the realm we call numbered two, a place within the Multirealms, a place that transcends between time and reality, hidden between all conscious thought! Does that help you understand?"

"Oh Sure, Thanks for clearing that up for me, I would never have guessed that."

"HAHA!" The Stone spoke, "Was that a joke, I just heard?" "Maybe," Jesse mumbled. "Good one," replied The Stone, "There may be hope for you yet."

"And the squirrel chase was kind of funny, now that I think about it."

"Oh, it was hilarious, would you like to do it again?"

"Very funny, I am starting to see why King Solomon was so smart, he had to keep one eye on you and watch out for everything else."

"Good, young warrior, having humor will help control

your fear. There is a lot more in these tests than the character chosen, so very much more, than just a story of a little blue bird. This is your journey, the journey of the Wonder, soon to be warrior. The Stones chosen Emissary to fight for the balance between light and the realm of darkness throughout all the Multirealms. Your first major training mission is that of a powerful warrior."

"However, no warrior known to man has ever been tested, as you will be Jesse."

You will enter into this journey and into this twisted reality of unusual characters, in which you must overcome the obstacles set before you. As in all realms, you must find, control and remove the evil and restore that realm."

"Wow, great speech" Jesse said sarcastically. "But I am still just a little bluebird here? I could still be squished like the centipede or eaten by, well most anything?"

"Are you afraid Jesse?" "DUH!"

The Stone thought for a moment and stated, "Have courage. Courage is not the absence of the fear within, it is merely the conquest of it. Nothing you encounter in this test will bring as much fear as the fear you impose upon yourself by the thought of entering into the unknown. Remember this, nothing is ever easy when it is important and all things are difficult before they get easier. The real power comes from within you.

It is the kindness which emanates from the heart, not something which a person can learn or acquire, it is something a person is born with.

Those who have it, will also see that in you Jesse, like a bright glowing light."

"I'll glow of it you say?"

"Yes indeed! Now in this test, you will need to hatch out of an egg, so you and this bird will learn to become one. This will be needed for you to learn, study and secure your hold on this realm, to save it from the darkness which has invaded it. Even if you know things, this bird will not and it is this tiny bird you must nurture and help grow. You must make lasting friends within this realm and learn all you can about this reality for this is just one of the many realms in which you will be assigned to protect."

"So, this is more than just a test?"

"Oh yes, everything concerning the Wonder, is never just a test!" There is no reality or test, in which you will travel too that is not as real as this one realm you know."

"So, you have a reason why I am to be a weak little, half sized bluebird in this reality?"

"Yes, the weakest must overcome and defeat the greatest of all evil!"

"Defeat all evil, I see, but that doesn't really make me feel any more confident."

"Now, if you are not yet ready for the big test then maybe another practice test first?" The Stone replied. "Maybe, it couldn't hurt?" replied Jesse. "That's fine." said The Stone.

"I have the perfect test in mind, but know this as fact, this realm is a world of rhymes and of deep thinking. You will not remember that you are a human in the test."

"All you will know is that you are this bug!"

"Really! Very funny," Jesse replied. "A bug world of rhymes I am to endure, and my mission is to find this thing, which I know not know for sure."

"That is correct," The Stone replied with a laugh. "Why am I rhyming already, I must say, this is petty?"

"Just getting you into the part which you must strive, to complete the mission and try to survive."

"This sounds a little crazy to me, but so does fighting Kumba unprepared. If this helps my ability to endure this fight, then on with the test to help give me incite."

"Tonight, it will begin, your strangest test yet."

To complete your mission, all the rhyming is set."

Eagerly awaiting his third test Jesse rolled over closed his eyes and began to fall asleep.

Think like a Bug Test

Once upon a summer's night a young firefly was born and came to life. He watched the skies and he became aware of all the wonderful creatures who roamed the air. There were birds that sang throughout the night with beautiful music giving much delight. There were many bugs who flew in the air and many more who couldn't go there. Also, many creatures were around, that could not fly and lived on the ground.

The young firefly had a name and it was Paul, he liked watching it all. He asked his mother to explain each creature, so mother did and described each feature. The birds could fly and most would sing, with lovely sounds and other things. They all lived together in the night which makes the world a glorious site.

"What about me, what kind of creature am I to be?"

"Well," she held Paul close and then said, "that we are just like our parents, you and me. We are bugs that soar up in flight, lighting up the dark places during the night.

That is the reason we must be sly and understand what is meant to be a Firefly."

Paul watched the sky and he could see many fireflies just the same as he. So up Paul flew into the air to shine really bright so all could stare at his light, but his light he couldn't share, because his light wasn't there. Paul became scared and did take warning, but the night was dark, many hours before morning. Paul came back down and told his mother; he had no light like all the others. He asked his mom where he might go, to find his light which had been stole.

Then she told him of a very smart bug, who was really quite old and to go there and ask for his help to see just how smart this bug could be. Paul flew and flew and there he found, this bug sitting and meditating upon a mound. With incense and candles burning many other bugs were also there learning. Paul came and sat in the circle then asked the smart one if he knew it to be right, as to where Paul could go to find his lost light.

"Lost your light the bug said winking and your here for a serious answer I am thinking? Is that correct, is that what you say and your wish is for me to show you the way?"

"Yes, oh smart one, if you know, won't you tell? The place in which my light fell?"

"What if I told you the answers you seek, are laying so plainly right at your feet, and what if I told you very sincerely and kind, that your light's not lost and that you are just blind?"

Paul shook his head and said "That can't be true and is this the best that you can do?" The bug did think for quite a long while and then turned to Paul and said with a smile. "I could tell you the answer and its simple my friend, but it seems obvious that I would simply offend. Then you would not believe me, so you would not mend or help you on your journey and it would not end.

So, to find the answer to seek your light there is only one way that would seem right. You must wait awhile till the end of the night and only then should you take flight. Over the waters and under the moon, this is where the answer will soon, reveal to you the one you must meet, who holds the answers in which you seek."

"How will I know him?" Paul did exclaim, "With so many bugs there, what is his name?"

"Knowing these answers will help very little, all I can do is tell you a riddle. So please listen closely and don't make a frown. This bug is different and flies upside down.

Don't look way up high, or anywhere around, not any place where other bugs are found. Just keep your eyes focused on what is below and as soon as you find him the answers should flow. Who stole your light, only this bug will know?

So, all the next day, Paul waited and waited and waited for night, for the sun to go down and the moon to take flight. Waited till the moon rose high and shown so bright. Then Paul started searching as he was told, flying around so brave and so bold. Remembering what the smart bug said, to find the right path is to be led, how to look and where to seek to find the one, who he must meet. He flew across the waters and looked all around. Then found the bug to which he was bound. Who could fly very quietly not making a sound and he would do all this upside down.

Paul shouted loudly down at the thief, seeing his light shining brightly beneath. To return the light the bug was holding, the light in which was so boldly stolen. "Give it back," Paul shouted down there, but the bug kept on flying to Paul's despair, as if this bug really didn't care. When the water had all passed Paul flew on over the grass. The one he followed had disappear, he couldn't find him far or near. Paul flew back near the water's edge and rested on a little hedge, which hung out over the reflecting lake, then Paul did realize his mistake.

It wasn't till he saw his reflection that he understood the smart one's objection, for me to seek and unfold, the things in which the smart bug told. To seek the answers and to unfold, the truth that my light was not stole. Believing it was the only plan in which Paul could see and understand. For down below him he could see another bug just like he looking up and shinning bright, he finally realized the smart bug was right. That his light wasn't stolen or even gone, he had his light all along. Now that the test was over Paul had found to pay attention and not be bound by false intention, for what we think and what we see, then to make judgments needlessly.

CHAPTER 10

Twilight Melodies

Jesse woke up that morning and The Stone said, "Congratulations Jesse. You passed your first test, to listen to those around you to achieve and complete the mission. Using only the brain of this bug was the purpose, and you did a Wonder- full job." Jesse had learned the lesson and he was so happy to get out of that Rhyming realm.

"That's cute," Jesse replied, "Thanks but why do I feel there was another reason why, you gave me this test?"

"Oh, I see, you have found me out. This test, while only using a fraction of your brain, had given the rest of your brain a time to rest. You do feel good this morning, correct?" "Yes, I feel great." "Then the adventure worked."

Jesse went down for breakfast feeling more confident about his new role and his training to being the emissary. Berry walked up to him looking very mad and hit him on his shoulder. "What was that for?" Jesse asked. Mom saw what happened, she also stopped and waited saying, "Yes Berry why did you hit your brother?"

Berry told them, "I went to sleep last night and wanted to visit my friends, so I climbed into Jesse's bed and when I went to sleep, guess what happened? I became some bug and my butt flashed all night like one of those Tow Trucks or some crossroad's caution light." This just made mom laugh. Berry says, "I'm glad you're all enjoying my misery!"

Mom laughed so hard she hurt then managed to the spit the words out, "tell me your dream again, please! Then Berry continued speaking, "Then everything I said rhymed! Like some stupid poem, it was TERRIBLE, just terrible. Every time I hollered out for Jesse, I would shout JESSE, then after that, I would say, "YOU'RE THE BEST-TY!" I couldn't speak without rhyming. What in the world is that all about? All I wanted was to visit my friends?" Mom stopped laughing for a sec asking her, "Now, how is that your brother's fault, if it was your dream?" "He knows!" Berry replied. Jesse just shrugged his shoulders with his hands in the air as if he didn't understand what she was speaking of, but of course he did.

"Enough, please, I don't care right now. I can't laugh any more, wait and let me catch my breath." Mom cackled. So, we all just set there quietly for a moment but only for a moment. Mom had to step outside for some air, she was still laughing so hard. Berry took Jesse's hand, whispering to the ring, "you said, if I was close to my brother I could see my friends again, it's in the book! So, you told me a story then. Shame on you!" Jesse held his hands over the ring, afraid it might say some remark in front of his mother as Jesse knew how opinionated the ring could be.

He then whispered in his sisters' ears, "What do you mean, it's in the book?" "Oh, nothing." his sister replied. Jesse snapped back, "Just remember, if mom finds out about all this, then I don't have to let you in my dreams, Is that clear?"

"Alright!" Berry said, holding her lips tight, shaking her face at Jesse in a childish manner, "But I better not miss anything else!"

Mom came back in the house and sat back down telling Berry, "Your dreams are not your brother's fault, now enough of this, lets please just have a nice peaceful breakfast."

Mom was still holding her chest, soar from all the laughing. As mom finally caught her breath, she gave out a big sigh of relief. Berry has always hated a quiet table, so after a few minutes she learns over and all that could be heard was a high pitch noise, "PoooOOT-T-tOOoozezeuuuooop-pip! ("Okay, maybe I missed an O or two, maybe even a T, you try spelling out a toot?") The sound did come from her general direction, so of course it was assumed! Laughter had returned heavily to the table and attacked us all. Jesse hurt with laughter, his only thoughts were, how much I love my family.

Mom announced, "I asked my sister to come over for dinner tonight, I invited Emma also." Jesse's lit up saying, "Okay Mom, that should be fun, can I help you with dinner?" "No thanks, Berry wants to help."

Dinner wasn't yet ready when they arrived. Jesse took Emma into his bed room and found out she was really good at playing Warcraft. She asked him if the ring stills speaks with him. Jesse held the ring up and it said, "Good day Emma. Jesse did well on his test." Jesse covered his hand over the ring as Emma asked, "What Test?" Before he could explain Mom shouted, "Come eat!" It was an enjoyable dinner. Afterwards Jesse brought Emma out to sit on the front porch, listening to the birds and crickets. Emma said, "Isn't that a wonderful sound, the country at night time?" "Yes, it is," Jesse answered, "You want to hear something else?" As she said yes, he placed his arm around her and told her to listen. "Listen to what?" she pressed. Jesse with a calming voice said, "Just listen." A swirl of soft wind blew Emma's hair back, her eyes lit up. Emma could no longer hear crickets and birds. She could only hear voices speaking and music playing. "I don't understand?" replied Emma. "That's singing and music you are hearing, I hear this every night," Jesse continued, "The ring allows me to hear strange sounds in the night, like this music, not sure yet where it comes from. Just by touching me you are able to hear it also." They held each other, listening to the music for a while, "That's amazing!" Emma told him, "So romantic, thank you for letting me hear it too. I haven't heard that song for a while." Jesse stood up holding out his hand and asked Emma, "Would you care to dance?" She blushed and said, "I'd love to."

She stood up and they danced to a slow song, coming from somewhere deep within the woods. They held each other close had a wonderful moment with a very romantic long slow soft kiss, their hearts beating as one in the pale lit moonlight.

Aunt Jane opened the screen door and stepped out, "Oh, excuse me." Catching them kissing, and turning her head

away. Then asking Emma if she was having a good time and that it was near time to leave. Jesse started turning a little red. Berry was watching out the window and shouted, "They're not ready yet Aunt Jane, they were KISSING!" Emma then blushed a little too, while Jesse stood in front of the window blocking Berry from seeing out. Mom and Aunt Jane giggled remembering their time of young love and romance.

Emma kissed Jesse on the cheek and he watched as they drove away. "You-hoo!" Berry giggled, making kissing noises at Jesse. Mom called out, "That's enough Berry, get ready for bed and leave your brother alone." Jesse decided to get ready for bed as well. Reminiscing the soft kiss and feeling good about his relationship with Emma.

CHAPTER 11

Trials of Wonder

As Jesse lay there in bed still thinking of Emma. The Stone spoke, "Are you ready for your test?" "Oh yes" Jesse answered, in a love sick voice.

"Good then, listen carefully, as an image appeared before them. This bird will be your warrior body for this realm. You must master this body and grow with it. This will take weeks within this realm maybe even months."

"I cannot stay in here for months, my mother would have a fit if I just disappeared like that!"

"Weeks in this realm are but hours out here, time runs different in each realm. Also, you must not use your human name and you must never tell any creature who you actually are and to use the name given to you."

"I see," Jesse nodded, "Please continue then." "Now Jesse your adventure will start." "You mean apparently, me and my sister's adventure will begin."

"Ha-ha, unless you want to get beat up every morning, I suppose so?

"Now let's begin!" Announced the Stone with a smirk.

Jesse found himself in a bird nest high up in a tree, freshly out from his opened egg. His younger bird brother

stuck his head out of a cracked egg shell. He was perky and silly, and oh so fat! "Berry, Berry, Berry," was heard from the newly hatched egg. Funnily, he reminded Mrs. Blue of a big blueberry anyway. Berry, you say? Okay then Berry it is, sounds like a good name, she thought. "Wait, is this Berry? My sister Berry?" She must have slip into my bed last night and why am I an extra tiny girl bluebird?" Jesse asked. The Stone replied "Females are the weaker of the two sexes, and you are a runt of a bluebird, only half the size of a regular bluebird. That is where your test begins, a bird half the normal size with the spirit of an eagle." "Well then," Jesse remarked, "What can I say?"

The days went by quickly. Every time Mrs. Blue brought in food Berry would step all over Blue on purpose in a haste to eat. "Now Berry, that is not the way to eat your food!" she reprimanded. "Mom, tell us a story," Berry pleaded. "How about the story of the chosen one?" "The chosen one?" Blue asked.

"Yes. The story goes: During a time of trouble, worry, and danger, when darkness covers the land and monsters hunt and seek the innocent, a mighty warrior will be born. The hero will rise to free the land and bring peace. He will know the future by his dreams and will have a mighty stature."

Jesse asked the ring, "Is this why I had to be born here? To fulfill a prophecy?"

"Well, it is part of why you must accomplish your mission, Jesse."

"But the story says, mighty! How can a tiny bluebird, ever be that mighty warrior?"

"I am not allowed to say. You must find your own way through many trials and learn this for yourself. Plus, I never said you would be the hero of any prophecy," The Stone teased, "Now, shall we continue the test?"

"That's me! I will be the hero!" Berry enthused. "Maybe it's me," Blue retorted, "It's me, Right, mom?" "Of course, dear. It is said that the hero will come when the time is dire. He will be as big as a tree and as blue as the sky. That's enough story time for now. I have to get us some food. You two behave." Berry laughed when Mrs. Blue left,

"As big as a tree - well, that leaves you out." "No, it doesn't!" Blue shouted. Let's fight it out then, 'mighty' warrior."

They would play whenever Mrs. Blue was out hunting for food. Berry chased Blue around the nest, sometimes pretending to be a bowling ball knocking Blue over. Berry jumped on Blue causing her to bounce up in the air and out the opening of the tree, falling down to the ground into a pile of leaves. Berry laughed, but soon wondered why his sister had not come back up yet. He peeked out of the hole, "Blue? Where did you go? Blue!"

Hearing the faint echo of her brother's voice, Blue blinked her tiny eyes. "Come back! Let's play!" Berry exclaimed. She looked up and saw how far she had fallen. It seemed like a long way back to her nest, which for this tiny bird, extended far up into the clouds. Well, this is a fine situation, Jesse thought. What would a bird do? So, Jesse climbed into the full story and started calling out loud, as his bird self, for her new mother. A faint voice whispered, "I wouldn't be hollering so loud. A snake might hear you."

She looked around but no one was in sight. Just then, a June bug walked close by. With her bird instinct she grabbed the bug in her beak, ready to swallow it when it pleaded, "Wait, do not eat me! I came over to try and help you." Puzzled, Blue quickly spat the bug out, "You can talk?!" "Of course, I can," the tiny bug said, as he wiped Blue's spit off. Blue apologized, "I'm sorry for grabbing you like that. It was like a reflex or something." "That's okay. I haven't spoken to a bluebird before, but you seem nice. My mom calls me Scooter. She says I move around so fast she can never keep up with me," the tiny bug explained, fidgeting with his hands behind his back.

"I like your name, Scooter." "Thanks! What's your name?" "I am called Jes…, I mean Blue."

"Nice to meet you, Blue," Scooter giggled, "You know, my mom says most little birds that fall from their nest usually get eaten up by a snake or a hawk. You should stay hidden in those leaves, and stop making so much noise." "Thank you," Blue said, then pointed to a long line of bugs marching forward, "Where are they all going?" "My mom says that every summer we bugs make the trip to Bug City because (Scooter mockingly mimicking his mother), it is a safe place for us to live, and Mom won't have to watch me every minute."

A few of the bugs came over: There was Bella the caterpillar, who was very sweet and nice, Cowboy Cracker, the trail boss, with his cowboy hat and handlebar mustache, and Sin-say Sam, a praying mantis that spent his time in a monastery. Believing himself to be a karate master, Sin-say Sam sprang when he saw Blue and did his karate chops, ready to fight. "Hold it right there, Sin-say Sam," Scooter explained, "Blue is my new friend and she doesn't want to eat you." "Well, lucky for you bird - or I might have whooped up on you," Sin- say Sam said, chopping and hacking a blade of grass nearby.

The Lighting bug brothers - Pip, Pet, Peep, Pat, Pot, Pill, Poo, and George - and their bossy sister, Piper also came by. During the night, the siblings scout ahead for any signs of danger and help light the path, when the six-foot long caravan moves in the dark. Large beetles carried stuff, as camels do in Egypt, guided by a trail boss who had made the trip several times in the past. Wagon trail, he called it. Like a cowboy in a Wild West movie, he rides on top of a beetle, cracking his whip while exclaiming, "Yee- haw! Keep moving!" Cowboy Corncob Cracker, or "Cracker", as everyone calls him. "Get back in line! Or face being left behind," he would yell out. He would often boast that he can break and ride any bug anytime, dead or alive. Jesse thought about how Cracker reminded him of Grandpa.

The group talked and talked and quickly became friends. Suddenly, a strange noise emerged from the woods. "We have to go Blue," Scooter muttered, "Stay safe and hidden." The scared little bugs hurried to their places in the caravan. "Bye," everyone whispered as they disappeared into the bush. Blue was left frightened and confused. "What could that noise be?" she wondered hiding in the underbrush. She glanced to where the bugs hid and saw that they were long gone. She felt all alone, at the mercy of whatever creature or monster that may be coming from where the sound came. If Scooter was right about the snakes she would have to stay put until her mother returns home.

Jesse didn't think getting eaten by a snake would improve his chances of completing his test, so he would take no chances. The noise continued, but did not seem to be getting any closer. Blue was becoming impatient. She hopped along, trying to stay hidden as she worked her way through the bushes. In front of her was a sandpit as wide as the caravan and half as deep. In it was a pigeon, squirming and cooing as it tried to get out. "Please help me!" It called out! Blue remembered all the stories about the birds in the woods that her mother told her. "Are you a carrier pigeon?" she asked. "Why do you ask?" The pigeon answered. "Well, isn't that a message tied to your leg?" Blue pointed. The pigeon looked at his foot and exclaimed, "Oh, golly, yes! That's right! I am a carrier pigeon and this is a very important message for the Great Horn. Whoever that is?" "Who are you?" Blue inquired further, "And aren't you afraid of the snake around the woods?" The pigeon panicked. "Snakes! Where is it? Where's the snake?" "Relax. No snakes here that I can see." Blue reassured him. "I'm scared of snakes," replied the pigeon.

"Now, who are you and why are you down in that ditch?"

"My name is Willy, Other pigeons call me Which Way Willy, because I never know which way to go when delivering my messages, and I always get lost."

The pigeon pouted and went sullen.

"They also call me names like dumb bird and make fun of me. But one day, I will deliver a message successfully, and then the other pigeons will like me."

"Oh, that's not nice. But it is nice to meet you, Willy. My name is Jesse, oh I mean Blue."

"Nice to meet yah. Now, little bird, do you know where I can find the Great Horn?"

"I'm sorry, but I do not know who or where this Great Horn is. Can you tell me what happened and why you are down inside that hole?"

"I took off with my message and was being followed by three red birds, when out of nowhere a big hawk began to attack me. Luckily, I escaped and landed here, but ended up in this hole by mistake! And now I cannot get out. Can you help me, Blue?" Blue told the pigeon, "I fell out of my nest, too, and cannot get back up either.

Maybe we can help each other out?" Willy nodded. "What exactly is keeping you stuck in this hole?" Blue asked while examining the pit.

"After I landed here, I tried several times to walk up to the sides, but I kept slipping back down to the bottom. I have been stuck here all morning, trying to get out."

"I see," Blue said. "Are you injured?" "No, I don't think so," checking his wings for damage. Blue was puzzled, "Then why don't you just fly out of the hole, Willy?"

"I can try!" Willy began looking around the hole and squinted his eyes. So, he flapped his right wing, and then his left, to make sure they work. Then with all his might he flapped them together and shot up out of the hole easily and onto the ground next to Blue.

"Thank you! Thank you! Thank you! I would have never thought of that!" Willy busted into laughter. "I suppose I need to go and deliver this message now, so goodbye!" "Wait!" Blue cried out, "Did you forget to help me?" "Oh, yeah. I forgot," Willy snickered,

"Now, hop on my back and I will carry you back up to your nest." In no time, the two reached the top of the tree where Berry was waiting and said their goodbyes.

Willy flew off, and likely went the-wrong-way-as-always.

Realm of Giants

Jesse woke up the next morning thinking of the strange test. While lying in bed his sister ran into his room and jumped on his bed. "Stop," Jesse whined. Berry still bouncing on the mattress laughed.

"Must keep jumping till you fall out of bed - just like you did in my dream." "What, same as in your dream?" "That's right." "You couldn't possibly be in the same dream." "You know better than that, Jesse. Now come on, Grandpa is waiting for you."

While toiling together at the farm Grandpa shared with Jesse an old Indian legend of the giants. In the story, a tribe of giants lived and hunted around this area, many, many hundreds of years ago.

Although these giants ranged in height from seven foot to ten foot, they came from another place. A place where a hole opened up between their world and ours, only large enough for the smallest of giants to squeeze through. After they came into this realm, the hole closed behind them and these giants were stuck here, until they can reopen the portal back to the giant's realm.

These giants terrorized the Indian tribes, attacking their villages and taking away the people. Devastated, the Indians sought help and called to the Great Spirit. Large granite boulders, weighing several tones were brought from a quarry which is over one hundred miles from these ruins. These red- haired giants formed the stones in a circle and a large opening in the sky formed. Out of this portal, one massive giant stepped through the portal, his face horribly disfigured, he growled saying, with a thunderous voice.

"We are back in the realm of man, let's hunt I am hungry!"

The giants separated across the land to find enough food to fill their bellies. One day the Indians heard something dark and ugly coming through the forest, uprooting trees and throwing them in the air. Everyone in the village ran for cover, hoping the giant, whose appetite was unquenchable, would not spot and eat them. The women hid in the lodge, they watched as the giant stuck in his enormous finger into the door of the lodge trying to collect the people. Tearing off the roof, the giant reached in and picked up the young women, swallowing them whole.

This infuriated the men as they watched the giant swallowing their people whole and then after destroying the village they watched as the giant disappeared into the storm. One of the warriors decided to fight the giant. Most were scared and didn't know how to defeat the massive being, but eight of the warriors followed, determined to free their women and somehow defeat the giant.

They followed the giant for days and planned a trap, digging a deep hole into the Earth, while one warrior taunted the giant, so he would give chase. For many miles the warrior named Cloud ran from the huge giant, the ground shaking behind him, his heart pounding.

The warriors could hear the giant coming, his smell traveled ahead and when the wind was just right, a horrible stench would have you hold tight to your nose. Cloud moved across the trap, EE-AA fast behind, he barely made it across the trap as the branches cracked under EE-AA's massive weight. Falling into a crevasse, trapping the giant, his snarling yellow teeth bared as his shouts filled the air like cannon fire. The warriors quickly filling in the hole, smothering the giant. Afterwards they cut open the huge belly, crawled in and found the women and girls he had consumed barely alive.

The tribe rejoiced after hearing of EE-AA's death, but this wasn't the end of the story. For after finding out about the murder of EE-AA, the other giants sought vengeance. They went to attack the village, but the tribe had moved, so the giant's searched, destroying any tribe they could find and feasting on their flesh. Soon the giants found the tribe inside a cave, which was too small for the larger giants to come in. A voice thundering loud shouted, for the men responsible for the death of their leader.

Cloud stood near the entrance and shouted, "We killed EE- AA and he is the largest of your kind, do you not believe we can kill you too." Becoming quite furious at the way Cloud spoke to them, they sounded an attack. The smaller giants came in and fought with the warriors, holding them back from coming inside, while the larger ones were digging the cave entrance wider, so they might reach and eat the tribe.

On this day the tribe's prayers were answered. From up in the sky a great storm came, a huge circle of clouds was roaring across the plains, lightening flashing as the winds blasted the ground so hard, even the giants held their heads away. Suddenly a swarm of Thunderbirds swooped out from the dark storm clouds, fiercely attacking the giants, with no way of fighting the huge birds and soon after tiring, they had no choice but to run away to escape the thunderbirds' wrath.

The ground shook and trembled, with every step some of the immense giants took, fleeing from the attacking birds.

The Thunderbirds spit fire balls, as they blast the giants, setting fire to the hair of many. They ran as fast as they could for these same ruins, which took the big giants three days to arrive and activated them, somehow. A giant hole formed in the sky over the ruins, where the larger giants jumped through to escape their onslaught of the fire spitting Thunderbirds. Once the larger giants made their way into the portal opening, one Thunderbird let her egg fly and land on the ruins, where a mighty blast broke the circle, leaving the stones on their sides. The Thunderbirds flew back into the heavy storm clouds and soon disappeared over the mountain tops.

The remaining smaller giants could not run as fast and it took them two weeks to arrive at these ruins, just to find them destroyed. Some years past and the story of these red-haired giants was told by another tribe. Telling how they cornered the giants in a cave, set a fire at the entrance and smothered the carnivorous beings.

"Wait a minute, the thunderbirds shot fire and dropped an egg bomb, really? "So, I am to believe there are real giants?" Jesse speaking softly to the stone, "Is any of this possibly true, or do you even know?" "These ruins have a great amount of energy and there is information on this on your internet, about Mud Fossils. This realm of giants does exist, which is the realm 607, which you have jurisdiction over, so in my opinion the story could be true."

"These very ruins you are standing was where it all happened. The Indians even marked this spot," explained Grandpa,

"These Thunderbirds have since been a good omen. "Have you ever seen one?" Jesse inquired. "I wish" Grandpa sighed. "No, I suppose it is just an old Indian legend."

A strange flickering of light, could be seen outside the front window as the family sat for an after-dinner movie.

Flames started to burst out on the front lawn. "Is that a fire?" Mom said, quite frightened. Grandpa and Jesse ran outside and saw Harry, Kurly, and Moe running away from the house. "Grab the hose!" Grandpa yelled.

A large, ashen pentagram, with four voodoo doll-shaped figures in the middle revealed itself after the fire was put out. "It's a curse!" The Stone yelled out, "He has placed a curse on this house and your family!" "Shush," Jesse mumbled, covering the ring with his hand so as not to frighten his mother even more.

"What could become of Kumba's curse?" he whispered. "Could be a lot of things, but nothing good I assure you," The Stone replied, "But since we do not know the incantation he used, all we can do is wait." "I am getting tired of all this waiting," Jesse exclaimed, "And what about my sister? How did she know the circumstances of these test?"

"She does seem extremely knowledgeable. She knows anyone who sleeps close to you will enter your dreams and the reality of the realm, you travel into."

"Can she get hurt in these different dream states, since she is not a Wonder?"

"This is a first for me, Lord Asher, the Wonder before you, always slept alone when he wore the ring for this very reason. Same with Merlin."

"You mean I am destined to sleep alone for the rest of my life?" "There are some things the Wonder must endure. You will understand this better in time."

"But I have this girl that I like very much."

"Jesse, there are thousands of realms in the Universe, each with warriors, but you were chosen as the only emissary. Your powers, once mastered, will make you invincible. But understand this: when magic is used, you become vulnerable. You can be killed. Kumba knows this all too well, and that makes him your most dangerous enemy. It is important that you learn all this while figuring out how to protect your loved ones."

"I see. So much to learn and understand." "Yes, this is why your training must continue!"

Jesse was just beginning to understand the extent of his power. He laid in bed that night listening to the music and spoken words from outside his window. He could hear the insects talking. He rose from bed, looked out the window, and cried out, "Shut up!" Everything became very quiet. "So," Jesse smirked, "they do understand me." Jesse closed the window, smiling triumphantly, and went to sleep to embark on another test, continuing his mission. Jesse inquired to the ring, "What is my purpose here in this realm, what am I supposed to do?"

"You must let this bird teach her new world, along with you. Remember nobody can know that you're a human, or the evil you are sent to find, will find you first, before you are ready. So, keep that secret for now and keep learning as a bird!"

The Hidden City

The day finally came when Berry and Blue were old enough to fly. Their mother decided to take them out for their first flying lessons. It was tough at first for the young birds, but their mother kept watch flying under them and pushing her head against their bellies to assist. Blue took to flying quite easily. This is fun, Blue thought.

A little stouter than Blue, it took a while for Berry to get the hang of it. Blue laughed as Mrs. Blue tried to hold Berry up, his big belly covering mother's entire head. She could not even see where they were heading.

Mother yelled out, "Keep flapping your wings, Berry!" but Berry did not hear a word as he let out a loud laugh. He stopped flapping his wings momentarily, to hear what his mother had said, this became too heavy for his mother to hold both their weight. The two hit the ground sending Mrs. Blue into a dizzying spin! Berry bounced and landed on his feet. "That was fun! Let's do it again?" Berry elated. After some practice Berry's flight became stable. "Now you two are finally ready for your trip to the park," Mother happily said.

The three settled on a tree branch where they enjoyed a sweeping view of the area. There was so much to explore and see from lush spaces to animals. "What's that over there and that over there?" Blue enthusiastically inquired. Their mother shared about pets loitering in the park, such as cats and dogs, and warned them to stay away for safety. "Humans sometimes throw bread crumbs for us to eat too," she said. Jesse mumbled under his breath, "I already know this stuff. Why do I need to listen to it?" The Stone replied, "Yes, Jesse the human does, but Blue the bird needs to learn it too. That is how you become one with your animal self. It's part of the test."

"Quick! Duck down!" Mother exclaimed as a flock of birds swooshed over their heads. "Who are those birds?" Blue asked. "Those are the red-winged blackbirds who live down by the airport. They taught themselves how to fly fast by watching the humans in their Jets doing tricks over where they live," Mrs. Blue shared. While Jesse knew the answer, he knew he must still play his part and ask, "Is this how humans fly?" Mother chuckled. "Only when they get inside one of those jets. Humans can't fly like us Blue. Now, go ahead you two. Fly around and explore, but be very careful."

"Mom," Berry getting frightened. "That cat is looking at me and licking his lips."

"It's okay, son. He is on a leash. Just stay away from it and you should be fine."

Berry was so heavy that he could barely get around, so he simply looked around to chat up other bluebirds in the park. Blue wanted to see the elusive Bug City that her friends had told her about. Just then she saw a bug crawling under a Holly bush, and she quickly flew down to investigate. The bushes were thick with thorny leaves wrapped in razor-sharp blackberry vines making it difficult for Blue to ease her way in. She came out into a small clearing in the middle of the bushes - and there it was Bug City!

"Wow, Jesse thought, "Seeing this city through this bird's eyes, is remarkable. Houses made of bottles and cartons stood everywhere. Ants marched along guarding the edges of the city while dragonflies patrolled the skies. Bugs, big and small, ran and played games with their families. It was like a human city but smaller. There were roaches who wore marching band uniforms and played joyful music as a crowd of bugs gathered to listen and dance. The scenery was not starkly different from the big park, except humans did not have an intoxicated Cowboy sitting inside an old beer bottle belting out songs from his good old Western days.

Blue hopped out into the clearing and made her way toward the middle. She startled all the bugs. "It's a bird! Run for your lives!" someone cried out. Everyone panicked and started screaming. They ran under any can or carton they could find. Within seconds all bugs vanished from sight. "Well, I guess that makes sense," Jesse sighed. Piper and her brothers flew over to investigate. After exchanging pleasantries, the siblings gave Blue a tour of the city before resuming her patrolling duties.

Bug City is full of surprises, Blue thought - and indeed it was. From under a leaf came Bella the Caterpillar who was chewing on yummy leaves. 'Hello, Bella. It's nice to see you

again. Would you happen to know where Scooter is?" Blue inquired. "Over that way, near the hotel. That's where I last saw him," said Bella as she was gulping down leaves. Blue flew across the opening to where Bella had pointed and found Scooter. "Oh my!" Scooter gasped, "Don't come swooping in like that, you'll scare all the bugs to death, quick come over here!" Scooter grabbed the head off a dead bug from a pile of trash then stuck it on to Blue's beak, "There. Now you look just like the rest of us. Just remember not to chirp." Grabbing Blue's wing he led her to the Puddle House Restaurant. A lady bug approached their table, "I am Bubbles, and I will be your waitress for today. What would you like to eat?"

"Give us two house specials and hold the hot sauce," Scooter told Bubbles while rubbing his belly and licking his lips. Bubbles yelled out to the cook, a grimy roach at the kitchen who spat brown juice from his mouth as he scratched his bottom "Two sugar cubes, dry, no sauce!" Blue thought about how pleasant Bug City was as she nibbled on her sugar cube.

On stage a group of can-can performers, the Chirp-ET, danced to a lively tune performed by a band of bugs. "This is the same music I keep hearing out my window every night," Jesse mumbled. "What did you say?" Scooter asked.

"Nothing. This is a nice song."

After their performance the lead dancer, Seniority Chirp, walked toward their table, and stared hard and long at Blue, "Buggy, is that you?" Both Blue and Scooter were stunned.

"I thought you died last week when that baby stroller ran over you?"

Bubbles also came closer and studied Blue's disguise, "That's right. He looks just like Buggy!" Panicked, Scooter intervened so as not to expose Blue, "This is actually his twin brother Pudgy." Señorita Chirp was puzzled, "I thought Buggy was an only child?"

Just then Cowboy Cracker strolled bowlegged over to the band and requested his favorite tune before approaching Blue and Scooter's table. "Good day, gents!" His tone and demeanor once again reminded Jesse of Grandpa. He then turned to Señorita Chirp, "How lucky am I? Of all of the Bug joints in all the world, you've walked into mine!" He then held out his hand, "Beautiful lady, would you care to dance?"

Blue bid her newfound friends goodbye as the song ended and went on her way back to the park. At the edge of the bushes, she was surprised to see the Cardinal Brothers - Moe, Harry, and Kurly - keeping watch as red birds. As in the human realm Moe was the biggest of the three, and was cruel and bossy. For some reason all three looked identical to those rapping gangsters Jesse had so much trouble with. Only difference is that Harry had a dark spot on his right wing and Kurly had a dark spot on his left wing.

"Hey, you, bluebird," Moe motioned to her, "How did you get into the city?" "Can't tell you," Blue replied. "What did you say? Tell us how or else!"

"No! I will not show you the way!"

Moe turned to his brothers and said, "You hear that, brothers? This bird wants all of the bugs for herself. Don't you think that is very selfish of her?" The other two, who were not very bright, looked at each other and nodded. Harry said, "That is indeed so selfish don't you think Kurly?" "Yes, that is selfish." Kurly looked at Moe and repeated the same words. Exasperated Moe said, "Shut up you imbeciles. You are not even smart enough to have bird brains." The two looked at Moe and said at the same time, "Why thank you brother." Moe just shook his head in disbelief. Harry examined Blue, "She isn't wearing our colors and is talking bad about us." "What do you mean? I didn't say anything about you," Blue remarked.

The three surrounded Blue, pushing her around from all sides, "Not so tough now, are you?" Blue was terrified as Jesse tried to calm the bird. She cried out for her mother. They kept pushing her, so hard that her neck stretched and that her eyes bulged as they squeezed and pecked on her head. "We can finally play whack-a-mole," Kurly joked as all of them left out evil laughs. Jesse thought of how similar they were to the three gangsters in town and wondered why things here in this realm seemed to perfectly match reality.

Blue's mother heard Blue's cries and raced to the scene. In Mom!" Berry cheered. Moe cackled while shouting, "So this bluebird is your child, Mrs. Blue? Where's that so-called commander husband of yours?" Kurly and Harry seconded, "Yeah where's that husband of yours?" "Oh, he's missing, isn't he? Maybe he got tired of you Mrs. Blue, or better yet, got eaten?" Moe jeered as all three continued laughing. Mrs. Blue did not answer, but glared at them with fiery eyes as she held the siblings' wings.

"Blue, Berry! It is time to go home."

The three kept taunting the family in the background. This made Mrs. Blue furious, "You want to fight some more?" "As if you can," Moe mocked, not believing Mrs. Blue could hurt them. Suddenly, a blue streak struck them from the back like a rocket shooting upwards. They did not know what happened, all they can see are two terrifying eyes coming straight at them!

Red feathers flew everywhere scaring away the red birds. "As they flew away, Kurly shouted -What's scarier than a monster?" "What?" Harry quizzed. "A Mom-ster!" "We will see you again little Bluuuebird!" chirped Moe.

They took off in a flash accidentally hitting the red wing squadron.

"Wow! You really scared the bird poop out of them Mom," Berry clapped. Blue felt proud of how brave her mother was that day as they cuddled in their nest. Berry looked up and said, "Did you see how quickly they flew away Mom? It was so funny!" Mom chuckled. "It was a little funny, wasn't it?" All three burst into laughter, so much that their bellies began to hurt. Blue turned serious, "Mom, why are some birds and animals so mean and cruel?"

"I used to wonder the same thing, Blue. But that's the reality, and what's important is we remind ourselves not to be like them."

"I want to make the world a good place to live in and make the bad birds behave. How can I do that mom?"

"Your father wanted the same thing. We need hope and courage."

"Mom that red bird called Dad 'commander'. What does that mean?"

"It is his rank, dear."

"Willy said his message was from the commander. Did he mean Dad?"

"I am not sure but we need to check that out. For now, you two need to sleep."

Mrs. Blue kissed them goodnight. As the night turned, Blue cannot help but have this feeling that change is coming, and that he is the one holding the keys.

CHAPTER 14

Zombie at the Door

Jesse woke with an earthy taste in his mouth, as if he had been eating worms all night. "Gag, Yuck! Why do I still taste, what the bird ate?" "Good" The Stone announced, "You are becoming one with the bird, this is good."

"So, the taste is a good thing you say?" "Indeed, it is!" Laughed the stone.

As he walked down the stairs, he could hear his sister telling Mom of her dream, "Here is something that came from my dream last night. I used to be addicted to Hokey Pokey, but I turned myself around.

Oh, and Kurly said he was going to eat the circus clown, but was afraid it might taste a little funny." Grandpa chuckled. Mom asked, "You remember this all from your dreams? And who's Kurly?" "Yes Mom. Kurly's one of the red birds, and they are more than dreams. I can prove it to you." "Oh really? How so?" Mom said.

"Tomorrow I will eat breakfast as my bird self.

"Well, that would be interesting," Mom told her, "Tomorrow you say? In that case what would you, as a bird, like for breakfast?" "Pancakes will be fine," Berry told her. Jesse spoke, "Berry, you need to stay away from those red birds. They are bad news."

"So, you know about your sister's dreams?"

Jesse quickly grasped for answers, "She talks in her sleep Mom." Jesse leaned over and told his sister, "Berry, you shouldn't sleep with me anymore. You might get hurt, so stay out of my room." "No!" Berry protested, "You keep me away from my friends, and I will tell mom about the man who is after you! Plus, a whole lot more!"

"So that's how you want to do this, huh? Blackmail?" "Please, Jesse! I have to go back. I will be good," she pleaded with big sad eyes and pouty lips. "Fine," Jesse relented, "but you do as I say, stay with the mother bird and keep away from any danger, okay?"

"Deal!" Berry agreed with glee.

At the Emporium Emma, Jesse, and Aunt Jane were straightening up the shop when suddenly some familiar faces showed up. "Look!" Emma pointed to the glass window. Kumba stood outside the shop while talking to Harry, Kurly, and Moe. "They're up to something, I can feel it," Emma said, "How do they always know where you are Jesse? Can he track your ring?" Aunt Jane took a hard look at the four. "Just where did that man come from anyway? I really don't like him one bit." "I know the feeling," Jesse agreed. "Look! His driver is getting out of the car. That is a big fella!" Emma remarked. "He doesn't look so good either. How come he still has that same shirt on with the tire marks across it?" Aunt Jane shared.

Kumba handed Shiver a can of paint as all of them marched forward. "Something isn't right. Lock the door," Aunt Jane told Emma. Shiver kept turning the shop's door knob, standing still and emotionless as swarms of flies surrounded him. "What do you want?!" Jesse shouted through the locked door. Shiver raised the can toward Jesse, grunted and simply kept tugging at the knob. "I'm going to call the police!" Aunt Jane shouted.

Jesse asked his aunt, "For doing what exactly? Standing at your front door?"

"No, not for that," Aunt Jane pointed down the street where Kumba had built a small fire while holding up his hands and chanting words. Shiver then began moving in robotic trance, painting symbols on the door and across the front window. When the police arrived, Shiver stood frozen outside the shop paint brush in hand. The windows were filled with strange words which seemed like a curse.

They tried to speak with Shiver, but all they got were grunts. "Come with us, sir," one of the officers ordered. He tried to pull his hand behind for handcuffs, but they were stiff as wood. "Raise your hands!" Sheriff Piper shouted. At once Shiver obeyed her direct command, and raised his hands in the air.

They then handcuffed him and ordered him to get in the car. He turned, walked over to the police car and got in. The two officers quickly closed the door behind him holding their noses, "What an awful smell!"

Kumba and the three gangsters were nowhere in sight, but Sheriff Piper reassured Aunt Jane, "We will find out more about him when we run his fingerprints. Don't worry. If you see that black limo, give us a call." Jesse and Emma talked among themselves, "He must have a connection to your ring," Emma suggested. "Maybe I need to stay away from you Emma. From this place. I don't want to see you or Aunt Jane get hurt," Jesse lamented. "Never. I'm a part of this now, have you forgotten?" She walked around the counter and snuggled with Jesse, "Do you really want to stay away from me? Wouldn't you miss me?" Jesse smiled and gave Emma a quick peck, "Not that I want to stay away." Emma held a finger over Jesse's lips. They stared deeply into each other's eyes, and without saying a word understood that they were in this together.

Jesse thought he was imagining things when he arrived home. He took a second glance, and saw the limo parked not far away from their house hidden among trees. He felt as though Kumba was watching him the entire time. "Is it because of the ring that Kumba always knows exactly where I am?" Jesse asked the ring.

"What if I left the ring here when I go out?"

"It's possible, but is it really worth all the risk over a girl?"

"For this girl? Yes. Also, maybe you are the wrong person to give me advice on relationships. You know, since you never had one at all?" Jesse kidded.

"Maybe you're right, but I still know of the dangers that come with the job of being the emissary," The Stone added,

"How sure are you that your family will be safe here with the ring, if Kumba comes here for it?"

"But what is safe? Here I have to worry about being safe from Kumba. Out there in the bug realms there are also dangers. There is nowhere, which is safe for any of us, if you think about it and why do these birds in the bird realm have some of the same names as the humans?" "Ah a very good question." The Stone continues. "Some realms coexist and are together but separate.

You can see these birds in the human realm, but cannot understand them. This is the same for the birds from their perspective, looking in on our realm. If both realms were fully connected, then this world would seem more like a Roger Rabbit cartoon. Since it is only partially connected, then humans and birds can be similar to some people in both these realms."

"Similar?" Jesse said, "They are almost identical to their human counterparts." "You will find Jesse, there are similarities and connections no matter which realm you visit, once you become aware and understand?"

Jesse laughed and said, "No I don't understand, but let's save that for another time."

CHAPTER 15

A Little Shiver of Doom

That night Jesse found himself back in the bird realm. He was starting to feel like he had more control there than he did in real life. "Where are we going today, Mom?" Blue asked. "After all that trouble yesterday, I can't believe you're this excited to be out there again," Mom replied, "Maybe we should just stay home today." Blue and Berry complained, "Why? Anyone who heard about you fighting those brothers would think twice about messing with us Mom." Blue shared, "Can we at least go to the airport to watch the planes fly?

My friend Scooter told me we should go, because he heard the humans are putting on a grand air show with their jets and planes." "Alright. We can go if your brother can fly that far," Mrs. Blue agreed before turning to Berry, "Honestly, son, you need to stop eating so much or you won't be able to lift a single feather off the ground." "Mom, why do you have to be so mean? I'm just big-boned." Berry replied.

The sound of a big plane flying overhead was so painfully loud that the little bluebirds felt frightened. Berry lost his balance from the jitters and fell on the ground. "I'm okay!" he shouted. The family watched as planes and jets, all in fascinating formation, came and left. Gliders pulled by other

planes floated on the air like eagles. Blue mimicked the planes as she practiced and dove from the skies. She was so focused on her flying that she did not notice A Red Wing squadron swoosh by. Thud! Blue was knocked to the ground. The Red Wing blackbird leader rushed to her side with the rest of the team following suit, "Are you okay?" "Yes. Who are you?" Blue asked. "My name is Captain Striker. These boys are called the Red Wing fighter squadron. We are training to become lightning fast like these jets above us." Mrs. Blue and Berry came over immediately.

"Is this your daughter, Mrs. Blue? I am so sorry. It was an accident. I did not see your little one. Sometimes it's hard for us to slow down."

"That's alright. You're not hurt are you Blue?" Mrs. Blue asked. Blue shook her head no. "We are sorry to hear about your husband missing. He is our friend and he's is our commander," Captain Striker apologized before turning to Blue, "Now little one you have to be more careful when flying, okay?" He continued, "Mrs. Blue we would be honored to have the commander's kids train with us, if they wish? We meet here every Tuesday and Thursday." This got Blue extremely excited, "Can I? Can I, Mom?" "Well, I guess there's no better flier to teach you and Berry how to fly than the Captain himself," Mrs. Blue replied. All of a sudden, a blackbird shouted the alarm, "Shiver is coming! Up there!" "Get into formation," the Captain ordered the squadron and quickly took off. Shiver pretended not to see the birds on the ground, and thought he would slip around them and come in from behind. "Come children. We must go now," Mrs. Blue said as she gathered the two. Shiver spotted the family rather quickly. "How tasty! A nice bluebird snack," he murmured. Shiver circled around and positioned himself where they could not see him. As soon as he saw an opportunity to strike shiver dove in for an attack.

Down he came as fast and hard as a heavy rain. Blue looked up and saw the evil hawk coming straight for them. She spread her wings to push Berry and Mom to one side just in time as Shiver glided past the family. Missing only by an inch he yelled, "I will get you, just you wait!"

He came back around for another attack chasing the family past the trees. He inched closer and closer, and even grabbed a tail feather from Berry! "Berry, watch out!" Blue warned, "Move faster!" Berry's heart pounded as he alternated running and flying. Just as Shiver opened his mouth to grab him Berry let out a huge poop. It hit Shiver right in his mouth stopping his attack. What an awful smell and taste Shiver thought as he halted to spit it out. Blue saw a big rock behind some bushes and had an idea, "Hey, Shiver!" Blue yelled, "Here I am your big meanie! Come and get me." Mrs. Blue felt fear in a way she never did before as she looked back and saw Blue taunting Shiver. She immediately flew up, coming behind Shiver as he dove for Blue.

"There you are!" Shiver exclaimed, "You can't get away from me now!" Like a bullet he shot straight for the tiny bluebird his evil eyes glaring. Blue stood very still pretending to scratch the ground and fluff her feathers. She was terrified, but she held her ground and waited. Closer and closer Shiver came with his enormous claws dangling in front of him and dark scary eyes darting through the air. Blue stuck her tongue out at him enraging Shiver. Mrs.

Blue tried to catch up to the evil hawk, but he was too speedy. Then just as Shiver was about to grab the little bird, Blue quickly flew straight into the bush then off to the side. Bam! Shiver was too big and too fast to make a full stop and hit the rock hard.

Mrs. Blue, who was right behind Shiver, smashed against his back. Shiver felt it and quickly looked behind. Seeing her on the ground he reached out to grab her with his enormous claws. Suddenly Captain Striker flew down right in the middle of Shiver's enclosing claws, like a surfer passing through a wave tunnel, and swept Mrs. Blue out of Shiver's clutches. Shiver let out an angry grunt as the bluebirds flew away with the Red Wing squadron back to safety. "This is not the end!" he shouted, "Trying to make a fool out of me, like your husband huh? You and your little family will be lunch one day along with anyone who helps you. Just like your husband's friends."

Mrs. Blue was so scared that she forbids the children from going out. For Jesse this was a waste of time. He should be out there learning and completing his mission.

"Mom," she asked, "how does Captain Striker know dad?" Mrs. Blue placed her wing around her, "Your father was a member of that Red Wing squadron. He was their commander."

"Do you remember that pigeon I told you about, Willy, and the message he was carrying that was from the commander? Do you think it was from Dad?"

Mom held Blue tighter. "I don't know. Maybe we could speak with Captain Striker about it tomorrow and see what he knows about this.

CHAPTER 16

Bluebird for Breakfast

Jesse woke up that morning complaining to the ring, trying to stay quiet not to wake his sister, "Is my sister really safe in this test?" "She will be when you learn how to control your Dimensional Power, like I said; once you learn how to control it you will achieve apprentice status, and become the Emissary of the Wonder stone and gain its full power." Jesse felt pressured knowing his sister is still in danger until he masters his DP. He went down for breakfast to find a bluebird on the table. Berry had flown into the house and onto the pancakes her mom made! Mom and Grandpa watched, completely stunned, as the fat bird stood on the plate eating pancakes just as Berry told them she would.

"I have never seen anything like this in my whole life," Grandpa said. Jesse waved his hands in the air, "Shoo bird! Fly away!" Mom raised her hand to stop him, "Don't scare the little bird, Jesse!" "That's right!" the bluebird shouted, "Stop scaring me!" Mom and Grandpa looked at each other in amazement. "That sounds like Berry doesn't it? I must be hearing things?" Mom said. Jesse jumped over to the table startling the bird. As it fell back it accidentally knocked over a glass of orange juice. The bird quickly drank it up until the bird was full then rolled over on the table showing its belly. Jesse quickly ran up to Berry's room and woke her up.

"Why did you wake me up? I was having the best pancakes!" "You're currently at the breakfast table as a bird, and Mom will never understand all this! You need to send your bird-self back to the bird nest before we get caught."

Berry seemed unbothered. She walked downstairs into the kitchen stretching and yawning, "Thanks for the pancakes." Mom looked confused as Berry motioned to the bird, "Come on other Berry." The bluebird flew up to her shoulder "See you later Berry," she said as she released it at the front porch.

Grandpa and Mom sat motionless at the kitchen table with their mouths open unsure of what had just transpired. You could hear a pin drop. Mom asked, "What is going on? Did you just call that bird Berry?"

"Remember, Mom I promised I would come as my bluebird self."

Jesse nudged his sister and mumbled, "Stop this. You're freaking them out!" "Fine!" Berry muttered as she sat down for breakfast, "Sorry about spilling the orange juice, Mom." Jesse rolled his eyes. Mom looked puzzled as she had already cleaned the mess before Berry came down.

"How did you know orange juice had been spilled?"

"Oh, I did that when I was the bluebird, remember? I told you yesterday I would fly in and have breakfast as a bird. Cool huh?"

Both Mom and Grandpa sat in disbelief. Berry leaned to one side letting out a fart. Everyone at the table looked at

each other and then back at Berry. Jesse grinned, "Quite the regular toot factory aren't cha?" Everyone giggled, and for a moment the strange situation at breakfast was forgotten. After breakfast, Grandpa noticed a package sitting on the front porch. He brought it inside the house saying, "There is no writing on this. No sender or anything." The Stone whispered, "Don't let them open it!" Jesse immediately covered the ring with his hand. "Who said that?" Mom asked. "I did," Jesse replied. Mom became suspicious, "And why not open it?" Not knowing what to say he shrugged his shoulders while Grandpa opened the box.

A horrible stench filled the air, and out from the package came flies. "My word!" Grandpa exclaimed, horrified to find a dead chicken inside. He rushed outside to throw away the carcass. "Who and why would anyone send us a dead chicken?" Mom said, panicked. Jesse rushed to his room. "Now, what was that about?" he said to the ring.

"That's voodoo magic. Opening the box inside the house has placed a curse on everyone."

"Darn!" Jesse shouted, "How many curses is that man going to place on us?"

"We must train Jesse, before things get worse." "How can things get worse than this?"

"Oh, they can, and they will get much worse, before it gets better!"

"Is there anything we can do to stop the curses?"

The ring gave Jesse specific chants for every corner of the house and around the barn. "This will create a barrier that will offer some protection. Then we can also cast a little curse of our own." Interesting Jesse thought, "What do you have in mind?" After a long day of setting protection spells throughout the house Jesse felt as if a load had been lifted with the spells in place. As he went to bed, he knew any further curse Kumba place will now be reversed and placed upon him.

CHAPTER 17

Blue's Clue

Mrs. Blue called out to Berry and Blue for a freshly caught worm breakfast. It was a lovely day with the morning sun peeking through leaves and into their nest. Blue inquired about the city and begged her mother for a look-see. "Why the interest in the city?" Mom asked.

"Well, you remember my pigeon friend Willy, Mom? He said he lived with other pigeons in the city in a big bird cage next to a place called 'zoo'."

"Yes, I know where that place is. I have been there before."

"Can we go there and check on Willy? Maybe ask him about that message?"

Mom agreed, "After meeting Willy we can visit the zoo." On their way to the city, they glided above the bushes around Bug City.

Mom agreed, "After meeting Willy we can visit the zoo." On their way to the city, they glided above the bushes around Bug City. Blue can see the three mean red birds in a tree nearby still searching for a way in. It was not long before tall buildings came into view with cars, houses, and people everywhere. Mrs. Blue explained how humans lived and worked in these buildings. As they flew closer to the zoo Mrs.

Blue pointed to a large pigeon cage, "That is probably where your friend Willy lives." They landed on a nearby ledge where several pigeons perched. "Do you know where Willy is?" Blue asked. The pigeons laughed. "You mean Which Way Willy?" one said. Another jested, "No good Willy?" A third one was more helpful, though brash, "Try over there in the corner. That is where he usually hides. Stupid Willy is afraid they might give him another message to deliver, and he might make a fool of himself again. So, he hides."

Blue found Willy sulking in a dark corner under a pigeon coop. He smiled as the family approached and greeted him "We're going to the zoo Willy. Would you like to come?" Blue continued, "By any chance did you deliver that message to the Great Horn?" "Not really. See, it's still tied to my foot," Willy said pointing to the scroll attached to his leg.

"I can take the message for you. Also, what did the commander look like?"

"Oh, he is a bluebird like you."

Blue felt a hint of hope. Somehow, he felt that the sender of the message was her father. She unfurled the message only to find unexplainable text written on it. "This doesn't make any sense."

"Oh, that's because it's written in code, so the enemy would not be able to read it. At least that was what I was told," Willy explained. Now I just need to find somebody to decode this message Blue thought.

Willy and the bluebirds enjoyed admiring the many animals from all over the world in the zoo. In one corner was a bird cage that towered as high as a low-rise building and housed several scary-looking birds. Mrs. Blue explained about the differences in how birds feed, "Vultures eat carcasses while golden eagles and hawks eat live animals and birds." Willy pointed to a hawk.

"That looks like the one that attacked me, only that is a girl and much smaller."

"Where is her mate?" Blue inquired. "Oh, she is alone now. The big male got sick last spring and died," Willy told her. "She looks so sad doesn't she Mom?" said Blue. "Yes dear. I know just how she feels," Mrs. Blue said pensively, "If it had not been for my two beautiful babies I would probably be as sad as her." "Come, I'll show you other good places to visit." Willy said quickly, trying to change the subject.

Willy took them to the town square where people threw breadcrumbs for birds and nuts for squirrels to eat. This delighted Berry who would eat till his belly couldn't hold any more.

Other pigeons gave Willy the dirty look and avoided him like a plague.

"Sorry Willy," Blue empathized, "They shouldn't treat you this way." Trying to break up the sad mood she said, "Hey what time is it when people throw breadcrumbs at you?" "What?" Willy asked. "It's time to duck your head of course," Blue answered. The two friends chuckled.

"This is really good bread Willy. Thank you for taking us here. "Of course, Blue, you are my new friend."

A young squirrel walked up behind Berry and bumped

him with his tail. "Watch it fur brain!" Berry yelled, but the squirrel went on to bump Berry again. "Get lost," Berry snarled. The squirrel kept bumping him. Not having it Berry jumped on the rodent, landing its back and holding tightly. The squirrel, much bigger than Berry, started running around going under park benches and around the water fountain. Berry held on tight to the fur on its back as it ran up a tree. Berry fell off the ground laughing, "What a ride!" He called the squirrel to return to play, but the squirrel stayed up the tree making a loud chatter. This seems all too familiar Blue thought as she sat down to watch. For Jesse it felt like déjà vu thinking Unbelievable! This is like watching a rerun of my first test, except this time I'm not the squirrel.

Willy also took the family to the market where ice cream vendors sell cones, and the church tower where they enjoyed the view of the entire city and planes taking off from the airport. All was beautiful and calm until a loud screech broke the peace.

"That's the one that attacked me!" Willy uttered shivering from fright, "Stay hidden." "He sure is big," Blue whispered.

"Children, we need to return to the nest as soon as that hawk is gone. Whoever he is he seems to be very angry, and we can't have him chasing us again like he did before."

CHAPTER 18

Mean Spell, Meaner Machines

Jesse woke to screams and the sound of loud machinery. Out on the lawn the tractor seemed to be chasing grandpa around the farm, transformed with front metal teeth chomping as it ran. "What's happening?" Jesse asked the ring, "Is it another spell?" "Yes, indeed," The Stone said, "Wait for it, the counter spell we placed over the farm should kick in any minute now." "Call Emma and see if Kumba is close by," The Stone advised.

Kumba had indeed performed a ritual that morning as Harry, Kurly, and Moe watched. "What's he doing fellas?" Kurly asked. "He's casting another spell on Jesse. Something about making their farm equipment come alive." Harry commented. "Wish he would make my old car come alive. It hasn't run for two years now," Kurly mumbled. Moe shook his head, "It doesn't work like that, Kurly." "Oh, so you know how it works?" Kurly responded. "Shut up!" Kumba yelled, "The spell is complete!" Jesse watched as the tractor chased his grandpa out through the corn field, fast on his trail. Suddenly a big wind blew over the farm, and within

seconds the tractor's motor shut down reverting to a normal toothless tractor. Grandpa heaved a sigh of relief.

Suddenly a heavy wind blew over the town. The limo had started by itself, and is now chasing those three gangsters and Kumba up and down the street." Emma told Jesse over the phone, "An unusual car chase was unfolding outside the emporium. "The limo's grill has transformed into teeth and kept chomping as it zoomed towards them. Like a shark after a meal! It's so weird here Jesse!" Soon the police arrived at the scene. As Harry, Kurly, and Moe were trying to dodge the car's constant attacks, the officers tried to block the limo with their patrol cars, but it came straight at them as if to plow through them. Kumba hurried inside one of the shops and locked the door watching the police cars being smashed like in a demolition derby.

Harry, Kurly, and Moe climbed on top of a parked car as the limo turned its sights to them. "I've been in so many bad fights, but this is the first time I'm in a fight with a car!" Moe hollered. The car bobbed and shook as the limo rammed it. "Kurly, do something good for once and offer yourself as sacrifice to the beast, so it will stop." "Why me? Why can't Harry do it?" Kurly asked in a panic. "Well obviously because he's much smarter than you," Moe replied as the car slammed against the hood of the vehicle once again. "How funny. I'm smarter than you," Harry stated.

"Well okay then," Kurly jumped off the car and ran down the street with the limo in close pursuit. Almost striking Kurly as he jumped up quickly climbing a light pole. Moe shouted, "What are you doing Kurly, get down from there."

"No way! Didn't you see the teeth on that car? I am staying right up here."

The limo suddenly mellowed down, and using its headlight for eyes sped out of town with the police in pursuit. Back at the farm Jesse felt good to finally have struck a blow at this man, but Jesse's thought this will just make Kumba try harder.

"Jesse, you know what that means" The Stone warns him.

"Yes, I know, I must train harder." "Good. Let's train some more, shall we?"

Jesse smiled, "Of course, and "Yes, yes, I know," Jesse interrupted the ring.

"It is another gorgeous sunny day in the Bug world, right?" "Now you're starting to understand!"

Kumba was seething realizing his spell had been reversed. His eyes grew fiery with rage. His fists closed tight, as he shook it in the air "I will get you, you little wannabe Wonder! You and that dam ring!"

CHAPTER 19

A Stank at the Dump

That night as Jesse prepared to go into the bird realm, he was desperate to find answers to the message that Willy carried. It was the only clue to the bird's father's disappearance. He knew he must train faster and not wasting any time getting to the root of it all.

"Mom, can we visit the Blackbird squadron? Maybe they have a clue about the code." Mrs. Blue wore a worried look as she examined the dreary sky and the heavy fog that covered the ground.

"It's cloudy and dim today Blue, I don't think the squadron would be flying now."

Blue looked down and turned incredibly sad, which pained Mrs. Blue. Sighing she said, "Okay. We can go anywhere you want, except the airport." She feared that Shiver would be waiting for them at the airport, and the squadron would not be there to help them. "Where shall we go then Mom?"

"How about we check out that Junk yard near the grasslands and try to find some insect larvae?"

"Sounds yummy!" Berry exclaimed, "I'm starving!" Jesse thought; when was his sister not hungry? They took off from the nest and soon came to a large pile of discards with

bulldozers digging the soil. They hopped under and around and found plenty of food to eat! "Over here," Mrs. Blue beckoned. Berry raised his head up with a worm still in his beak, "I am going exploring Mom, if that's alright."

"Sure dear. Just stay close, and keep a close eye for Shiver."

Blue was sifting through piles when she heard movement in the rubbish. A bug with a tie and glasses emerged. "Well, hello there Miss Bluebird! Aren't you the most beautifully colored little bird!" he exclaimed. Blue inched toward the bug to shake his hand. "Now stop right there. If you are here to eat me, and you take one step closer that wire cage will fall upon you and trap you here." "Oh," Blue said, "I am not here to hurt anyone (in her mind she thought especially not an old dried-up bug as him!)

I eat berries and larvae and I have lots of bug friends. So, thanks, but no thanks." "Phew," the bug heaved a sigh of relief, "Well, in that case little bird let me fix that trap first so you don't get hurt." "Are you some kind of smart Bug?" Blue asked with a puzzled look, "And by the way, my name is Blue."

"It is a pleasure to meet you Blue. I am a harvest fly or a cicada. You can address me as Professor Harvard Fly. I was named after the school I attended in my younger days. As you can see by the red crown jewels on my head, I am a member of the Royal Order. I like to build and invent things."

"What kind of things?" "I'm glad you asked. Like this one over here."

The professor gestured Blue to follow him. He was happy to show off his inventions. Blue flew over excitedly to ask, "What is it, Professor?" "Chirp into the small end of that cone," the professor told her, motioning to a piece of plastic from an old kazoo. Blue positioned her beak into the hole. "Yes, that's right, into that small hole," the professor said, then held Blue back, "Wait! Remember what I said, chirp real softly." Blue looked at him strangely, then leaned over slowly to chirp softly. The sound came out booming at the other end so loudly that it made Blue jump! "Wow!" She exclaimed in excitement. "Now watch this," Professor Fly walked over to the small end and vibrated his sides to make a high-pitched sound. Blue held her wings over her ears as the vibration echoed as loud as the jets at the airport.

"Wait, what's that over there?" Blue asked as he pulled back a cloth sticking out of the debris. It was a jet airliner like the humans use, though this one was too small for humans. Professor Fly explained, "It is a small model airplane that I am currently working on. I'm repairing the missing tail. The wings are still good and make a nice shelter when it rains or when danger is nearby." Blue agreed, "It sure is roomy inside for you, but I am way too big to fit into that little door."

A large, scruffy cat jumped up onto a heap of trash spotting them, "Well, what do we have here? Who is your very tasty-looking friend, professor?" The professor motioned to Blue to ease her way toward a small drain pipe. "Morning Stank," he greeted nervously, "How can I be of service to you today?" Stank licked his paw staring at the two and acted like nothing was on his mind. But in his mind, he was thinking how nice a juicy bird would be after eating rats for such a long time.

"May I come a little closer?" Stank asked. "Oh," said the professor, still trying to discreetly instruct Blue to move toward the small pipe, "you already have the best view of the whole dump from up there." Stank stood up and stretched his back. Blue and Professor Fly were almost taken by surprise as he leaped to pounce on them nearly grabbing Blue. They dove right into the pipe while the junkyard cat was trying to reach his claws into the opening. "Why are you running from me? I just wanted to shake your hand to say hello," the cat meowed. "Stank, don't you remember the last time you came here and caused trouble and were trapped in a cage?" Professor Fly reminded him.

Stank jumped back a little and looked above his head for a possible trap. "That's right! If you don't leave, I will not let you out of the trap the next time I capture you.

Blue here is my friend and you better leave us alone, or I will pull this string in my hand and you will be trapped here forever," the quick-witted professor warned. Stank got nervous looking in all directions for a possible trap. "Fine!" he relented, "But the great king snake told me if a bluebird shows up here, I am to eat this bird and anyone who tries to help her." "Is that right?" Professor Fly asked, turning his head to Blue to see if she knew anything about was Stank was saying. "But I don't know any king snake," Blue replied, "Who is this king snake you speak of?" Stank replied, "I cannot tell you anything, or he would do something terrible to me!"

"Well would you rather be in one of my contraptions again for two days and have the rats poke you with sticks and make fun of you like that one time?"

Stank looked around for traps again and said, "I'm going to go. I have other things to do anyway," and took off quickly. Blue was astounded, "Wow! That cat would have eaten me and you scared him away! You weren't afraid one bit, were you professor? Professor Fly placed his arm around Blue's shoulders and told her, "It's not always about how big you are little one or how frightened you become. Sometimes it just takes a little wit to overcome your fear, and be able to fight back against a much larger or more powerful enemy."

"Thank you, Professor Fly. I will remember this!"

"Don't worry, Blue. If he comes back, I will catch him and make him talk then."

"Thanks Professor. Maybe he will have a clue as to what happened to my father."

Just then Mrs. Blue arrived, "Come Blue. I saw a cat over there, and I think it's time for us to leave now before he learns we are here!" "Okay Mom," Blue said, winking at Professor Fly as the wise bug winks back.

"Bye, Professor Fly! See you next time!"

Blue flew over to her mother ready to go home.

"Did you see your brother? We need to look for him."

"Berry, where are you?" the two hollered. From a distance Blue can see Stank digging hard into a heap full of garbage as if searching for something. She heard her brother calling for help in the same spot. "Over there! Mom!" Blue cried out.

The two tried to make Stank leave, but the cat simply dug faster determined to catch Berry. Mrs. Blue frantically flew over the cat's head and peck him. Meanwhile, Blue went back to the professor. He instructed Blue to grab the kazoo then climbed up on Blue's back to save Berry as quickly as possible.

"Here Mrs. Blue. Chirp as loud as you can into this tube," the professor told her. As they flew over the cat's head Mrs. Blue chirped as hard and as loud as she could. Her chirp was much louder than Blues, echoing throughout the air. This startled Stank causing him to jump ten feet off the ground. The frightened cat sped off to the woods nearby. A bulldozer dumped trash on top of the spot where Berry was still hiding. Berry continued crying for help underneath the mound. "Berry!" Mother yelled. Professor began shaking a small bell into the air. "What's that going to do Professor?" "You'll see."

Hundreds of rats came from all parts of the dump and gathered around the professor. "We have a situation here," the professor explained, "A bird was trapped by Stank, and we need your help to rescue him." "Anything for you, Professor," The rodents said as they began digging and scouring the garbage. Within a few minutes Berry was zipping out of the mound with hundreds of rats pushing him up like lava spouting out from a volcano. The scared bluebird was laid in front of the professor. Mrs. Blue Mom was ecstatic. She hugged every rat and gave the professor a peck on his little head. His face turned bright red.

CHAPTER 20

Dark Crow Magic!

Jesse woke up the next morning to a familiar awful smell coming from the sheets. "Oh, Berry! Not one of your farts again!"

He lifted the covers, trying to fan the smell away. Berry smiled and jumped over to give Jesse a big hug and began to thank him for not letting that cat eat her. Jesse hugged her back.

"You don't think I would let anything happen to you, you little fart machine?"

After breakfast Jesse went to his room to play his game unit, Berry walks by the door and ask Jesse, if he has seen her game boy. "No Berry, you didn't leave it in here." "What is a Game boy?" The ring asked. "It's like the game I am playing on TV, but compact." "Is that real life in that box, is it magic?" "No, this is a computer game, just for fun." "You do know what a computer is, right?"

"Of course, I know, I am a prime example of one, but I was unaware that humans had these things yet?" "If you have been dormant all these years, then that would be understandable. The computer can fill in all your missing time, like wars, government, life, if that is something you would be interested in?"

"So, humans have computers now, can you show me?"

"So there has been a war, during my absence?" The stone asked. "More than one," Jesse replied. "We have had two world wars, well a lot has happened, since your time away. Okay, look here at the computer screen, this is called the internet, you can look up anything."

Jesse set the ring down on some books, level with the screen. Jesse turned the pages as the stone watched. "Can you hook me up to this computer?" The stone inquires. "Not sure how to do this, can you receive frequency waves?" "If I feel these wave I can connect." "I have an idea." Jesse took the ring and headed to town.

On the way Jesse picked up Emma, to take her to lunch. "Aw fast food, so romantic, she jokes." "Laughing," Jesse says, "Sorry, I came here for the stone." "Just joking, whatever the stone needs?" They walked into the malt shop; Jesse asked the ring if he could connect to the free Wi-Fi. "Yes, but this might take a while." So, they ordered lunch and spoke while the ring was very silently downloading information.

While sitting there, Kurly walked in, handed the counter some money to pick up their take-out order. "Don't look now Jesse, I think they found us again." "No, it looks like he is picking up an order, probably doesn't even know we are here."

Kurly looked around and saw the two and walked over. "Well, he does now." Emma whispered.

"Well how are the love birds?" Kurly asked. "How can you act so normal and then try to torment us?" Emma shouted. "Nothing personal, it's just my job." "So is Kumba on his way?"

Jesse asked. "No, I'm not going to tell him, he is busy anyway, chanting over a bucket of simmering coal and chanting his voodoo stuff." "So how much is he paying you?" "Suppose to be enough for us to cut a record and become rap legends." "So, he hasn't paid you anything?" "Not so far, he hasn't." "So, you're working for this evil man and he isn't even paying you, sounds kind of like a bad deal." Kurly replies, "When you put it like that it does sound kind of bad, but it really isn't anything personal guys, it's just that we need the money for our record deal." "Nothing personal! Jesse and Emma said in unison. Just then the stone woke up from his downloading, saying "I am finished." "Good we can go then," Jesse remarked.

As they were walking out the stone remarks, "Much has happened sense the 19 century, I must say and this internet holds so much information."

"So, you have downloaded the whole internet?" Jesse asked. "Why is there another internet I have yet to see?" "No,"

Jesse replied, "We only have the one." "Good, then yes, I am up to date. Remarkable how many new things there are in the world now?" "Kurly heard the ring speak and just stood there and started, then as the two waved bye to Kurly, him not saying a word, as he watched the two love birds leave.

Kurly went back to the apartment and mentioned he saw the two at the malt shop. Kumba overheard and ordered the three young men to go after them. "They already left, not sure where they went." Kurly commented, then whispered to Harry, "Jesse has a talking ring and it downloaded the internet."

"Man are you insane?" Harry continued, "There is no such thing as a ring, which speaks." "I'm telling you there is!" Kurly fired back.

Jesse went home and there the Stone brought up a possible problem. "This internet holds amazing knowledge, we cannot let Kumba learn of it or find out about this, it could be very dangerous for you Jesse, if he does." "What do you have in mind?" Jesse asks. "We need a spell, which Kumba won't recognize."

"How about a spell where he won't see or hear anything about the internet?"

"Trouble is, if we placed a spell like that, he would see the images as foggy, which he would then recognize it as a spell, so by doing this, he may find the internet even faster than if we did nothing." "I see, so we take a chance on Kumba finding out about the internet, because we are trying to hide it from him?" The stone suggest, "We need a weakness of Kumba to place this spell upon." They thought for a while and Jesse spoke. "I see no weakness in the man, all I see when I look at the man, is his enormous ego, believing he knows everything."

There was silence for a moment, the stone spoke. "That's perfect!" The stone replies, we will hide the spell in the man's personality. Of course, this will magnify Kumba's temperament tenfold and he will believe he knows everything and reject any words containing internet."

Jesse asked, "So this will make Kumba meaner and more boastful, are you sure it is worth all this, just to keep him from maybe finding out about this one thing?"

"When I downloaded your internet, I found where many objects of magic are kept. If Kumba knows about these objects, he would disappear for a few months and collect these items, then return. There are two in this town alone and any one of them would increase and magnify Kumba's powers."

"Wow, okay, I'll give you that one. We will do it your way." Jesse agreed. So, the stone prepared the spell. Multiplying Kumba's ego, where he will listen to nobody. Jesse then said. "I guess we better prepare ourselves for more attacks, since we have made Kumba a madder than mad, madman, so to speak."

Meanwhile back at the gangster's apartment, Kumba shouts out firmly, "My spell is ready, we will send that boy and his entire family, a little invasion of crows to eat up the harvest." The gangsters stood still and then heard a commotion outside the window, they ran over and watched as thousands of birds were flying past their window, all heading for the Mason family farm.

What is all that racket outside?" Jesse noticed. Berry looked out the window.

"Look, Jesse! There are crows everywhere!"

The siblings quickly ran downstairs to see what the commotion was about. Jesse saw Mom and Grandpa chasing after the birds.

"These crows are eating up all my corn. I tried setting off fireworks to scare them away. Usually it gets rid of them, but they don't seem to be afraid of anything! I don't understand this!"

Jesse whispered to the ring, "Do you think Kumba is behind this?"

"Certainly, a form of revenge for us putting a spell on his car. Back in the nineteenth century New Orleans had a similar crow attack. I am pretty sure this is the same thing," The Stone continued, "It's said that Marie Laveau, once Kumba's master, knew how to channel crow energy. Do you see Kumba anywhere?" Kumba was nowhere to be found, but nearby, Jesse spotted the three gangsters behind some trees. The Stone rushes Jesse, "Quick! This is the perfect time to send our spell, since we can hide our spell, in Kumba's Crow spell. Raise me high and repeat these words."

"Celestial Magic, hear this call, reverse this spell back from whom it falls. Add a spell and do it in haste, hidden from the eyes of the person it is placed." Send it back to the one who spoke this curse and make his life, increasingly worse!"

"Now he will not listen to anyone's wisdom and believe everything told to him, will be a waste of his time.

As soon as Jesse said the words there was utter silence, as if everything existed in a vacuum; a bottle with the lid tightly sealed. Not even the wind blew. The crows swirled above and circled the farm, soon the crows took off heading straight for town.

The family watched in amazement as the three henchmen ran as fast as they could back to town as crows flew right behind pecking and clawing at them.

Jesse immediately called Emma to share what happened. She answers and shrieks "Jesse! Kumba is across the street with his hands raised chanting something, but crows are everywhere here in town, I never seen so many at once."

Kumba looked up and his eyes grew wide as the crows descended upon all of them. Kurly had a tennis racket and was swinging it into the air, Moe had a ball bat. Harry was just running away with many crows hard on his trail.

Kumba stared over at the store and could see Emma looking out. He stared at her with nothing but pure hatred in his eyes. She could see Kumba raise up his arms, then out from his hands a bright red blast of lighting, the crows all fell raining down on the roof tops and covering the streets with their dead bodies, as Kumba holds his stare at Emma and the Emporium.

"You should see this, Jesse; things are crazy over here and that man keeps looking over here like he wants to kill me!"

Jesse started getting worried about the spell they had placed, thinking Kumba could get much meaner and said, "Please be careful Emma, and let me know everything he does, if anything." Jesse instructs her over the phone.

The whole family picked up what was left of the corn from the crow invasion. Tired Jesse laid in bed listening to the music from the Bug Realm filling the air as it does every night. It was time to train in that world once again and he found himself getting excited at the possibilities as he shut his eyes.

CHAPTER 21

A Fishy Encounter

It was cloudy again with heavy fog covering the ground, Blue was eager as ever to visit the Blackbird squadron hoping to finally get some answers. Mrs. Blue did not agree, "I don't think the squadron would be flying in this weather Blue. Maybe I could take you both to Symphony Pond near the outskirts of Frog Bottom Bog."

"What's a bog?" Berry asked. "Isn't that one of those pet humans have with wagging tails? The ones they take to the park?" Berry inquired. Mrs. Blue laughed, "No, that's a dog sweetheart. A bog is a place that is always wet and with spongy soil with lots of grass and peat moss. Lots of creatures live in the bog like big toads, frogs, spiders, water bugs, mice, snakes, and mosquitoes. There are also large predators that you should watch out for like the Lynx, which is a type of wild cat. There are also birds there like the stork." "Wow that sounds like a wild place!" Berry exclaimed, "And is it safe Mom?" "Yes, as long as you do as I say. Can you do that Berry?" Mom asked. "Sure, as long as there is food there," Berry rubbed his belly, "I'm awful hungry." "Yall must be careful and watch for the big bass they call boss. From what I heard he eats small birds near the water's edge, so you need to pay attention where you are." Mom pleaded.

Symphony Pond is a mere ten-minute flight across the grasslands, where bats, coyotes, giant frogs, and other animals, all were ruled by a monstrous king snake named Kumba. This snake shows no mercy to anyone who enters his kingdom. Kumba, Jesse thought looking over at Berry, both with their eyes wide. Both wondering why the name Kumba was also in this realm? They landed near the pond where Mrs. Blue showed them how to stand very still and quickly catch tadpoles as they came to the shore. "These tadpoles are yummy!" Berry said with a big smile across his face. "Yes, they are!" Blue agreed, "Do I have to eat the water bugs Mom?" "Only if you want to Blue."

Berry noticed a tree nearby with a bunch of mosquitoes and flies, so he went to investigate. It was a sticky yellowish sap running down a tree with many bugs stuck in the mess. What a mother lode of bugs! Yummy! He thought. He grabbed a bug, and got his beak stuck in the sap. He pushed himself away from the tree to break free, and now he has sap and dead bugs all over his face! "Mom, help!" Berry cried out. "Oh, Berry! You look like a bugsicle!" Mrs. Blue giggled, "But don't worry. It's just tree sap. It will wear off. Let's get you cleaned up."

Berry and Mrs. Blue were so busy cleaning off the bugs that they didn't notice two small frogs moving closer to them. The frogs were eyeing the bug stuck to the sap on Berry's leg. One stuck its tongue out to collect the bug on Berry's leg. "Let go you bug-eyed toad!" Berry squealed. The frog tried to let go, but its tongue was stuck to the sap. Berry mumbled, "Fog, yet go of ma yeg!" The second frog snapped its tongue out to grab some bugs stuck to the sap on Berry's head. Berry was being pulled in two directions by the frogs! The frog jumped pulling his tongue in quickly and suddenly he had Berry's head inside his mouth. "Mom, help!"

Mrs. Blue came over and tried to pull the frog off of Berry's leg, while Berry pulled in the opposite direction. After a tug of war, the first frog finally broke free, and Mrs. Blue tossed it to the pond.

Berry came rolling down the ground with the other frog still stuck to his face. Mrs. Blue cannot help but laugh. "It's not funny, Mom. Stop laughing at me!" he demanded as she tugged and tugged. She resembled a mother taking off a child's shirt when the child is holding it tight. Mrs. Blue tried once more to rid Berry of the other frog. With one hard yank the frog popped off like a plunger after sucking at a drain.

Blue chuckled a little as she watched from a distance, but then she noticed something moving in the water and hopped on over to see what it was. The water swirled in ripples, and then as Blue got closer, she could see a strange silver creature swimming underneath the water. Then it disappeared! Blue inched closer and looked all over trying to locate it. Suddenly, like a flash of lightning the creature sprang up creating a fountain that soaked Blue all over. She shook the water off her feathers and looked fluffy. A thud sounded from the ground behind her.

"Mom," Blue called out, "Can you come over here. This fish is flopping on the ground?" Mom called back, "That is just a small fish dear. Nothing to be scared about. Not much bigger than you are dear." Blue walked closer staring as the tiny fish that wasn't much bigger than her after all. All of a sudden it stopped flopping. Faintly, the poor fish called out, "Mother, where are you?" "Poor thing!" Mrs. Blue gasped. "Please help me get back into the water," the fish pleaded, "I can't catch my breath and Mother would get mad if she found out I swam near the shore again."

Mrs. Blue was startled to see two big eyes watching them from the water. She grabbed Blue and stood between the two. Soon several smaller pairs of fish eyes were staring at them from the pond. Peeking from behind her mother Blue asked, "Who is that?" Mrs. Blue took a step backwards as the two big eyes came closer rising slowly out of the water and toward the shore. "Mable! I told you not to go jumping around the shore line!" Said the eyes that are now accompanied by fish lips and a stern voice to boot.

"Flap around and get your tail back into this water right now before them birds start eating you!"

But it was no use, Mable was too tired and almost breathless. "It will be fine mother fish. We'll help your daughter get back into the water." Mrs. Blue reassured, heaving a sigh of relief. Using their beaks, the Blues began pushing her easefully into the pond head first, and soon she was swimming toward her mother. The water came to life when all her brothers and sisters cheered. The mother fish wrapped her fins around Mable. "Thank you so much for your help," she told the family. Little Mable was ecstatic too, "Thank you for saving me!"

"My name is Blue and this is my mom and my brother Berry."

"My name is Molly," said the mother fish, "and these are my children. You should all come sometime for the evening chorus and listen to the symphony. They have fantastic harmony, and everyone around here always comes to listen." Mrs. Blue seemed thrilled about the idea, "Why that would be nice! We would love to come back for that." The two mothers had a lovely chat. Exchanging stories about life in the park and in the pond, while the children, birds and fish, played by the edge of the river.

Amid the stillness there was a big splash and out came a large silver hump heading straight for the shore. "Look out!" Mable shouted to Blue. "That's my father! He eats much bigger birds than you," Mabel warned. Blue and her mother grabbed Berry. Unaware of what was happening he yelled, "What? Why did you pull me away? What's going on?" Blue pointed to the large fish eyes coming their way. "Holy Moly! That's one giant fish!" Berry exclaimed. "Yes, that's my daddy," Mable said to Berry, a bit proudly, "I'm glad he didn't eat you, though." "Please don't worry about my husband. He may be the boss fish in this pond but I'll talk to him. He won't come after you or your family again," Molly assured them as she gathered her children to swim to the deeper ends of the pond.

The bluebirds saw the big bass, Boss, swimming back and forth near the shore. His eyes were still focused on them. Molly approached him and scolded him loudly, "Leave them alone Henry. They are my friends now, and they helped rescue Mabel a while ago."

"Don't call me Henry. Other fish are listening!" Boss spoke back.

"You better do as I say, Henry, or you will sleep in the grass tonight!"

This mellowed Boss down, "Okay Molly. You don't have to shout, geez. They just look so delicious that's all." He stared at them as if in a trance and swam away. "Come on children," Mrs. Blue told Berry and Blue. "Let's go home now. "Some Boss fish he is," Berry chuckled.

CHAPTER 22

The Origin of the Stone

As Jesse awoke, he was eager to have an uninterrupted date with Emma this afternoon. Jesse found that wearing the ring, Kumba could follow him anywhere, but without it there was no way for him to protect himself.

"So dang if I do and dang if I don't!"

"Basically yes," The stone replied. He left the ring in the drawer thinking a few hours for a movie date in town won't hurt. Berry was in Jesse's bed looking out the window when the ring spoke, "Hello little one, would you like me to tell you the story of how I was created?" She pulled out the ring from the drawer. Her eyes grew wide with excitement. She put hands under her chin replying, "Yes, I'd like that. I like stories!"

"If you close your eyes I will project the story into your mind," The Stone explained. "You mean like watching a movie?" "Yes, just like that."

Berry closed her eyes and at once she heard the ring's voice in her mind along with vivid images of its creation.

"This story begins close to three thousand years ago in the arid desert of Africa where the lush valleys were plentiful, and the fresh breeze coming from the Nile River greeted the people every morning. Life was good and the people who lived there were happy."

"Wow!" Berry shouted, "I can really feel the air and the wind. I can even feel the sand on my toes. It's like I'm there! This is so amazing."

"Yes, my dear. There is more to tell. Let's continue," The Stone replied.

"I was created with the understanding of a thousand realities, because of a King's wish for understanding and wisdom. For this reason, only, I was born. My very heart was taken from that of a star. My shape formed from the image of creation. I was a new form of life, a conscious sentient being with my own thoughts eager and ready to serve the one whom I was created for. A seemingly just and righteous king. That person was King Solomon over the years he began to change and summon those from other darker realities."

Berry asked, "Like in the bug world?" "A different realm yes, but much darker than the bird's world you have come to know," The Stone continued. "These beings look so strange. Those are some big lizard people!" Berry blurted out, "Oh, I'm so sorry for interrupting. Please continue."

"The beings summoned by Solomon were forced to work under his rule. The people didn't know what to think about these creatures. Some said Solomon used monsters. The people called them Jinn or demons. They possess magic of their own, but none had power over Solomon due to my protection. I felt it was wrong that he kept these beings enslaved making enemies of them. I spoke to Solomon about this, and was ignored for the most part.

One particular being was called Asmodeus. He was a shape shifter. Solomon called him the king of demons. Which in turn kept the people from questioning his rule. Asmodeus worked continuously day and night, year after year. Solomon would say that if he let them off for a day they may never come back. Asmodeus grew tired of his captivity and begged for his freedom. Solomon refused many times, and kept him in his service. Meanwhile I became known as the seal of Solomon. They also called me the ring of Solomon, or the wondrous many-sided stone. I became highly sought after. A symbol of power to many."

The Stone continued, "Around the year 950 BC King Solomon became crueler ruling Jerusalem with a steel hand. He ordered the construction of a temple in his name, and assigned a formidable magician named Khaba to oversee its construction. The workforce became an ill-behaved vicious bunch. One unruly Jinn named Bartimaeus was among them. Bartimaeus was assigned to hunting bandits in the desert. A job he greatly enjoyed. Capturing and torturing humans made him feel incredibly powerful over them.

His wickedness caught the attention of Solomon. One day King Solomon asked Asmodeus, "What could make demons have more power over man?" Asmodeus answered, 'Our mighty stature was made possible by magic. If we had power over this magic, or had its curse upon us removed, together we could all rule humans and be incredibly powerful. Allow me to show you, wise King. Allow me to hold the ring, and I will demonstrate how this could use the ring to free himself from Solomon's hold over them, he pointed the ring at the king, trying to make its power work for him, but found that he could not control its power!

He started growing and became a giant. Growing twenty stories high with large bat-shaped wings appearing on his back that caused a great sandstorm as they flapped. Asmodeus was frightened knowing he couldn't use my power and he certainly couldn't give the ring back to Solomon for fear of punishment. He panicked and threw me as far as he could, tossing the Stone hundreds of miles away, sinking deep into the ocean. Where I was quickly swallowed by a fish.

Since Solomon no longer possessed my magic, he was overpowered by Asmodeus. Asmodeus placed the king inside his mouth as revenge, and spat him across the air like a cannonball sending him four hundred miles away to another land. Then the demon changed his form and disguised himself as King Solomon.

'Now king!' As he laughed, 'There is the answer to your question of how demons can have power over man! Take the power then rule in your place,' the demon laughed.

Time past, Asmodeus realized that he could be more powerful should he retrieve the ring, and was regretful for tossing me into the sea. He told all travelers who ventured to King Solomon's lofty palace that the seal of Solomon was lost at sea and anyone who could retrieve it for him would receive treasures beyond their wildest dreams and even replace him as king. I was glad to break free from my servitude. Only to be awakened when a truly special person or if magic comes

close. I slept in the belly of one fish or another for centuries, but lived in many other realms during my slumber."

Berry spoke, "What a terrific story! It's like seeing a fantasy movie! That Asmodeus was the biggest lizardman I have ever seen, and wow, to see King Solomon get spit out like a cannonball from a giant's mouth, with my own eyes. But ring you said you were asleep for centuries. When did you finally awaken?"

"That was when Merlin brought an army to the sea and summoned the fish for them to eat."

"Oh…tell me about that one too!" Berry excitedly requested. "Let's keep that story for another time," The Stone replied, knowing Merlin's story was a little more complex for a young child like Berry.

Leaving the ring at home seemed to have worked. Jesse and Emma had a wonderful time at the movies. There was no sign of Kumba or his minions, but when Jesse arrived home, he found carvings on the fence. This was the first time he had seen those markings.

"What do these symbols mean?" he asked the ring.

"It's another spell used in the past to summon evil spirits and ghosts to a dwelling."

"Great. I leave for a few hours and I come home to this." Jesse shook his head exasperated, "Whatever, I'm heading back to training now in Blue's realm. Wake me if anything attacks: Bugs, birds, demons, ghosts, wizards, Kumba or his henchmen, or whatever may come!"

CHAPTER 23

Symphony Pond's Twilight Serenade

The Blue family landed in a field where birds search for worms and bugs. Blue spotted some mice playing and went down to greet one, "Hello, my name is Blue." The young mouse scurried off to the grass and peeked to say a meek hello.

"I haven't seen you here before. My name is Clifford."

"Hi, Clifford. Yes, it's my first time here, my mom and my brother and I are here to watch the concert."

"Are you a hawk? My mommy says I'm not allowed to speak to hawks. Especially the mean one called Shiver." Blue chuckled, "No Clifford I am not a hawk. I am just a little bluebird. I've heard of Shiver all right, and yes, he's a big meanie!"

Clifford came out of hiding, "Okay. Then you can come and play with us, but keep an eye out for Shiver. He often comes here to deliver animals as gifts to the king." Two other small mice appeared from behind the grass.

"These are my sisters Clair and Flower."

While playing peek-a-boo and chase Clifford showed Blue all their hiding spots. "This is where my mother said I should hide if Kumba or Shiver comes."

"I've heard that name before. Who is this king?" Blue asked. "You're either new or not from around here, are you?

Everyone here knows who the King is."

"Is he some kind of monster?" Blue asked, collecting information as the ring had instructed. "He is the biggest, meanest, worst monster of them all!" shouted Clifford, "He slithers through the grass and sneaks up very quietly and strikes very fast! We always have to listen and watch out for him." "Oh my! Is he the one you call the Snake king?"

Clifford nodded. "Yes, he is the worst of all snakes. The other mice call him The Terror of the Grasslands. He captures mice and keeps us in a cage for fun, or eats us for his dinner. I heard he eats little birds and frogs too."

Blue wore a worried look on her face. "Blue you said you're watching the concert? It's getting dark. It's almost time for it to begin" Clifford shared, before pointing to a hill overlooking the pond.

"Look, over there! The mice are already gathering. We can see the whole pond from there. It's the best place to hear and watch."

"Yes, my mom says we can stay for the concert." Clifford took her by the hand and says, "Well, come on then. Let's go get us good seats! Come, come!"

The hillside was quickly getting crowded with mice and all kinds of creatures of the forest. The water in the pond began churning and lighting up. Frogs rested on water lilies croaking away. Crickets and birds of all shapes and sizes perched on trees chirping in harmony. Many of them

traveled far just to see the symphony. The entire pond came alive with sound. The air was filled with excitement as Blue, Berry, Mrs. Blue, Clifford, and his sisters sat together on the hill.

A large stork with a funny bow tie flew down to a little island near the edge of the pond. Everyone then became very still and silent.

"That white bird is the conductor." Clifford continued, "He comes nightly to start the symphony. He won't start until everyone is quiet."

"What's a conductor?" Blue asked. "He's the one conducting the orchestra. You'll see. Now shhh," Clifford whispered while holding a finger in front of his lips. The stork raised his wing holding a small stick while studying each performer to see if everyone was ready. He heaved a deep breath and was about to start when a little plop was heard in the water. The conductor sighed in frustration. Mable stuck her head up from beneath the water, "Whoops! I'm sorry!" She ducked her head back in the water with only her eyes visible above it, and tried to remain still.

The stork looked sternly at her then toward Molly to signal her to keep her children quiet. He shook his head, and raised his wing once more. He pointed to the frogs with the lowest bass voices. After counting to three the frogs let out a rhythm of low croaks. Crickets joined in the musical as Woodpeckers pecked on a hollow log creating drum-like sounds. The conductor pointed to the bird chorus, and they began to sing in unison;

"Sand man, bring me a dream
Make him the cutest that I've ever seen."

Blue watched as birds lined up beautifully and swayed in groups: crows cawed, doves cooed, robins chirped. Lighting bugs flew in the sky above forming mesmerizing patterns that looked like fireworks on the fourth of July. It was an amazing night for the bluebird family just as it was for everyone present.

As the final song played a shriek was heard. Panic suddenly set off at the pond. Birds flew away from the trees frantically. Frogs jumped into the water, while rodents took to the hillside to hide in the grassland.

"What's happening?" Blue asked Clifford. "Go home Blue! King Kumba is here!"

For some reason, Blue was curious about how this feared monster looked. After all he knew that name. A large snake slithered out of the grass and swam into the water. He was trying to grab and eat any frog or fish that crossed its path. It crawled up onto the podium where the conductor stood, raised his head and announced! "Why has the music stopped? Hiss…I never said anyone could leave! Hiss…I am your king and you ought to obey my commands!"

Very slowly Blue and her family flew up and away from the scene as the serpent continued to rant. Berry asked, "How dumb is that snake? Nobody's going to let him eat them of course!" Mother tried to shush Berry by placing a wing on his mouth. But the snake king overheard Berry's snide remark.

"How dare you make fun of me bird! Laugh as you wish now, but I will catch you one day soon and play with you right before I eat you all!

Let's see who's going to have the last laugh! Hiss…"

Mrs. Blue shuddered at the thought. "Quick, Berry! Blue! Let's go." The snake continued, "A Berry huh, that sounds like a yummy name! I will of course remember you three"

Within a few minutes the family was back safely in their nest. "Blue asked her mother about why the snake was like that? He also has figured out that this snake was the other half of Kumba's magic. The one he must do battle with and defeat.

"Do you remember when you and Berry were left alone, and Berry would order you around?" Mom asked. "Oh yes." Blue replied. "You see, this snake believes the same thing. He thinks that because he is bigger and stronger than everyone else that he has the right to make himself king and do as he please."

"That's not right. Just because he is bigger doesn't give him the right to abuse other animals."

"That's true Blue. The mean and strong will always try to control the small and weak. So, we must always be wise and careful and just stay away from King Kumba.

Now, can we all do that?" Berry and Blue both nodded.

CHAPTER 24

Romancing the stone

Berry was the first to wake the next morning, "What a beautiful day," she remarked, humming the Lone Ranger theme song on her way down the stairs. "Good morning sweetheart! No bluebirds this morning?" Mom said, giggling.

"Not this morning Mom. Jesse told me to stop doing that. I don't mind, I got to listen to a symphony last night. All the birds and bugs and frogs made music."

"That's great! I'm glad you're no longer having your nightmares."

Out in the barn, Grandpa uncovered a handsome Harley motorbike to Jesse.

"Wow! Grandpa I didn't know you had one of these! This sure is an awesome bike." "Glad you liked it, Jesse, because now it belongs to you."

Jesse's eyes grew wide. "You're kidding! Thank you, Grandpa!" "I am getting too old to ride it anymore. Now you don't have to walk to town or borrow a car for your date."

Jesse wasted no time and went to the Emporium straight away. "No ring today?" Emma asked. "No, I figured I'd leave it at home again, so we won't be tracked. This day is just for you and me," Jesse smirked. From a hideout across the street,

Kumba was furious at Harry, Kurly, and Moe for not being able to track Jesse's whereabouts. "Where was he yesterday?" Kumba shouted. "We searched everywhere for him yesterday, but we couldn't find him" Moe complained. Kumba said to Harry, "How about you, you imbecile? Kurly interjected, "His name is Reel E. Harry, boss. We all have hip-hop names."

"I don't care what you call yourselves! What I care about is that you do your jobs, and right now you aren't!" Kumba yelled once more, "Even the chauffeur has more brains than you three combined! If only you three had his brains!"

Harry and Kurly looked at each other and made faces. Kurly said, "No thanks, boss. That man never eats and he stinks." Kumba glared at the three.

"You better not lose that boy again, or else!"

"We won't boss. You can count on us," Moe assured him.

Once Kumba left the room Harry turned to Kurly, "Kurly, I am not sure this job is worth it." "It's Kurly 2 cents to you."

"This Kumba guy is going to turn us into zombies like Shiver, I think."

"You think so Reel E. Harry?" "Yes, I do and sure, I'll call you 2 Cents, as that fits your brain capacity."

"Are you making fun of my stage name, Mr. Reel E. Harry? Well, your stage name just makes you sound all hairy like a "You know my name means (Harry 'reels in the chicks) Mr. 2 cents."

"Oh, still making fun of my stage name, are you?"

"No, not at all, I really don't give 2 cents about your name, braw."

"And you're a hairy ape!" "Yeah, yeah. Very original."

Amid the banter, Moe shouted, "Stop with the stage names, would you?"

Moe wore a serious look on his face as he looked out the window. "What you looking at Moe?" Harry asked. "Isn't that Jesse on that bike?" Moe asked. Harry and Kurly ran up to the window. "Nice bike!" Harry blurted. "Oh yeah," Kurly agreed, "That's a really cool ride. Do you think he'd let us ride it, Harry?" Moe shook his head, "You two are real idiots. We're supposed to make that boy's life miserable not admire his bike!" "Oh yeah. I forgot." Kurly replied.

Kumba walked into the room after having eavesdropped on the conversation. "What's a bike?" he asked while looking out the window. Emma came out of the shop and climbed up on the bike. As they set off to a nearby river Kumba was raging,

"What are you idiots waiting for? Get them!" "There is no way we can keep up with him on a bike man!" Moe complained.

"If you three had bikes, could you keep up then?" "Of course," replied Moe.

"Then take me to where bikes are sold."

So, they did. "Wow! These bikes are cool!" Kurly remarked, revving up his new dirt bike. Kumba ordered them at once, "Now, go find that boy and make him miserable, or you will be!" The three nodded as they rode off. Harry looked back and saw Kumba showing the motorbike salesman his watch.

"Why does he show everybody that watch?"

Moe said, "Haven't you noticed he never brings out cash?

That's some sort of Voodoo spell he puts on them with that watch- looking device. That's why we are still working for this guy, so he won't put a spell on us and turn us into a frog or something much worse."

"Oh, I see. Well, anyway these bikes can surely move, they're great!" Harry replied. Moe nodded, "They sure are, aren't they fellas?" The three laughed together. "Keep your eyes open. We better find them before he makes zombies of us!" Harry enthused. "Right" Kurly agreed.

Passing the tall trees leading to the forest the two young lovers enjoyed their pursuit of a romantic adventure. Holding tight to Jesse, Emma welcomed the soft breeze and the sun's warm light. They pulled up to a popular lovers' lane. Jesse asked, "Did you see any signs of those guys or Kumba?" "Nope. None at all," Emma answered, "Isn't this nice? Just you and me, no ring to get us tracked." From a distance, Jesse spotted a cave up the hill. "Lots of kids go there. It's kind of cool. You want to check it out?" Emma asked. "Sure. Seems fun," Jesse replied, not minding the storm brewing overhead. "Story has it that pirates hid their treasures in this cave. There are also stories about Bonnie and Clyde staying in this cave one time," Emma shared.

Upon entering the cave the skies grew darker and the rain started. They were both glad to make it inside the cave before the rain came. Jesse was amazed at the sheer size of this cave system. It went on for miles like a labyrinth. From inside the cave Jesse spotted Harry, Kurly, and Moe surrounding his motorbike. Pointing at the three he said, "Oh great! Now we have stalkers. How did they even know we were here? I left the ring at home."

"Isn't this the bike Jesse was on?" Kurly asked. Harry pointed to the couple standing at the mouth of the cave. "There, up there, there they are by the cave's entrance!" The skies above began to darken. "Hurry up you two before the rain comes down any harder!" Moe commanded.

The three made their way through the damp cave trying to decide which path of several to take. Harry said, "My clothes are getting dirty! You know how expensive these jerseys are?" Moe was annoyed, "You want to go back and tell Mr. Kumba you quit because you were getting dirty?" "He has a good point Harry," Kurly agreed, "I wouldn't want to tell that scary man that. None of us wants to join Shiver in zombie land!" "Okay, point taken," Harry

"This way Jesse," Emma whispered as she led Jesse by the hand further into one of the cave's tunnels, "We can hide in here." "Is there a back way out of here? Or do they have us cornered?" Jesse asked.

"I don't know I've never gone this far in, but they are not giving us much choice!"

Moe listened to the silent whispers echoing through the cave. "Fellas, they went this way."

Jesse and Emma went deeper and deeper, trying to stay ahead of the three. Jesse saw a ledge up high. He and Emma climbed it and laid there quietly as they peeked and listened to the three underneath them. Jesse looked up and saw a small hole where rain was seeping in. He poked at it and could see a small way out. They then started digging to make the hole bigger, but made a loud noise from the fallen mud.

"We see you warrior boy!" Moe yelled, "Where do you think you're going? You're trapped up there!" The three threw rocks up to Jesse and Emma while threatening them.

Emma and Jesse fought back. Throwing balls of mud at the three to slow their ascent to their position. Using their hands, they dug quickly further into the hole increasing its size. Suddenly the roof started to cave in, and a gush of rainwater came rushing down along with a massive chunk of mud falling below. Flowing down covering the cave floor below. The three were covered with mud that kept them slipping over each other. Step by careful step Jesse climbed up through the hole and immediately pulled Emma up, as soon as he climbed out.

They rushed to block the hole with stick, rocks and mud stopping Moe, Kurly, and Harry from following. They all gasped and tried to run away back to the cave's entrance. The young couple found themselves on a ledge the rain was pouring down. Jesse studied the long overhang to the ground below and stated "That's a long way down!" "Yes, it is," Emma replied, her heart pounding. Both peered down wondering how they would be able to climb down safely when the ground beneath them started moving.

Emma screamed. Suddenly a mudslide came rushing down toward the two. Before Jesse and Emma could move the mud took them sliding off the small cliff and down a narrow winding slope? As they slid down the hillside, they hit a small ramp that threw them up into the air and off another embankment.

Jesse hit a pile of mud slowing him down before stopping his descent. He landed 30 feet down the cliff near another overhang still 20 feet over the river. Emma was sliding right behind Jesse a little to the right and moving at a very fast pace. Jesse grabbed her arm as she zipped past. It was just in time before she fell over the edge of the embankment. Emma hung over the edge tightly gripping Jesse with one hand and the other hanging by her side. Jesse stood up and tried to grab both of her hands to pull her up, but more mud crashed down the slope, hitting Jesse as he holds tight to Emma. The two were soaking wet and suddenly the ground gave way beneath them. Down they went sliding along the hill like a ride at a water park. Jesse went down still holding Emma's hand, they slid quickly down the embankment, flying off the sides, splashing into the river below. The two swam toward one another unable to stop themselves from laughing at their sheer luck.

"That's the most fun I have had in a long time!" Emma squealed. "Me too!" Jesse smiled.

Hand in hand they swam toward the riverbank and walked toward where Jesse's bike was parked. They noticed three bikes parked close by. With no other bikes or other people around Jesse had a feeling the bikes belonged to the three gangsters. Emma, feeling naughty said, ""Hold on a moment!" then cut the gas lines to all of them. Jesse hastily cranked up his bike. The two young lovers laughed as they sped off.

Emma looked behind and could see the three all covered in mud trying to crank their bikes with little luck. "That should hold them awhile." She snickered. "Hopefully," Jesse exclaimed, "Now let's get back before the rain gets worse!"

The three watched as Jesse and Emma left, they tried to start their bikes, then Harry noticed shaking his head, "My fuel line has been cut." "Yeah, they cut all three. We're going to have to push the bikes home," Moe said. "Kumba is not going to be happy with this is he Moe?" Kurly asked. "No, he isn't!" Moe replied.

CHAPTER 25

Wizards, Dragons, and Crabs, Oh my!

The next morning Berry turned over to wake Jesse up and talk to him about the dream realm. Berry was thrilled, "It was so fun. Thank you so much for letting me be in your dreams Jesse!" "No problem," Jesse smiled.

"Are you going to see Emma again today?" "Yes, we are going to the park for a picnic." "What about that man?"

"They don't seem to know where I am. Just where the ring is. That's why I will leave the ring here. Can you keep it safe?" "No problemo!" Berry exclaimed. "Will be happy too!" While Jesse rode to town to meet Emma, Berry pulled the ring out from the drawer for an adventure of her own.

"Hey, ring. You promised to tell me the rest of the story about Merlin the Wizard."

"Oh yes, I did, didn't I?" replied The Stone, "Well okay, I suppose there is time. I stayed asleep, dormant for many centuries deep in the ocean, stuck within the belly of one fish after another. Until one day Luther's mighty army set up camp on the beach in siege of Morgan Le Fay's castle. Merlin was with that army. His magic woke me from my slumber. I could feel it and he could feel mine. He cast a powerful spell. Waves

began rising. With each wave hundreds of fish washed upon the shore. Thousands of soldiers scooped up the fish with their arms and began praising Merlin. The men gathered the fish and started setting up camp, preparing everything for their sieged- on Morgana's castle. I was in the belly of one of those fishes." Berry's eyes grew wide in amazement.

"That's awesome. Tell me more about the fishes!"

"One fish had light shining out its mouth and eyes. Merlin picked up that fish and cut it open. There I was, emitting this blinding light like a sunrise illuminating the night into day. I was awakened, anew and back into the human realm after such a long time. Merlin studied me and asked, 'What do we have here?' He was not even surprised to hear me answer! He has read all about me in ancient scrolls. We spoke that night, and I felt right away that he was a good man. All the while Morgana was observing Luther's army less than a mile away from outside the window of her castle. She had been tracking their movement and has been expecting them for two days."

"Who is Morgana?" Berry asked.

"She was a sorceress who possessed magic like Merlin. However, she took a darker path and was consumed by greed to obtain more power."

"I see. And did she see your light in the night sky when Merlin cut the fish open? I bet it could be seen for a hundred miles."

"That's right little one. She did. Then she readied her troops, spreading her men along the ridge overlooking the beach, not waiting till morning, figuring Luther's army was tired from the march. She ordered her men to fire their arrows on the five- thousand-man army below."

"And you could see her up on the ridge?"

"Let me show you," The Stone said, reflecting an image of a green fire bursting at the sorceress' feet as she chanted incoherently. "Oh my!" Berry cried out as she stared up at the projected image of the story shown as a reality within her mind.

"We could hear her chanting over the fire and see flames against the night sky. Up they rose shooting over Luther's army and striking into the ocean. The waters glowed in the same glossy green light as Morgana's flame. Hundreds of white glowing eyes could be seen across the shimmering water, slowly heading for shore.

One soldier walked out into the waters holding two of the eyes saying, "They seem harmless." Then out from the swirling waters a great claw emerged as many watched. The claw grabbed the soldier and held him up in the air by his waist. The men panicked and ran. His screams were heard by all. Then a second claw splashed out encircling the neck of the soldier, and with a quick snap his head fell off. As the crab creatures emerged from the waters crawling out to the shore, they grew to frightening sizes. Morgana watched as the monsters she summoned swept through the invading army attacking and snapping soldiers and driftwood in half. Loud crunching like the snapping of wood and Bones could be heard.

Then hundreds of giant crabs were ascending the shoreline, attacking Luther's army like a late-night buffet.

It was horrible to watch as the army battled the monsters. Hundreds of arrows started to rain down over them. "Merlin called the army to prepare for battle. Morgana ordered the archers to keep shooting. Thousands of arrows poured down like rain upon the cornered army. Shields up! Was heard.

Now at that time I had never seen creatures such as these. The power Morgana used to summon these creatures was not one, I was familiar with. Merlin was determining how to fight off Morgana's attack, saying, 'I need a dragon, but none are near, they are all too far away to help us with this onslaught of creatures.' This is when I spoke up, 'If you hold me up then I will bring you dragons!'

Merlin held me up and with it a realm of my own opened. You could see a giant circle in the night sky, daylight shining from within it. At this point hundreds of giant crabs were on shore. As the men fought back at the beast an enormous shadow could be seen coming from the portal. A mighty dragon shot straight out from the circle, dark he was, as dark as the night sky and screeching out a horrifying cry.

He fiercely descended on the crabs shooting fire from his mouth as it burned a line along the water's edge, slowing the crabs attack.

Two more dragons came flying out from the hole in the sky and started to feast on the crabs. The larger dragon flew up to the cliff and landed in the middle of Morgana's army. He blew his flames amidst them, and the screams from the men could be heard. Many falling off the cliffs above as we watched them burn.

The soldiers moved away from the ocean and took cover. Morgana ordered her troops to retaliate and thousands of them descended on Luther's army. They came from all directions. Merlin's army fought back first with arrows, then swords. At one time five men saw death in the grips of the dragon's claws! The other dragons picked up soldiers, took them out for miles and dropped them into the ocean. Many sank from the weight of their heavy armor.

Morgana's army fired arrows at the dragon, but none could penetrate their thick scales. Within minutes hundreds lay dead on the cliffs above, and Morgana had no choice but to order her men to retreat. The huge dragon picked up three men in his mouth all at once and started chewing. The sound of metal armor crunching is a noise unheard of by these soldiers. The dragon could see Morgana returning to her castle. He let out a large belch and armor and body parts sprayed out from his mouth, clanking as they hit the ground.

The dragon seeing his target moved along the ground towards the sorcerous. Morgana casted spells to slow the dragon, but it kept coming. While the other two dragons were still spraying their fire on the hoard of crabs, roasting both the crabs and men. How fierce the dragons fought, always seeming to know what they must do next. The large dragon kept moving toward Morgana raising up his massive wings. The soldiers were towering beneath the mighty creature. As he flapped his wings the force sent men flying off the cliffs.

Once she was in reach he blasted a river of lava toward her, which quickly disintegrating everything it touched. Burning soldiers as they tried to escape the infernal. The dragon ever continuing up the path after Morgana. 'Hurry,' she shouted. Morgana was only feet away from the castle door. Some soldiers stood ahead holding the castle doors waiting for her to enter. While many others were still coming behind her trying to escape the dragon's advance, but with no avail.

Morgana made her way in and ordered her general to close the doors behind her, seal the castle, and make ready for more attacks. They could hear the loud horrible screams outside the doors from the ones who didn't make it inside the castle. Rumbling wind of flames battered against the castle doors, like the bellows of a large Kiln, the dragon blasted the door with a heavy force. Inside they could feel the extreme heat burning hard against the massive beams, and watched as the doors metal hinges melted before them.

The big dragon took flight calling the other two to join. They flew around the castle blasting it, setting much of it to flame. I began to glow to stop the dragon's attack. They then flew away from the castle and circled overhead.

In protest King Luther shouted, 'Why stop now, let's destroy her once and for all, let's finish her!' There was silence for a moment, then I spoke as King Luther and Merlin both watched and listened. 'If revenge is what you seek, then no help from me will you receive? You won today, King Luther, take the victory, before even larger things crawl out from the oceans deep. Treat your wounded and leave this place in victory.'

King Luther stood silent for a moment and started laughing, then said, 'Merlin what you say makes sense. We shall retreat and fight another day! 'But the king continued, 'Never again throw your voice into an object just to prove a point to me. Come my friend, let's go home.'"

"I've seen enough of these images. There is too much blood! It's like being inside live TV, my eyes can't take it anymore." Berry closed her eyes saying, "Tell me when the fighting stops, please." "Sorry little one. The story is almost over," The Stone assured her, "So Morgana escaped to the safety of her castle, barricading herself inside and tried to figure out what new magic Merlin had found. The dragons flew back into the portal which closed shortly afterwards. And that concludes my story!" "Whew!" Berry heaved a sigh of relief.

"This was the first time I saved Merlin's life and Luther's army. I stayed with Merlin for many years. My magic gave him the power to speak with and become many animals. He could also change the appearance of a person to look like another. Which he used with Luther and later King Author. Merlin possessed all the wisdom that came from my journey just as Solomon once did. This made Merlin greatly feared by his enemies and even Morgana. She learned what I was and desired me deeply enough to rage many battles with Merlin to obtain my power. Merlin knew that the sorceress would not stop her relentless pursuit, until she possessed my power.

Morgana in her quest searched for a weapon which could equal my powers. She found a way and opened the 7th realm.

Retrieving the Ruby jewel to create her own medallion of power. She then took her dear friend, a powerful good white witch named Bella, and cut out her heart. Imprisoning her within the medallion for eternity. She renamed the Medallion the Rubella charm, so she could have a sentient conscious living charm as Merlin has by combining the purity of a white witch's soul to a powerful magic Jewel.

Berry became anxious, "What happened next?" The Stone continued, "Years went by and there were many fights with Morgana, she became very powerful, so much so, that it was best for Merlin to leave. He called the Lady of the Lake to protect me and keep me safe until a new Wonder warrior was found. He then turned himself into a bird and simply disappeared from this world."

"Wow. That was a great story! You sure are old, aren't you?" The Stone laughed, "I suppose that is true."

In town Kumba's minions found and surrounded Jesse and Emma pushing their chest up against him. Moe inspected Jesse's hands as his two brothers pinned him against a wall, "Shame, you don't have it on you. Let's show him what happens to those who do not obey." The three beat Jesse from all sides as his fear crept in. Emma screamed and Harry pushed her to the ground. People began to gather around the five until a police car with its blaring siren pulled up. The gangsters immediately took off. After a conversation with the police.

Jesse dropped Emma off and headed home.

"How is Emma?" Jesse's mom asked, worried as she applied ice over Jesse's bruised eye.

"She is okay Mom. Just a little shook up. They were after the ring. When I told them I didn't have it they did this."

Jesse's Mom was furious, "Can I do anything else for you son?" "No Mom. I'm fine. Thanks," Jesse insisted. He proceeded up to his room and recounted the events. He realized being without the ring was much too dangerous. "I need to finish the training and learn how to defend myself," Jesse told the ring, "What else can I do?" "Analyze what you learn carefully. Then question everything you learn and put it into practice intelligently," The Stone replied.

CHAPTER 26

City under Siege!

Over the summer Blue became friends with many creatures in the forest and visited them regularly. She became so good at flying that Captain Striker promoted her as a top flier, and even let her fly with them as a member of the Red Wing squadron. Meanwhile the three cardinals had bandages all over from thorns and traps trying to get into Bug City. Professor Fly had captured Stank in one of his traps. The rats were so happy that they brought the professor whatever they could find in the junkyard.

Life seemed good for Blue, until one day she woke up shivering from the cold wind. "Mom, it's so cold. What is happening? Mrs. Blue wrapped her wings around the small ones to keep them warm, "This looks like an early cold spell. The seasons are changing. Cold winter is upon us, and it will stay that way for a long time. Food would be hard to find worms, bugs and insects." "You mean they will all be gone Mom?" Blue inquired. "Well, most bugs, insects, and even worms burrow deep into the ground all winter and come back out during spring when everything becomes warm again."

"If that is true Mother, and if this is an early spell what will happen to the bugs in Bug City?" Blue asked. Mom looked

Blue in the eye, "If the bugs are not in their winter homes before it gets really cold those bugs could be in trouble."

"Oh my. I have to go see my friends then and ask them."

Blue quickly flew off to Bug City. When she arrived, no bugs were in sight. The Puddle House Restaurant was closed. All the bugs were huddled inside the motel. Blue knocked on the door. Scooter opened the door, his body shaking from the cold and his voice shivering, "How are you Blue?"

"Why are all the bugs still here Scooter? Doesn't the caravan head back to the woods before cold weather comes?"

"Yeah, Mom says normally we would have already left by now but those mean cardinals are on the prowl for every bug who has tried to leave. They are guarding all the exits to Bug City, so we are trapped here."

"What can I do to help?"

Scooter looked glum. "Nothing I reckon, unless you can make those red devils go away, or help find us a way to get back to the woods in secret. It is getting way too cold for the caravan to make the trip. Other birds are also hungry. We will surely be eaten if we go, but freeze if we stay here."

"Stay warm in the hotel," Blue said. "Let me see what I can do."

Blue tiptoed on the bushes out of the city. She could hear the cardinals scheming to catch any bug who tries to leave. She flew above them and tried to talk them into letting every bug pass. "Why would we listen to you Blue?" Moe replied harshly, "There are no fruits in the farmer's orchard, the worms are almost gone in the junkyard, and the only food left is hiding in that bush. We are staying right here till we can eat them, so go away, or we will beat the heck out of you again! And this time your mom is not around to help you, trouble maker!" "Yeah, she's a trouble maker isn't she Moe?" Kurly agreed, shuddering. "Moe?" Harry muttered, "I'm freezing. Can we go now?"

"Shut up, you imbecile! You want to starve? We're not going anywhere! Keep watch!"

Blue thought hard. Professor Fly might have a suggestion on how to save the bugs. She flew back to the junkyard, where the professor was busy working on his model airplane. "Oh, hello there Blue," he greeted, "You want to see my latest invention?" "Maybe later professor. We have an emergency," Blue shared the bugs' dilemma with the professor. The Professor reflected long and hard then pointed to the model plane, "Well, we could fly them out there." "How?" Blue questioned.

"Well, I suppose I could attach some string to the plane to be pulled. We would need a big bird to pull it, some lights, and a way to keep the plane straight since the tail of the plane is still missing."

"Great!" Blue exclaimed, "You go fix that tail and get the plane ready then. I have an idea, but I will need my friends to make it work. Stay busy while I find some help."

For the plan to work Blue needed the red birds away from Bug City. She wasted no time and visited the Red Wing squadron to ask the Captain for help. "I see that is a dilemma," The Captain continued, "Tell me what your plan is."

"Well, we do need a big bird to pull the plane, and I have just the right friend: Which Way Willy."

Blue returned to Bug City and gathered the older bugs to share the idea. "That might work," Scooter remarked. Blue asked Cowboy Crackers, "What do you think?" "Well," he replied, "it sounds as tough as walking through a plate of molasses, and what do we do about those three bullies?" "I have something in mind that should keep them busy," Blue spoke, "Okay, Scooter. Now that you know the plan tell the other bugs. Remember to keep it a secret among us, okay?" Scooter nodded.

Behind a shrub a curious creature was sporting a bug mask on his beak just like Blue once did, and eavesdropping on the conversation. As soon as the bugs heard the plan they quickly dispersed. The creature flew off to the spot where the cardinals were waiting. "Guys! I know what they are planning," Kurly said, peeling the mask off his face.

"You mean that mask actually worked?" Harry asked. Kurly stuck out his chest proud of his accomplishment, "Of course. I told you I'm a world class spy." "Shiver hates Blue," Moe quipped, grinning, "He hates Blue more than he hates us." "Well, I hope you're right about that," Kurly said, "Come on. Let's go and tell Shiver about Blue's plan. He will surely thank us and with his help we can have all the bugs we can eat." "What a great idea," Kurly praised Moe, "A bug sandwich does sound scrumptious!"

The three flew up the side of a mountain cliff where Shiver resided hovering just above his home being careful not to get too close. "Shiver," Moe shouted, "We have news to tell you!" "What do you want?" Shiver roared, "You are bothering me!" Kurly shouted down, "It's really important. We're sure this will interest you." "Go away you bothersome birds! There is nothing you can say that would be of any interest to me. Go away before I eat you!" Shiver growled angrily. Moe remained determined, "We just thought you wanted to know about what your friend Blue is planning but if you're not interested, we will be on our way." "Blue!"

Shiver zipped, seething in anger, grabbing two of the cardinals with his large claws, "What is it? Tell me quickly or I will eat you!" All three were terrified. Kurly nervously pleaded, "Please, Mr. Shiver. If you could just calm down and promise not to eat us, we will gladly tell you about Blue's plan, and help you get rid of that troublesome bird." Shiver loosened his grip. The brothers shared about Blue's plan to fly the bugs out of the city to their winter home using a contraption that Professor Fly created. Shiver smiled devilishly, "Interesting. Her father was always a bothersome trouble maker. Him and those black birds, but now that you birdbrains have told me why shouldn't I just take care of you like I did the Commander?" The cardinals shuddered in fear, "Well, we did help you capture the Commander and we told you of this little bluebird's plans. But we never said which day Blue decided to execute her plan."

Shiver didn't like being outsmarted, but had no choice but to agree. He raised the two small birds close to his face giving them a terrifying stare, "I will be there, but this better not be a lie and you better not get in my way!" He then threw them to the ground, before flying back to his cave.

217

CHAPTER 27

The Oracle on Main Street

Jesse awoke the next day to find the ring glowing and flashing inside the drawer. "What's wrong?" Jesse asked. Answering, The Stone states, "Remember when I said Kumba had to have some powerful magic to be able to locate you this fast?" "What of it?" Jesse replied. "It is worse than I thought, if he holds Morgana's charm!" The Stone continues, "We must find out if this is true Jesse, for if he holds this ambulate his powers will double every full moon."

"Oh, good grief, really, this means his powers have doubled once already and there is another full moon just a week away." "We need information and must find an oracle. There is one person in town who can help us Jesse and we must not waste any time. But first, we need the hair of a dead man."

"Why do we need the hair of a dead man?"

The Oracle will demand a gift and the hair of a Wonder would make some very nasty spells. We can use it to trick her."

"And how am I supposed to get hair from a dead man, you want me to dig somebody up?"

"Does this realm not have an undertaker?" asked the Stone.

Main Attraction
HAIR STUDIO

"So, I just walk in there and ask for some dead person's hair?" "Unless you have a better idea, Jesse?"

"I know." Jesse remembered, "There are shrunken heads in the emporium. I'm pretty sure they are dead, will they work?" "Yes, should work fine," The Stone said.

Jesse walked into the Emporium and asked Aunt Jane to see the heads. She gave them to Jesse and he quickly ran his comb through a small shrunken head taking some hair. She gave him an awkward look as he did this. "So, you just wanted to comb their hair?" Aunt Jane asked curiously. "Yes, Aunt Jane, I know how this looks…Thanks got to go now," speaking hastily. "No, you go right ahead Jesse, no judgment here." Aunt Jane replied.

"Now this is important Jesse, do not speak of the hair we collected. The Oracle will eventually ask for it. Jesse quickly placed the hair on a new comb and put it in his pocket. He rode his bike to town following the ring's directions. As they pulled in front of the town's beauty parlor Jesse comments, "Am I getting a haircut or are you wanting a wax job?"

"Very funny, but not the ladies in the shop, the lady out front feeding pigeons, she is our oracle."

"Help me to understand?" Jesse questions, "You have the wisdom of a thousand realms, right? But you still do not know what the power is that Kumba holds."

"Guessing doesn't count. That's why we're here to find this out!"

"She seems normal to me," Jesse suggests, as the lady stated "Good morning," Jesse asked her how she was and they conversed a short while. "You must have made a mistake," he said to the ring. Jesse turned toward Mrs. Hawk and asked, "Are you the Oracle I seek?"

"Oracle? No boy, I'm just feeding these pigeons."

"Well," Jesse remarked, "Apparently there is no oracle here." "No, I do not believe this is a mistake!" The Stone spoke, casting some words to bring forth the Oracle.

Mrs. Hawk sat straight up and started shouting, but it was not her who speaks. "Who summons me to this realm?" "It is I, Jesse Mason, who calls you."

"What gift did you bring?" replied the Oracle. Jesse thinking about the hair said, "Gift, I brought no gift."

"Then away with you and leave me alone!"

The Stone spoke, "Hello Mathilda." "Who said that?" The Oracle shouted. "You know me, Mathilda." Thinking for a minute, she says, "Yes, I know of you, Stone of Wonder, but never have I heard you actually speak before. So, the tales are true, you are Merlin's magical ring? Well in that case, find me a younger woman to live inside and I will grant you a vision!"

"Ridiculous," Jesse announced. "We're not going to bring you a body for you to live inside of!"

"Then I will take that magic ring as payment young man."

The Stone interrupts, "So, you do know me? Well, I know you too Mathilda and I know your secret. I will bring you nothing and you will help us anyway, if you wish to remain in that body."

"I have been around for over five hundred years, staying

connected to this realm using unsuspecting victims like this lady here before you."

She suddenly transformed into herself into a hideous old hag of a women, exposing the true face of a witch. Jesse jumped back at the site of her presence. She started floating up above the bench and said, "I know you're here to banish me from this human host I possess." The old witch cackled and took off floating down Main Street. "After her Jesse!" Shouted the Stone.

She cackled as she cast spells back at Jesse and anyone she passed by. The stone repelled and absorbed most of her attacks, as Jesse ran after her. Mr. and Mrs. Shows were driving their truck, Red Velvet down Main Street. "Yuck, to pretty and white." Zap' "Yes, that's better." The Oracle laughed. "Black Velvet, now that's a ride!" she then turned their truck into an electric toy car and them into monkeys. As she flew on casting spells she turned to Mrs. Tindall and zapped her friends into chickens. Then poor Mrs. Jorden was turned into an elephant, while her sisters, Kinni and Cindy, watched in horror as they became clowns, in full make up. The town was starting to look more like a circus as the chase continued.

She turned and cast a spell, finally a direct hit on Jesse, transforming Jesse into a pig. Jesse let out a loud squeal. The Oracle laughed even more saying, "Sweet ham for breakfast." The stone quickly cast a reverse spell turning Jesse back to himself.

"You're a soul sucking witch and I though we ended you, you old hag. Remember we can take you out of this lady's body and send you to a realm of darkness."

"Not if you can't catch me, Wonder-stone!"

Jesse formed a lasso with the stone's power and encircled the rope around the floating witch holding her tight in midair. Suddenly the Oracle takes off flying with Jesse holding tight to the rope. He was raised up off the ground and began floating in the air under her. Grabbing a light pole with one arm, still holding the Oracle, he asked the ring, "What do I do now?" "Hold on!" The Stone blurted out, laughing as hard as Jesse has ever heard him laugh. Jesse was mad at first, but then realized how ridiculous this event was. They both started laughing causing Jesse to lose his grip on the light pole. She took off around a corner dragging Jesse right across the hood of Sheriff Piper's car. She and Deputy Broady were sitting in the car, making eye contact with Jesse as he rolled over their hood, not believing what they were seeing.

"Isn't that the Mason kid?" Sheriff Piper asked. "I believe it is, but isn't it too early for Halloween?" replied the deputy.

"Yes, it is and tell me which Halloween did you ever seen a witch flying down Main Street?"

Soon with a police car following, lights flashing and sirens blaring, Jesse continued getting dragged down one street then another. Still swinging on the end of the rope running into building after building as the old hag turns the corner.

Jesse demanding the ring to "Stop laughing, there is a police car right behind us." Answering The Stone says, "Use the rope as a lasso and heard the witch like riding a horse." Jesse did and it worked. Cutting down an ally trying to escape the police car for obvious reasons. "Where are we heading? "Jesse inquired.

"Turn down here past the elephant and head back to the beauty shop Jesse." The Stone instructed.

When they arrived, The Stone spoke again "Enough!" Bringing the Oracle to a complete stop, as the stone caught and held her motionless in the air, struggling to get free, she shouted "LET ME GO!"

"Watch you old witch, here is where I will send you if you don't help us!"

As he showed her the fiery realm. Knowing she couldn't fight the stone, she then said firmly, "What do you want, Wonder stone of destiny?" "We need some answers and have summoned you to enlighten us?"

"Alright, I will help you. No sense getting so testy a girl just wants to have some fun. Go ahead then Stone of Wonder ask your question?"

"We wish to know of what power Kumba now holds?"

She reached up, hands spread out and says, "I must concentrate, yes, oh my, your enemy holds much power. He holds the sister ambulate, the Rubella charm, Morgana's magic."

"Wait, did Kumba hold this charm when he was vanished by the last Wonder?" The Stone questions.

Looking at the stone, the Oracle continues, "Yes, but you knew this already, didn't you?" "Mind your business you witch, you're not hear to ask questions." The Stone replies.

"Ah, the brilliant Stone of Wonder doesn't know the answer."

"Yes, I sent Kumba into the nether realm and although Kumba was unaware of time the ordeal past quickly for him. The Rubella was wide awake all this time."

"Yes, and she is pissed seeking revenge against you, Stone of Wonder for locking her up."

"What else can you tell us?" Jesse demanded as he pointed the ring at the Oracle.

"Easy boy, I'll get to it! I see a full moon, yes, the next full moon your battle is set to take place. Much, much power this man has collected. Not even the stone's power may be enough for you to survive the ordeal I have just envisioned!" the oracle continued, "There is nothing but trouble in your future young warrior. Beware the Snake! He will attack from two realms at once and it is you Jesse Mason who have a destiny to either save them all or perish! Heed these warnings young warrior!

There I have answered your questions, now you must pay me for this service as magic always requires a price!"

"What is the amount of money you want?" Jesse asked, as to not have a curse added against him. "No money" she laughed saying, "Let's see, you will not bring me a body, and you will not trade for the ring. How about a kiss young man, yes, a nice juicy slobbering kiss?" grabbing Jesse's arm and puckering up making kissing sounds. Jesse turned his head almost throwing up, gagging. "No!' the Oracle said laughing, "Well then, how about a simple lock of your hair, just a few strands will suffice." Jesse reached into his pocket and pulled out the comb and handed it to Mathilda. "Yes, yes" she cackled, "Now the debt has been paid, leave me be in this body as you said you would."

As the police car was pulling up, the stone rushes her, "Go quickly! We need you no more!"

"Alright, alright, I'm going, don't get your panties twisted."

The Stone cast a spell and the animals and the vehicles returned to their former selves just as Sheriff Piper drove up.

She turned the siren off and got out of the car saying "How long have you been sitting here Jesse?"

"You know my name Sheriff?"

"Don't see how I can forget it right now."

"Just sitting here officer, speaking with Mrs. Hawk." "Can you confirm this Mrs. Hawk?"

Mrs. Hawk raised her head slowly and said "Sheriff, didn't see you there, how are you doing?" Sheriff shook her head and told the deputy, let's go. "But wasn't that Mrs. Hawk floating down the street? Wasn't it her and what about the Elephant sheriff, you just want to forget what we just watched?" Deputy Broady questioned. Sheriff Piper turned to Jesse and said, "I don't know what is going on Mr. Mason, but I'll be keeping an eye on you." Broady asked, "Aren't you going to arrest them Sheriff?" "Just get in the car," she says, "I am not going to read in the paper tomorrow that I arrested two people, one boy and one witch for floating down the street!" After the Sheriff left, Jesse wondered, "So this Rubella charm, you already know of it?"

"Yes, I was aware of her when I sent Kumba away. I could have left her here, but she is too powerful. I knew I had to go away for a while and couldn't in good conscience leave her here in the hands of man."

"Her, I thought you said it was an amulet, a thing, not a person, or a she?"

"Jesse, just as I am a sentient being, created by a super intelligent race who resides in Realm two using technology unknown in the other realms, they gave me life. While The Rubella charm was created with magic to live and become as a sister to Morgana. By using strong magic she became aware of other realms and connected to the one we call number seven, where a different form of magic is used and technology is abundant. Using this realm along with her magic, the amulet became alive and was given the name "The Rubella". For all unknown reason she considers herself as female much in the same way I consider myself male."

"Wait a minute, she is a conscious female amulet and you are a male living stone. Do you have some history with this female pocket watch, I am unaware of?"

"Yes, I know Rubella very well and yes she could be a little mad about me sending her into that nothing realm."

"Okay I think I understand now, you couldn't use your wisdom to figure this out, because of the amulet being a female and females think more with emotions in their calculations, is that about, right?"

"Maybe." announced the stone, "but as you said, I do not have much experience with the human ritual of dating and this is my first time dealing with a vengeful magical female amulet, I am at a loss. Plus, when Rubella and I first met I had no knowledge of magic except what I learned later from Merlin, and was not the master which I am today"

Jesse went over to see Emma and told her of the event. She met Mrs. Hawk when she first came to town. She was a lively good-hearted woman till her husband passed. She remembers a time when the police stopped her and she told them her name was Happy-Butt. After asking her three times about her name he then asked for her driver's license. He tells her mam it says here your name is Gladys. She responded, "Well Glad-ass, or Happy-butt, officer, what's the difference?" Which mad them both chuckle a little.

In their hideout Kumba's henchmen lie waiting for their orders. "I'm changing my name to Hip Hop Harry! Sounds cool, doesn't it?" Harry said. "Better than Reel E. Harry," Kurly replied, "I've been thinking about changing my name to Kurly 2 Cents, or 3 Cent Kurly. What do you think?"

"I always knew you were worth more than 2 cents, bro." "Thanks man, see I put it in front of my name instead of atthe end.

It makes sense. Or should I say it makes perfect 'cents'?" Harry said, trying not to laugh at his own pun. Kumba and Moe walked in. "Have you seen them yet?" Kumba inquired. "Sure did. They walked by about twenty minutes ago. They looked so happy holding hands. Ah, love is in the air." Kurly swooned. "You idiot!" Moe yells, "You were supposed to tell us when you see them!" Kumba leaned in close to Kurly with an intense gaze and threatened, "Next time you mess up I will cast a spell on you so you will remember. Now will you three get off your butts and do what I am paying you to do!"

Moe peeked around the corner of a building and announced "There they are, walking around the Emporium." Harry asked, "What's the plan Moe?"

"Let's jump out and scare the bejesus out of them. Now on the count of three – one, two, three!"

They jumped out of the corner, but both Jesse and Emma were nowhere in sight. "Where did they go?" Kurly asked. "Split up and look for them," Moe ordered. Kurly walked down the road, around a corner and came face to face with them. "Morning, lovers!"

Jesse looked at Emma then asked, "Are you here to cause more trouble?" "That's what he is paying us for. Just not sure why."

"You mean you are getting paid to harass us?" "Suppose to be, but I haven't seen any money as yet. Emma asked, "Then why are you doing this?"

Moe sees Kurly, his back obscuring the two lovers. "Hey, Kurly! Do you see them?"

Kurly stayed silent for a second, making Jesse and Emma nervous. Then states, "Nothing here Moe. Must have gone the other way. You two better split. If Mr. Kumba knew I let you go, I would be in deep crap!" Both heaved a sigh of relief. "Thanks?" Emma replied. "But why are you helping us all of a sudden?" Jesse asked.

"No time to explain bro, but if we don't do this we're toast."

As Jesse and Emma left, Kurly was still watching adorning a sad pitiful face, afraid to go back to Kumba after having failed him once more. He looked at Emma and mouth the words – "Help me!"

Back at the hideout Kumba was furious. "We couldn't find them Sir," Moe explained. "Then why are you back here? If I find out any of you are helping them I'll make frog soup with your corpse!" Kurly swallowed hard and stuttered, "Frog soup?

"You don't want that, do you boy?" Kumba asked. "No, sir." "Then get out there and look for them!"

CHAPTER 28

Bug City Airliner

Blue and the Professor discussed how the model plane should arrive at Bug City just before dark. They had built a harness for Willy, and fixed the plane's tail with old tape from a box and some sticks. They placed the kazoo cone under the tail so smaller bugs could come into the plane from the back and the larger ones can come through the side door. Once everyone has boarded the Professor would place the microphone back into the cone as a plug. Captain Striker flew down.

"Blue, the team found Willy trapped in a sandpit trying to walk out of it.

He was supposed to come here, where did he go?"

"Not sure," striker replied. Could you please find Willy again and bring him here personally? If not, he would most likely stay lost."

The Captain found Willy flying aimlessly trying to figure where to go. He rushed him to turn around, leading him to the Junk yard.

"How much longer Professor?" Blue asked. "We're almost there Blue," said the professor, "Go and make sure the bugs are ready. If the coast is clear we should arrive on schedule. I will explain to Willy what he is supposed to do and harness him. We will meet you in the city by nightfall." Blue flew to the Bug City hotel and went over every detail with the frightened bugs.

The cardinals were keeping a close watch around the bushes surrounding Bug City making sure that none of the bugs could escape. Shiver just arrived perching on top of a towering tree. It was almost dark when Captain Striker and his squadron landed just outside the bush surrounding Bug City.

"Are you ready to proceed Captain Striker?" asked Blue. "Yes, my squadron is ready. Are we all set?"

Willy can be seen up above, pulling the plane behind him and coming in for a landing. Suddenly the plane started spinning as it descended. Hitting the ground with a flop. The professor came out the door all dizzy from the ride. Upon inspection he saw the tape holding the tail had come off. Without it there is no way to guide the plane. "Everyone, we will have to cancel the trip. The Phoenix needs fixing." the Professor announced. Blue looked at the tail. "I think I may have a way to fix it. Just back the plane under the bush to Bug City while I look for Bella." Blue then prepared Captain Striker, "It is time to proceed with your part of the plan. Please keep those cardinals at bay." "You got it," Captain Striker said, "Fall in squadron!" They got into formation, and then dove fast towards the cardinals zooming in a circle over them.

Each member of the squadron pecked hard on one of the red birds' heads as they swished past them. This sent the red birds in a frenzy, scurrying away. But hunger made the brothers persistent. Each time they tried to circle back Captain Striker shouted orders left and right telling his team to press on. Shiver watched patiently. If they are planning to fly the bugs in that contraption I just need to wait and attack them once they are up in the air. Then I'd have me some juicy pigeon, and a bluebird for an appetizer, he thought. "Okay, Scooter. Time for you to bring out the bugs," Blue ordered. The bugs swung the hotel doors open running toward the plane as quickly as they can. "Bella!" Blue cried out. "Where are you girl?" Blue hoped she had made her transformation into a butterfly, because it is their last hope to save the bugs. From out of the hotel door came a colorful butterfly. Blue flew alongside her and told her of the plane's missing tail. "Can you hold on to that stick? Use your wings to guide the plane." Bella nodded. "I'll try!" She grabbed tightly onto the stick while Piper and her brothers, four on each side, held on to the wings in front. "Crank them up!" Piper shouted, her and her brothers began to glow brightly.

The bugs boarded the plane quickly. Some of them were very fearful because they have never flown before. The Professor told Blue that Willy kept going the wrong way. Blue called for Cowboy Cracker.

"Do you think you can ride this bird and keep him flying straight?"

"You can bet your sugar cubes I can!"

"Professor let's fit Willy with some reins and a saddle for Cowboy Cracker"

"Yee-haw" Cowboy Cracker said excitedly, as he climbed up on Willy's back. "Alright everyone," the Professor yelled, "Buckle in and hold tight!" He turned to Blue and said, "All secure and ready to go!" The Red Wing squadron were succeeding at keeping the cardinals away. "Okay, everyone ready? You know what to do?" Blue asked. "Yes!" everyone in the plane said in unison. Cowboy Cracker patted Willy's neck. "Who's a good boy? Who's ready to fly?" Willy raised his head and stood in attention while waiting for the go signal.

Blue was to stay in place over the top of the plane where she could speak with everyone: Bella operating the tail of the plane, Cowboy Cracker in front, and the Professor inside all ready to do their part. Blue checked the sky for the Cardinals and saw Captain Striker keeping them quite busy. "Everyone let's get this show on the road," she hollered. The air was filled with anxious voices, the sound of little violins playing, and the glow of the lighting bugs along the wings.

Cowboy Cracker stuck his spurs into Willy's neck and hollered, "Giddy up!" Willy and Blue both started flapping and the plane started bobbing off the ground steadily up to the sky. "It's working!" Piper exclaimed. "Perfect! Bella, turn your wings a little to the right," Bella does as Blue says, "Now, keep going straight." The mighty team of blackbirds flew right behind the model plane as the three cardinals, now tired but still relentless, hurried and tried to catch up to the craft.

Shiver watched as the plane flew up into the air and took off as soon as it did. The sun was almost setting and the skies grew dimmer, but it was easy for him to follow the lightning bugs. He positioned himself high above their heads where he followed the small aircraft. Captain Striker's senses were quick and sharp. He glanced and immediately saw the hawk above and ordered some of his squadron to protect the plane. Shiver dove straight down toward the little plane. Getting faster and faster by the minute. Just then a member of the Red Wing squadron came in front of Shiver's attack and sounded the alarm. The squadron did their emergency formation and charged upwards toward the formidable beast, faster than they have ever done in the past. Each member clawed into Shiver's skin, forcing him to let out a pained screech.

Blue looked up to the sky and said, "Oh no! It's Shiver! Fly faster Willy!" Cowboy Cracker stuck his spurs even harder into Willy's neck, "Yee-haw! Giddy up! Faster! Shiver is right behind us!" Willy had flashbacks of Shiver's earlier attacks and his enormous claws, and felt a sudden surge of adrenaline. Cowboy Cracker's hat almost flew off of his head and everyone in the plane swayed sideways as Willy picked up the pace. As the squadron kept Shiver busy, the cardinals circled around to catch Bella. Each of them took turns snipping at her and trying to get a bite of her butterfly's wings. Sin Say Sam heard Bella's frightened screams and hurried to the top of the plane's tail using his karate moves every time the cardinals came near.

Squeals filled the plane as it whirled around trees and

passengers were tossed from side to side. Blue shouted, "We need some help Professor! The red birds are chasing the plane and are about to eat Bella!" The professor took to the microphone and started making a loud sound using his kazoo. It made a loud blast, louder than it did back in the junkyard, the cardinals quickly flew away from the plane. Captain Striker flew down to Blue.

"I have two men down. He is still coming at us, and we can't hold him much longer!"

"What do we do Captain?" Blue asked.

"He can see the plane because of the lights. If we turn those lights off there are fewer chances he will catch you."

Shiver broke away from the squadron of blackbirds and headed for the plane. Shiver plowed through the cardinals knocking them to the ground. He yelled, "You guys are useless! Get lost and never show your face again or I will kill you!" Afraid of Shiver's wrath the three quickly dashed away. Blue shouted triumphantly. "Three down and one to go!" Blue thought since she outsmarted Shiver once before she could do it again! "Captain, I have an idea. We need to make Shiver mad as a distraction. Can you fly up and inform Cowboy Cracker to wait for my signal?"

It was so dark if not for the lighting bugs one wouldn't be able to see their hand their front of their face. Willy felt frightened making him turn in the wrong direction once again. Cowboy Cracker calmed Willy, "it's okay boy. Don't be scared, just close your eyes and go where I lead you." Willy nodded and followed his instructions to head straight for the bushes to set the trap. Shiver was closing in fast and licked his beak in anticipation of his bluebird meal. "Faster, Cracker! Fly faster!" Blue commanded, "Head for that big tree!" she turned to Piper, "Are you and your brothers' ready?" "Yes, we are!" The Professor shouted, "We're already here!" The bugs held on tight to their seats with their eyes glaring, and mouths screaming. Blue pointed out the perfect spot for Cowboy Cracker. "Over there is the perfect place for our trap," she directed, "Keep heading over that very large bush, the one in front of that tree. That's the spot."

As the plane made its way towards the tree, Blue hollered, "Okay everyone. Get ready! Here we go!" She mouthed a countdown as Shiver was about to swoop in. Cracker maneuvered the plane left then right and in a loop. Then he steered it straight down. "Five, four, three, two, one – now, Cracker!" Blue shouted, just as the plane flew a few feet above the ground. The Professor instructed the bugs to scream as loud as they could to produce the loudest racket the kazoo cone ever made.

Shiver screeched from the deafening noise and became disoriented. When he closed his eyes the lighting bugs shut off their lights and let go of the plane while staying in formation. Cowboy Cracker turned the plane to the side away from Shiver. Shiver shook his head trying to gain composure but as soon as he opened his eyes the plane was gone.

Piper and her brothers turned their lights back on pretending they still have a hold of the plane. Shiver regained his senses and saw the lights. "There you are!" He snarled. He was flying towards the siblings at an incredible speed. Seeing this they flew towards the trap. Piper and her brothers formed a target circle in front of the bush. By the time Shiver realized it was too late. He flew into the trap. He had hit the tree hard breaking branches and making a loud thud. He tried to stand up hoping to continue attacking but his head spun and spun. Everything went dim as his eyes rolled.

The siblings searched for the plane, but could not find it where it was supposed to be. From a distance Cowboy Cracker can be heard hollering, "The plan worked Blue! The hawk is down!" they quickly followed suit in that direction. Everyone cheered and clapped for them.

The roaches started playing "Hallelujah" in celebration.

"Grab the plane and turn your lights back on Piper," Blue said, "We need to figure out where we are and see where we are going!"

The cardinals saw what happened to Shiver. With the threat no longer in sight they followed the siblings' lights. "Watch out!" Captain Striker shouted! "The brothers are closing in fast!" "Cracker fine a place to set the plane down? We'll take care of this," Blue ordered. Cracker pulled back the reins, "Open your eyes Willy, we need to land." Willy began shaking a little.

"I am afraid to open my eyes. I think it's better if I just keep them closed."

The cardinals seeing shiver was now out of their way, they devised a plan of their own. Two of them came over the top of the plane to fight the remaining members of the Red Wing squadron, while one slipped underneath and went after Cowboy Cracker using its beak to bite the reins. This knocked Cowboy Cracker off his saddle and made him fly up into the air hitting Bella off her spot. She lost her grip and was left holding on to the stick with only one hand. Cracker yelled out as he fell towards the ground, "Help!"

Captain Striker swooped in to catch Cowboy Cracker just in time before he hit the ground. "Ye-haw!" he cried out as he held on to Captain Striker's back and waved his hat in the air. "I…I can't hold on much longer Blue," Bella pleaded. Slowly, she lost her remaining grip, causing the plane to lose its tail, spiraling out of control. The bugs screamed in horror. Bella felt dizzy as she spun in the air. Willy's feet began to get tangled in the string that connected him to the plane. The plane started to go down fast. Willy's eyes were still closed and he just kept flying away. Blue tried to hold it up, but it was just too heavy for the little bird. The plane twisted in circles barreling ever faster toward the ground. Blue flapped her wings frantically to slow the plane's descent. Striker grabbed the tail to help slow the plane down as it crashed to the ground. The plane screeched and bobbed stopping just a few inches off the water of Symphony Pond. Inside the plane there was utter silence. "Did we make it? Is everyone alright?" the Professor asked, looking out one of the planes windows, his glasses off his face still dizzy from the ride. "

Yes!" Blue shouted "But Willy is gone and I am not sure where we are."

Bella clapped her hands with glee as they opened the plane door, and all the bugs poured out. Some sliding down the cone at the back of the plane, while others were cheering and thanking Blue for saving them, but as the bugs looked around, they began to wonder. "This isn't our winter home," Scooter told Blue. The clouds began to part and moonlight shone upon everything. "I know where we are," Blue surmised as the bugs left the plane.

"This has to be Symphony Pond."

Everyone gasped, "Everyone, stay away from the water's edge and be very quiet." All around there was silence. You could only hear the sound of the breeze blowing gently through the trees. The pond began to bubble, and a croak was heard. "Frogs!" a bug shouted, the crowd ran back frantically into the plane, afraid of being eaten. "We must leave this place fast," Cowboy Cracker told them as he climbed off Captain Striker's back keeping a careful eye for possible danger nearby, "Blue we have traveled way off course and the Professor says the plane is damaged. It will take days to repair it."

Blue kept silent examining the situation. She knew that without a plane they were in serious trouble. They must both head south to find a way across the pond. Coming face to face with large toads, or go around the edge and face other dangers even before they make their way through Kumba's grasslands. Captain Striker, who knows this area well, is concerned.

"Blue, I don't think either way is a good idea. It isn't safe anywhere around here."

Blue knew this was the truth. Choosing either one, meant that they could all be eaten.

CHAPTER 29

There Be Monsters in Them Waters!

Up in the air Blue could hear thousands of frogs sounding off in the thick grassy bog, "We have no choice our best chance is to cross the pond." The Professor exclaimed as he examined the plane, "We cannot fly the plane Blue. There's too much damage and both wings are broken, but if we can find something to seal up these holes, we might be able to use it as a raft and float it across the pond."

Blue thought hard and remembered the tree sap that her brother had gotten stuck into once before. "Let's build a raft then." She said and told Piper and her brothers were to collect some sap to plug up any holes. Captain Striker agreed, "Great idea, but we must hurry. My squadron is keeping those cardinals busy, but with the moon coming out those trouble makers will not take too long to find us."

Everybody began patching up the holes with sap and tying twigs and sticks to support it underneath. Just as they were pushing the raft into the water it seemed like the whole pond was waking up. Frogs and fish could hear the sound of the broken plane splashing into the water. "It floats!" The Professor said, relieved. "We need to hurry!" shouted Captain

Striker, "Those red birds have spotted us and my squadron is getting very tired.

They can't hold them back for long!"

Watchful eyes emerged all around the raft from out of the water. "Frogs everywhere!" The professor warned, "We must move now!" Blue and Captain Striker pulled the raft with a cord and it started moving through the water. Suddenly a frog jumped on top of the raft then another. They croaked calling on to their comrades until the entire raft was surrounded by hungry frogs. It got harder and harder for them to pull the raft as more frogs jumped on top of it. The raft began to get heavy and the threat of sinking became real. Blue found a stick and shooed the frogs away. The raft began leaking from the inside. Professor and Cowboy Cracker immediately tried to seal the holes up. "Help!" the bugs cried out as more water seeped. A tiny voice then came out from the water. "You need help?" It was Mabel! "Yes, Mabel! We are in trouble" Blue begged, "Could you grab one of the strings in front of the plane and pull us toward the other side before these frogs make us sink?" "Of course!" Mabel obliged.

From up above the red birds spotted the aircraft. "There they are!" one pointed. Moe dove straight for them grabbing and holding Blue down with his claws. Captain Striker let go of his string at once to help Blue fight off the red bird. "What are you going to do now bluebird?" Moe grinned. The professor got a hold of his kazoo and sounded it as loud as he could behind Moe. The kazoo just sputtered with bubbles pouring out. Moe laughed, "Your noise maker isn't working anymore, is it?" He then kicked the Professor into the frog-infested water.

"Nothing will save you now, Blue! This is the end for you and your bug friends!"

Everything seemed in vain. All the bugs were crying desperately while the squadron was wounded and getting weary fast. One frog jumped and landed on top of the plane causing part of it to go underwater. From inside the bugs could see more frogs staring back into the plane's windows. Their tongues slapping against the glass. Harry pecked on top of the plane trying to break it open so he can eat the bugs inside. "Say goodbye Blue," Moe said with a devilish smile while pecking at Blue's head. "Wait," Blue pleaded, "Can I just say one more thing?" "Say your final farewell?" Moe laughed. "Piper," Blue cried out, "remember the story I told you about my brother Berry and the tree sap?" "You mean how it was stuck to his legs?" Piper asked. "Yes, that's right. Maybe these red birds would like some of those sap bugs?"

Piper understood and took off. "What bugs are those?" Moe asked, salivating over the thought of more bugs. "You and your brothers want bugs, don't you?" Blue continued, "We will give you plenty if you spare my life and my friends'."

"Is this some kind of trick or are you just stalling?"

"No, no. See here comes Piper and her brothers with those bugs just for you and your brothers."

Piper and her brothers started throwing the dead sap-covered bug parts at the cardinals. Consumed by hunger the brothers were hypnotized by the bugs coming their way. But soon they were covered with sap. "What's all this sticky stuff?"

Moe questioned angrily, "This isn't going to save you." Moe looked at his brothers. One had its head stuck inside the plane after making a hole in it trying to grab a bug. The other was squeezing Blue around her neck. "Let's finish this," Moe said.

He reared back to deliver a hard blow to Blue's head.

All of a sudden something grabbed Moe's neck from the back, and then pulled back hard. "What is this?" he shouted. Hearing his brother's scream Harry pulled his head out from the small hole inside the aircraft and came over to help. But like his brothers something grabbed and pulled his head yanking him off the plane and into the water. The frogs had not eaten bugs fell into the water. Some of the sap-laden bugs were stuck to the cardinals' feathers, and the frogs wasted no time in having a go at them. Their tongues latched on the red birds left and right allowing Blue to finally break free from the red birds' grip.

"Mabel," she called. "Can you call your dad?" Mabel looked strangely at Blue. "Are you sure?" Blue shouted, "Yes! Hurry!" The three red birds were trying hard to rid themselves from the frogs, slinging them back into the water. "Hey fellas," Blue yelled, "You want to see a magic trick?" The three were seething. "We'll be free in a minute! Just you wait!" Moe retorted. They were almost free and began to laugh as they moved toward Blue again. Just as two of the cardinals broke free a large splash was heard nearby. The waters around the plane started swishing back and forth. The raft started wobbling as the pond churned. Blue smiled and muttered under her breath, "Here comes the magic!" "What kind of magic trick is this" Hairy asked "A disappearing one." Blue answered.

A high wall of water shot straight up out of the murky pond along with what seemed like a large streak of silver. The three cardinal's eyes popped out in terror screaming at the massive fish in front of them. Harry and Kurly flew up at once holding each other tightly as the big bass opened his enormous mouth. Moe stood frozen, his mouth hung open unable to move. In a split- second the big fish jumped over the plane and sucked the red bird into his mouth, diving back into the deep waters. After seeing their brother's demise, the two birds flew off as fast as they could. The raft was once again afloat. Mabel's head popped out of the water, "Are you okay Blue?"

"I was sure glad to see you girl! I thought I was a goner for sure." "My dad was actually sleeping, but my mom insisted that he help. I think that fat juicy bird he just ate made him a little less grumpy."

Molly came right behind Mabel, "Are you alright my dear?" "Yes, Ma'am, thanks to your family," Blue replied. "What are you doing in our pond with a plane full of bugs in the middle of the night anyway?" Molly asked.

"Such a long story! I would love to tell you all about it someday, but right now we really need your help. We still have a long way to go."

"I see. What can we do to help?" Molly asked.

"Could you please help us get this plane over to the other side of the pond and away from all these frogs? My friends are inside and we are trying to get them home."

Molly looked at Blue, smiling and shaking her head, she said; "Blue you are a strange one. You make friends with fish and now you are trying to save bugs. I have never met someone who cares so much for what most birds eat for breakfast." Blue chuckled, "Well, I am just trying to help!" "Henry!" Molly yelled out. The waters churned and there he was. "What is it, Molly?"

The bugs inside the plane could see the enormous fish and were huddled in the middle believing this was their end.

"Push that plane across the pond and over to the other side for our friend Blue. And mind your manners." "Yes, dear. But I am going back to bed after this."

Henry swam back to the edge of the pond and started pouring through the water like a torpedo straight for the plane. Picking up speed as he charged forward. "Hold on tight!" Molly shouted. Everyone in the plane huddled together, nervously holding on with all their might. Some began to scream, while the roaches started singing:

"Way down upon the Suwanee River, We're still not home To a place where the fish won't eat us That's where we want to roam."

The big fish hit under the plane raising it up out of the water like a surfboard carrying it speedily across the water and tossing it on to dry land. The plane rolled over a couple of times till it came to a halt at the banks. "How's that Blue?"

Molly asked. Blue replied with glee and gratitude, "Wonderful! Thank you so much Ma'am! We are all very grateful for your help. But the bugs cannot thank you personally, because they are afraid to be eaten by a fish or a frog. They really are so thankful!" Miss Molly laughed, "That's okay dear. Tell them they are welcome.

"Yawl look very tired and should rest here for the night. Mable and I will keep watch." Blue was ecstatic, "Really? Thank you!" Scooter sat by a fire with Piper and the others. "How are you, guys?" Blue asked. Scooter laughed, "Well, this was quite the adventure I can tell you that." Sin Say Sam scratched his head a little, "I would like a little less adventure and a little more of our winter home." "I agree with that," Cowboy Cracker said. Professor Fly nodded his head in agreement.

Out of know where, Bug circus's Famous Ringmaster Domino Fatty walked out of the grass, "Well wasn't that exciting to see and was it worth all the trouble," he kept on, "What is so special about this winter home anyway? Why is it better there than where I live?" Scooter looked over at Domino Fatty and said, "To answer your question Fatty, our home is where we all stay because it is nice and warm, and it's a great place to live and play when the cold winds blow outside. Home feels safe. At least that's what my mom says." The rest of the bugs nodded. Fatty nodded too, "I think I understand now why you want to go there and why just any old place won't do. I feel the same way about my circus."

All the bugs curled up closer to the fire. Scooter looked at Blue and asked, "Blue, things are so scary here. Are you sure you are going to be able to get us home?" "I wish my dad, the Commander, was here to help me," Blue sighed as she pondered what to do next. "Did you say the Commander is your father?" blurted Domino Fatty Flea. "Do you know where my father is?" Blue pleaded. "Sorry Blue. I have no idea, but I remember the mice talking about King Kumba having the commander in a cage. We can ask them tomorrow." Jesse knew then and remembered his dream about Kumba the king snake having Blue's father in a cage.

This is where Blue must go to save her father and defeat the evil snake.

Blue was up early and flew over the field where they must continue their travel. While trying to find the safest path for them to follow she saw her friend Clifford.

"Hey, Clifford. You have grown since the last time I saw you." "Oh, hello Blue. What brings you here?" "I need your help to travel through your field to bring my bug friends back to their winter home." Clifford was quite surprised.

"I didn't know you had bugs for friends Blue. But sure. I will be happy to help in any way I can."

"Great! I have another question for you about Kumba. They say he has prisoners in cages. Do you know anything about that?"

Clifford nodded his head in sorrow, "Yes, everybody knows about that. I have seen the cages myself." "Is my father there?" Blue asked. "Well," Clifford replied, "there are many blackbirds there and mice. I believe I also saw a bluebird there. But it is a heavily guarded place. Every time Kumba wants to make a statement he brings out prisoners and eats them in front of everyone or tortures them." Blue felt anxious and hopeful at the same time. "Thanks Clifford. This is the best information about my father's whereabouts so far. But first, I must get my friends to their winter home."

"Where are your friends now?"

"They're at Symphony Pond right now," said Blue. "I will meet you there and show you the safest way across the field," Clifford replied. Blue flew back to tell the others and to introduce Clifford. All the bugs were awake and sitting around a small campfire the professor had built. Captain Striker was there with only one member of the Red Wing Squadron. The rest were too injured from last night's fight. "Has anyone seen Willy?" Blue asked. Everyone looked around and shook their heads.

"Okay, here's the plan," she continued. "Captain Striker you and Sergeant Swift take Cowboy Cracker and Professor Fly and find Which Way Willy. Check the city for him. That is where his home is. Tell him of our situation and that we need him. Bring him back here and have The Professor hook him up once more. Then meet us in the field. The bugs cannot remain here. The frogs haven't eaten since the cold spell. We don't want to risk it. Clifford and I will find a path. We will start marching there on foot. Piper, you, your brothers, and Bella will keep watch from up in the air for anything that might be hiding in the grass especially King Kumba."

Everyone agreed. Cowboy Cracker and Professor Fly climbed on back of the two remaining blackbirds and left to find Willy. Clifford told the bugs to follow him, while Piper checked the path ahead. Off they went to cross the scary jungle ahead. Blue stayed by the water and called for Mabel to say her thank, "I will miss you Mabel and I will see you real soon." Blue gave Mabel a light peck on the head and flew off. Blue caught up with the bug caravan as they followed Clifford through the tall grass. They took many turns and worked their way around hungry toads and their families. Blue was glad Clifford was there to help. He knew hidden paths around the field and served as the perfect guide.

Clifford took the bugs on a path toward his home where they came upon a small clearing. He held his paw up for them to stop. He looked all around his home, but everything was unusually quiet. None of his family was out playing as they usually were. All the other houses surrounding his were in shambles. Suddenly a big snake started slithering next to them. Clifford turned around toward the bugs holding his finger in front of his lips. The snake was so big that it seemed like it spanned forever. Blue saw the big snake and she knew it was King Kumba. She landed quietly and spoke with the mouse. Clifford began to cry a little. Fearful that Kumba had eaten his family. Blue wrapped her arms around Clifford and assured him, "Don't worry Clifford. I am sure they are just hiding somewhere. As soon as the bugs get home, I will help you find them." Once the path was clear of Kumba, Clifford led the group in the other direction.

During the search for Willy Captain Striker and Cracker visited the hole near Blue's house where the two first met. They also checked Bug City and the woods where they escaped from Shiver. The Professor and Sergeant Swift checked the airport and the area around Shiver's nest before heading to meet up with the Captain and Cracker in the city. Shiver was in his nest resting. He was all bruised and bandaged. While he was laying there looking up at the sky, he spotted the Professor riding away toward town. What that bluebird did caused such embarrassment, he thought. He decided to follow them in hopes of being led to Blue.

In the city the Professor spotted a large cage with lots of pigeons roosting and went down to speak with them. There they found Willy hiding near the back of the pen. He was still shaken up over their harrowing escape from Shiver. They told him what had happened and how much they still needed his help. Then out of nowhere Shiver zoomed in and landed on top of the cage. He was so large and muscular that it sank a little from his weight. All the pigeons and the Professor jumped into the cage and shut the door. This angered the hawk even more. "Tell me where that bluebird is hiding! I have a score to settle with him," he demanded. The birds kept quiet and just huddled together in fear. "We're not telling you anything!" the Professor cried out. Shiver squeezed his claws into the cage wires ripping it and roaring "Fine, I will find her After Shiver left the pigeons shared tales of their own encounters with Shiver and how they wished they could do something to rid themselves of this monster. Professor

Fly was studying the bird cage as this was the first time, he had seen anything like this. He noticed netting hanging on the wall and asked Willy what it was used for. "The pigeon caretaker used to be a fisherman. These are nets he used for fishing," Willy answered. An idea hatched in the Professor's mind, "That's very interesting." He then climbed on to Willy's back asking him to help save the others. "I am too scared," Willy replied.

"So, you're just going to sit here afraid and let Shiver eat your friends?"

"Blue's in trouble?" Willy asked.

"Yes, and she needs you, Willy. We all do."

"In that case, I will help," Willy told them as he stood up mightily, "Blue would help me if I needed help." The other pigeons were amazed at Willy's courage to leave the safety of the pigeon coop and face an angry Shiver.

They all headed back to Symphony Pond to collect and fix what was left of the shattered plane. "What's the plan?" Cowboy Cracker asked the Professor. "Well, I am going to figure something out as to how we can use what's left of this plane. Cracker can help me, while you go and locate Blue and tell her we will be there as soon as we are able. Then report back here," the Professor ordered. "Yes, sir," Striker answered. The Professor began removing the broken wings off the plane and fitted them underneath to create a sled. Then he tied some rope from the sled and attached it to Willy. Cowboy Cracker mounted Willy getting ready to pull the sled through the grass to the caravan.

CHAPTER 30

Hot & Extra Spicy

The sled worked better than expected, and the gang was speeding through the grass in no time. Cowboy Cracker spotted Captain Striker from a distance motioning for them to head toward him. "Giddy up!" Cracker shouted as he sank his spurs into Willy's neck, "we are in a hurry to catch up with the bugs." The sled jerked forward as they sped up sending the Professor flying to the back. Their speed made such noise that King Kumba heard them coming. That sounds like a rabbit heading this way, he thought. He coiled himself and readied for a strike. As the sound drew closer and louder, he hissed and flicked his tongue in excitement. Over his head, Willy suddenly whizzed startling and distracting him. The sled came tearing through the grass hitting Kumba, then traveling up his long slender body like a skier hitting the slopes off of the snake's head.

The sled went flying into the air. "Yahoo!" Cowboy Cracker shouted as the sled hit the ground smoothly and continued plowing through the grass. The Professor climbed out covered with grass. King Kumba still thought that a rabbit had hopped over him and kept searching. He found the sled's tracks that parted through the grass and followed where the trail led. "Our ride is here!" the bugs cheered as Cracker made a full stop at their rendezvous. "This is amazing! You actually turned the plane into a raft, and now a sled!" Blue exclaimed. The Professor blushed, then turned serious, "I think we have a problem. We encountered the snake, and now I am pretty sure that it has been following us." "We need to load up the bugs quickly and keep moving. I'll keep an eye out for that king snake Kumba," Blue said.

As Cracker and the bugs head on to their destination Professor Fly clambered onto Captain Striker's back as backup. Blue saw Kumba slithering through the grass and closing in on her friends. "You're Highness!" she shouted. King Kumba stopped and searched for the voice. "Up here," Blue called out. The big snake looked up and hissed, "What do you want? I am busy chasing a rabbit for dinner." He studied Blue's face and recognized him from their previous encounter. "You think I am unaware of who you are, bluebird? I know this realm better than you, boy! Hah! The ring sent you into battle against me as a bluebird? A weakling?" Jesse felt a bit of panic. How did he know this bird was him? He thought.

"I know you are a boy in the human world and I know that brother bird in your realm is your sister. You are a fool to bring her into my realm!"

Jesse realized that this snake was the magic from Kumba trapped in this realm and it is this snake which he must defeat. "Think Jesse think," Blue whispered as she acted calm and collected, "I am told you know where my father is." "Your father? What father?" "The Commander. How interesting.

How did you know he was my prisoner? Some mice told you, didn't they?" "So, it's true? You do have my father as a prisoner."

"He is mine forever! To do with as I wish, fool. Now out of the way before I eat you!" "You silly snake! That's not a rabbit. It's just a bunch of bugs!" "You don't fool me bird! No bug can make these kinds of tracks."

King Kumba recoiled and snapped his big jaws trying to catch Blue. After three close attempts he snarled and sped off. Captain Striker and the Professor showed up, and Blue shared what he had learned from Kumba.

"I have an idea Blue. Stall Kumba for as long as you can.

I'll fly back to the junkyard and collect something to help us."

Blue quickly caught up with Kumba and grabbed his tail. He jumped up in a fit. "If I catch you, I will swallow you whole," he boasted. The snake took off once more determined to catch what he believed was a rabbit dinner. Blue tried a few more times, angering Kumba. Then she flew ahead to catch up with the sled to warn Crackers of the snake's fast approach.

The two remaining cardinals were watching from a nearby tree. Harry asked, "Look over there. Isn't that Kumba chasing something? I think he might be chasing that bluebird." "No," said Kurly. "That's a rabbit he's chasing but it has no legs?" "Well, what would Kumba call a rabbit with no legs?" Harry joked. "Dinner!" They uttered simultaneously and laughing. "Look at them go, ripping their way through! Still can't figure out how that rabbit can move so fast without legs and all?" Kurly remarked.

Captain Striker and the Professor flew back from the junkyard with a stuffed rabbit that they had filled with extremely hot pepper sauce from the trash. As they flew their way to the sled, they could see the snake below them. The Professor explained his idea to Blue while tying the toy to a string behind the sled. Seeing Kumba only a few feet away the Professor cried out, "Go!" Willy looked back and saw the enormous snake and in reflex he quickly took off away from the frightful snake.

The bugs jerked and flew to the back of the plane from the sheer speed. Kumba got closer zipping his way through the grasslands while keeping an eye on the stuffed rabbit thinking, I knew it! That bird was lying to me. I will catch that bird later and make her pay for her lies!

Blue flew alongside Cracker and told him to slow down so Kumba could catch the stuffed rabbit. As soon as they did Kumba leaped forward grabbing the rabbit and quickly swallowing it whole. "Fly fast, Willy! Kumba has taken the bait." The Professor announced as he reached back to cut the string where the toy rabbit was attached.

The sled hit a bump causing the professor to drop his scissors. He frantically attempted to cut the string by hand. Willy flapped as fast as he could, but the string became tighter and tighter as Kumba pulled the toy. "Blue, a little help! I have nothing left to cut the string with." Blue turned and shouted, "Hold on!" Kumba's eyes widened as he saw the string, realizing the other end led to him. He started to panic, but it was too late. In an instant, he found himself being pulled behind the sled. The big snake's body flung from side to side against rocks and briers along the path.

The string became entangled in grass finally breaking. "Well, he took the bait." The Professor announced, "Maybe he will now stop chasing us." When they looked back though Kumba was back on his belly and was still coming fast. "What now Blue? We are almost at the bugs' winter home," Cracker queried. "I have an idea." Blue quipped and landed on the ground behind the sled. She waited along the path for the big snake to arrive. Upon seeing him she jumped out. Kumba was a little shocked that Blue was standing right in front of him.

"Not scared that I am going to eat you and all your friends, eh?" "Like you did with Clifford's family?"

"Hah!" the snake told Blue, "Those pesky mice got away, but you won't!"

Kumba reared back to strike. His eyes turned red and out from his mouth came a loud belch and red flames. He panicked yelling, "What is this? Am I on fire?" His vision became blurry and he tried to gasp for cool air into his mouth. "How did you like that hot sauce we added to your rabbit?" Blue mocked, "It's a spicy seasoning, and don't you think, your Majesty?" The snake blew another big fireball out of his mouth. He rose above the tall grass crying in anguish, "Water! Water!" He took off faster than lightning and headed for the pond to cool off his flaming mouth.

The group watched Kumba until he was out of sight, then caught up to the sled in the woods. All the bugs came out and cheered as they finally made it home after the long tiring journey. They found the opening to Moss Cave and proceeded inside for a little celebration. Blue told Clifford about the good news about his family and promised to help them. As the day ended Blue said her goodbyes and told them that she would see them again in the spring. Captain Striker and Sergeant Swift left for the bird hospital to pay their injured comrades a visit and Willy returned to the pigeon coop as a hero. Blue carried Professor Fly back to his junkyard before finally flying home to see her family. She was so excited to share adventurous Journey with Berry and Mom.

CHAPTER 31

Ethereal, the Demon King

Jesse woke up feeling good, believing his test was over. After all he did get the bugs back to their winter home, a tremendous feat. Downstairs Mom had a wonderful breakfast of sausage, scrambled eggs, and biscuits. At the breakfast table the family discussed an errand that Jesse would help Grandpa with, and then he had a lovely shopping date with planned with Emma. Things seemed to look bright, but Kumba was relentless in his evil plans.

Kumba donning a voodoo robe was busy with an incantation as Shiver was painting a pentagram, drawn on the floor. The gangsters entered in. Moe nervously said, "You wanted to see us boss?" My name is Kumba! King of voodoo and the mystic arts!" he growled, "You three and Shiver take a candle and stand around the circle. One at each point where the stars meet. We're performing a little ritual." Moe and Harry picked up a candle each and did as they were told. Kurly started easing toward the door trying to slip out when Kumba made eye contact with him and belted, "Where do you think you're going? Get your candle and stand on your spot!" Kurly had no choice but to abide. "Moe, what are we doing? This doesn't feel right," he whispered. Harry agreed, "There is nothing right about any of these fellas."

"Quiet!" Kumba shouted as he continued chanting words in his Creole accent. The room turned dim and a strong gust of wind blew around them. Kurly slowly tried to drop his candle on the ground to make a run for it when Kumba said, "If you leave the circle of protection now, the spirits I have called will devour your soul boy."

"What?" Kurly was in disbelief, "The spirits?" "Yes," replied Kumba. "I am summoning Ethereal, the demon king. If you break the circle, he can collect your soul and take you to his realm, and I assure you, you do not want that."

He continued chanting. Dark ghostly shadows appeared in the room one by one until they were all completely surrounded by the dark figures. "Moe? Harry, what are these things?" Kurly shuddered in fear, from being face to face with these apparitions. "Don't break the circle Kurly, or we'll all be toast."

"Quiet!" Kumba shouted angrily. "I call on Ethereal, the dark one. Come to me and grant me your power oh mighty king." A thunderous voice - "WHO SUMMONDS ME HERE?"

"Crap!" Kurly mumbled. Kumba continued, his eyes still closed. "I ask you for your powers, oh great mighty one of darkness!"

One of the spirits came face to face with Kurly, who went pale as ashes and whispered, "Moe?!" "We all see them Kurly. Just don't break the circle!" Moe replied. The dark voice

spoke once more.

"Why should I bestow on you that power which I hold?"

"Oh, dark one, send me your power to vanquish my enemies from this realm."

Silence fell in the room as the boys stared at each other. Kurly whispered, "Is he talking about Jesse and Emma?" Harry Replied; "I think so?"

"Who is this enemy you speak of?" The demon king commanded!

"The stone of Wonders new warrior," Kumba shouted. The demon King continued, "Awe, the light has awakened and has chosen a new warrior, the enemy of all darkness. I will join with you wizard, live inside you and I will give you what you seek, my power, take it all and let it serve you!" the voice resounded.

"Destroy he who shines light into all the realms, and then cast shadows onto them, so I may dwell in your realm as I wish!" Then the spirits became a column of smoke, which Kumba held out his hands and the smoke started twisting around, which shone brightly as Kumba's absorbed all the smoke disappearing into his outstretched hands. The powers, given by the Demon King was now his to control.

Kumba opened his eyes and turned to them. "Behold, the magic I now embrace!" A shimmering purple light glowed around Kumba as he cackled so loud, Kurly felt chills down his back. "I am now more powerful than any human on this planet! I will kill that warrior and his whole family! The room trembled in fear. Kurly blew out his candle and tossed it on the floor and shouted, "I'm through with this man. I never signed up for ghosts or evil spirits!" Moe agreed, "Yeah, this is way too much. You need to find some new henchmen to work for you. We're done! We are going to tell Jesse of the monster you are! Come one, fellas!"

"Leaving, eh? I'm afraid I cannot allow you to leave, knowing my plans." Kumba said, wearing an evil grin. Kurly made a run for the door, but was frozen where he stood. Moe was frantic, "What have you done to him?" Kumba stood close as he slung red sparkles over Moe and chanted dark words. Kurly was frozen and couldn't move, all but his eyes, which tried desperately to look behind as he heard Kumba cast his spell over his friends. After a minute, Moe shook his head and asked, "You wanted to see us boss?" Moe had forgot what the three had witnessed! Harry and Kurly remembered everything, but besides being terrified, they tried their best to act normal.

"The Henchman, that would make a great name for our hip hop group, don't you think Harry," Kurly asked. "Whatever you say 3 cents." Harry replied. "Will you two shut up?" Kumba demanded, "Find that boy and hurt him badly. Do you understand me? Now do as you are told." "Hurt him? I thought you told us not to harm him, as you need him alive?" Harry quipped.

"Well, now I want you to hurt him really bad, I am tired of waiting on that boy to give me what is mine! If that means leaving him black and blue then do that. Now get out there, find that boy, and make him bleed!"

They all nodded. "Let's go. This place gives me the willies," Harry remarked. "Do we really have to beat him up? I kind of like Jesse and Emma," Kurly sighed. "You heard the boss" Moe intervened, "Do you want to go back and tell him you don't want to work for him anymore?" Harry interrupted "No way! I don't want to be a zombie." "We better do as he says fellas. The man's crazy," Moe remarked. "Yeah," Harry agreed, "We better go find Jesse. I'm tired of that man." "Me too!" Kurly replied. "Since we don't know where Jesse is how about we check out the dirt track at the edge of the town? If he isn't there, we can ride our bikes for a while."

Jesse lost track of time helping out his grandfather. He rushed to get ready and while sprinting downstairs he slipped the ring onto his finger, yelling out, "Got to go Mom! I have a shopping date with Emma!" He hopped on his motorbike and zoomed to pick her up. From their hideout across from the emporium Kumba stood in a bad mood thinking, that boy seems to outsmart those three every time I send them after him. As the gangsters returned, Jesse and Emma began to walk down the street. All three jumped out grabbing Jesse's arms forcing him into the alley. Emma broke free and ran back to the emporium to call the police.

"What are you going to do now, Yankee fan?" "What do you want?" Jesse asked. "Just hand us that ring and we promise to not hurt you, even though we were told to," Kurly said. "We'll even leave that sweet girl of yours alone…maybe?"

Moe said laughing. "You better not touch Emma, or else!" Jesse demanded. "Look who's making demands. Hold him still," Moe ordered. They could see Emma coming from around the corner. "Well, too late. I guess your girlfriend is going to get hurt after all. So, surrender the ring now! Hit him, Harry!"

Two of the gangsters were holding on Jesse's arms when the ring started flashing many colors. Suddenly, he could not feel their hands upon him. Leaning back Harry tried to hit Jesse as hard as he could, but when his fist reached his face, he let out a loud pained cry.

"He broke my hand!"

The two other brothers were stupefied. "What do you mean? You barely touched him!" Moe said. Jessie realized his Dimensional Protection, or DP, had kicked in, like the old hag said it would. He could no longer be hurt by any force. He flung his hands into the air easily throwing the two holding him more than ten feet away. They landed hard against the concrete, groaning in pain. "I don't want to do this anymore fellas! Come on, let's get out of here!" Kurly cried. Moe agreed, "That girl called the cops and I'm hearing sirens." They started limping away from the alley. Emma ran toward Jesse. "Are you okay? The police will be here soon." Jesse, without so much as a scratch on him, nodded.

Sheriff Piper saw the three brothers limping down the street. She shook her head. "Got what you finally asked for, fellas? Seems like you crossed the wrong guy this time. The next time you cause trouble, its jail for you," she warned. Emma was confused, "How did you beat up all three of them at once?"

"It's the ring! Now, we won't have to worry about them any longer. I have been given the ring's power, but right now I just want us to enjoy our time together," he explained, placing his arm around Emma's shoulder.

The three reported back to Kumba at once. "I hit him as hard as I could and he didn't move an inch, but he broke my hand," Harry explained. Kumba said, "He is getting more powerful. We must devise another plan." "How can we get the ring if we're up against this kind of magic, Kumba?" Moe asked. Kumba wore an evil smile across his face, "I know a way. We will take the ones he loves and use them as bargaining chips." "You mean kidnap them? But that's prison time if we get caught," replied Moe. "You believe that is the worst thing that could happen to you three?" Kumba cautioned. The three looked worried. "But that Jesse broke my hand. I don't believe we can hurt that boy anymore; he is as tough as nails." Harry told Kumba.

"So you want to leave my employment?"

"Yeah," Moe replied. "We're through. Find yourself some other goons." "Fine. But look here first," Kumba said, pointing at the enchanted red diamond in the middle of the Rubella, which favored a watch. Moe glanced at it and poof! He was mesmerized by the amulet, his face expressionless and gray, Kumba had turned Moe into a zombie - pale, emotionless, and in a stupor just like Shiver! Kurly and Harry stood in horror watching their friend Moe get zapped by Kumba's Voodoo. "Shiver, is this what happened to you?" Kurly asked. For the first time, Shiver turned his head toward Kurly, opened his eyes wide and spoke, "Help mee…" he grunted. In a snap Shiver turned back forward, his face expressionless once more. Kurly shouted "Crap! Now we have a Moe zombie instead of Moe Money. I told him we should have run away!"

Kumba turned his gaze on them. "Now, does anybody else want out?" "No, not me, boss." Kurly said terrified. Kumba continued, "The boy received his power of protection. He can no longer be intimidated." "So, you don't need us anymore?" Harry felt somewhat relieved, "we can stop now and go home, right?" Kumba glared at them.

"Okay, I will take that as a no," Harry muttered. "Shut up!" Kumba yelled. "It means that we have to take his sister and use her to trade for the ring – or better yet, his girlfriend."

"Let me get this straight. You mean you want us to help you kidnap Emma? Emma, across the street Emma? The girl I went to school with since kindergarten Emma?"

Kumba gave Kurly an exhausted stare, "Do you have a problem with that?" Though he was against it, Kurly looked at Shiver and Moe and thought of what could happen to him if he was to say no. He shook his head and said, "Oh, no Mr. King, sir. I am fine with that, yes sir. Just making sure who we're talking about."

Kumba's sinister voice echoed as he laughed, "I must have the ring at all cost. Anybody who gets in my way will get hurt!"

Harry waved his hand in front of Moe's face and received no response, "Kurly, what are we going to do?" "How should I know? All I know is we are in deep trouble. We either do as he says or he will zombiefy us," Kurly said, poking his finger against Moe's cheek, "Look – nothing. Moe is gone, man. Nobody home in there just like Shiver." "I didn't know all this would happen. We just needed a little extra cash to record our album. I never signed up for kidnapping. And now Moe's a zombie!" Kurly bellowed. "But do we even have a choice?

I mean, that guy can turn us into a frog or something. Have you seen the owner of these apartments lately? His wife came by here twice looking for him. Just that big bullfrog sitting in his chair behind the counter, right?" "You don't know that for sure."

"Oh no. How many frogs have you seen wearing glasses?" "What if we tell Sheriff Piper?" Harry suggested. "And go to jail for conspiring to kidnap someone, and have that man turn me into a bug or something worse? Do you even think the police will believe us when we tell them about the zombies and all this magic stuff?" Kurly responded. Harry scratched his head, "Well, you have a point. What about these other realms he speaks of? He could maybe send us to the bird realm and we would be one of them and then maybe, we'll be okay?"

Kurly turned and suggested, "You're so stupid Harry, have you ever heard of real bird cardinals getting a recording contract? Look at Moe. He can't rap. He can't even speak. We'll be lucky if we survive."

CHAPTER 32

Innocent Hearts Beware

Now that Jesse had acquired his dimensional powers, he was able to connect with Blue whenever he wished. He flew to town and overheard Kumba speaking with the gangsters.

"We need a hostage. His sister Berry is in the shop with her aunt. We will take her."

He saw his human mother and Aunt Jane walk out of the emporium, leaving Berry there with Emma. Blue flew in through the door as a customer left and landed on the counter. "Oh, what a cute little bird!" Emma gushed. Berry held out her finger, and Blue jumped onto her hand. "This is Jesse," Berry said.

"Jesse? Why would you think that?" "I just know," Berry replied. Blue spoke, "Yes, it is me." Emma was shocked as she turned to Berry. "See? I told you," Berry giggled. "How is this possible?" Emma remained stunned. "The ring did this to me, but that's not the problem," Blue explained. "You're a bird! And that's not the problem?" Emma replied. Jesse continued, "We haven't got much time. Kumba is planning on kidnapping Berry and maybe you as well. I spied on them as a bluebird, from the rooftops.

I overheard them planning it, so they can force me to give up the ring to Kumba." Emma looked out the window.

"Those gangsters have been watching the store from across the street all day. And that Kumba has been speaking with them the whole time."

"You must hide. They are coming," Jesse warned. Just then the door swung open. "Is the owner in?" Kumba asked with Shiver right behind him. "Not at the moment," Emma replied nervously, trying to pretend she is unaware of Kumba's plans, "They will be back very shortly." Kumba and Shiver walked in looking for Berry, who had quickly hidden behind a bookshelf. "What do you want?" Emma asked. Kumba pulled out his watch, "I am interested in selling my watch. Look closely. What do you think?"

Emma only glanced for a second as the watch twisted back and forth. Then at once she did not move or talk anymore. Blue flew up on a high shelf.

"Quick! Put her in the trunk! Let's go," Kumba ordered Shiver. Shiver slung Emma over his shoulder and did as he was told. Kumba looked at Blue perched high on top of a shelf.

"I know your sister came in here. Where is she?"

"You leave this place and let Emma go!" demanded Blue. "Oh, I'm afraid I can't do that, unless you freely give me that ring. As for your sister I no longer need her, do I? Since I now have your heart!" Kumba remarked, letting out an evil laugh, "You know where I will be. I am sure the ring has told you.

You bring the ring to me at midnight in the park near the ruins, and your Emma will not be harmed. But if you don't, I am sure my three associates will have a lot of fun with her before I end her life!" he laughed once more and left.

Berry heard everything and was furious. "What should we do, Jesse?"

"Open the door, I need to follow his car. Also call the sheriff tell them what happened and stay hidden."

Sheriff Piper arrived at the store to find Berry all alone at the emporium.

"Did you recognize the men who took Emma?"

Berry replied, "Have you seen that Kumba riding around town? The weird guy that always wears strange clothes?" "Yes, I do. Was he the one who took her?" Sheriff Piper asked.

"Yes, him and that big smelly man who drives the car. They zombie-fied Emma! Then he scooped her up over his shoulder and put her in the trunk! He was trying to find me. Then he saw Jesse sitting up on a beam, he spoke to the bluebird in the shop and told her he didn't need Berry as hostage anymore because he had Emma."

"He spoke to a bluebird?" Sheriff asked.

"Yes, and the bird warned us about that strange man. That he means us harm." "You got all that from a bird? Quite an imagination you have their little girl."

Berry frowned, "Why don't you believe me? I'm telling you the truth!"

"Alright, I think we got what we need. I'll leave an officer here to stay with you until your mom and aunt comes back.

Just stay put and tell the officer if you need anything."

Sheriff Piper turned to the other officers, "Have we not stopped that limo before or questioned this Mr. King fella?" One officer answered, "Yes, we did. I pulled him over for reckless driving one time."

"Did you give him a ticket?"

"Yes, I did, I think I did, should be on your desk, Mam."

At the police station, they searched the desk and could find no such report. "I know I pulled him over and gave him a ticket!" the officer insisted. "Then what happened?" Sheriff Piper asked.

"I stopped them and walked around the car asking for a driver's license and registration. That Kumba guy sat in the back. He was quite rude, and I remember telling them both to step out of the car and I handed them the ticket. But come to think of it, that's all I remember now. Next thing I remember is getting coffee and donuts at the malt shop. How can that be?"

Sheriff Piper wondered the same thing. "We have a kidnapping and no idea who the kidnappers are, or who exactly that Kumba is. So, we have nothing, is that right?" "Maybe that big fella in jail might know?" one officer interjected. "He was let out some time ago," Another officers sighed as they looked at each other. Sheriff Piper lost it, "Well we have a kidnapping, and we lost our only witness and we don't have a single clue except a bluebird who talks! So, get out there and start looking for that car!" Jesse asked the ring what he should do.

"Kumba must not get a hold of the stone. Otherwise, the world will be in danger."

"But he has my girlfriend!" Jesse exclaimed.

Mom and Berry had just arrived back from the shop. Berry wasted no time and handed Jesse an old book. "What is this?" Jesse inquired. Berry looked down on the floor and murmured, "That is Lord Asher's diary. It will tell you everything you need to know about Kumba." "That's great." Jesse told her. "Where did you find it?" "It was in Aunt Jane's store." Berry replied.

"How long have you had this?"

"Since the first day the ring came to you."

Jesse was in disbelief. "Berry! Why would you hide this from me?" "I didn't know it was about your ring at first, then when I did, you didn't want me to sleep in your bed. The book tells me how to be in the same dreams that you were in. You were trying to stop me, so I hid the book. I'm sorry Jesse," Berry explained.

Jesse shook his head while flipping through the pages of the book. "How to transform into another dimension." He looked at Berry and said, "I could have used this earlier." Berry bit her lip in embarrassment. "Sorry Jesse." On another page he read: "How to protect yourself." I could have used that too, and on this page, "how the ring works and what to expect."

"Berry, this book has everything I need to understand the ring's power, its weaknesses, my responsibilities, and how I can harness my DP. It's all here! How can you not tell me about this?!" "I'm sorry." Berry pouted. "That's alright Berry, at least you gave it to me now, when I need it most." "So you're not mad?" "No little sister, I'm not mad."

Jesse continued to turn the pages and sees something about Kumba. Lord Asher writes:

I met Kumba when he was still a slave to Marie Laveau, a well-known voodoo practitioner. Kumba watched her and developed his magic abilities. He became so infatuated with Dark magic and mastered the dark arts so well that Ms. Laveau gave him his freedom out of fear. I met him at the Wizards Temple, better known as the Masonic Temple. We became good friends. That is until one day, while standing by the waters of Lake Pontchartrain, the Lady of the Lake surfaced from the waters and walked up to me and handed the ring to me. She called me the Wonder. Kumba didn't show it, but he became obsessed with acquiring the ring for its powers. So much so that I had to leave the ring at the temple, guarded at all times, just to keep it safe and out of his evil hands. Kumba became the leader of a large army of Dark Magic practitioners, and soon was well-known and feared by all in New Orleans. He became more obsessed with power as time passed. Reading ancient writings and any book he could find to gain more knowledge about the ring. He is now a master of voodoo and wizard magic and cares for nobody and nothing. He doesn't seem to have any weaknesses except for one. He is allergic to animal hair, especially those of cats. I once watched the man swell up like a red balloon after petting a cat. He was in the infirmary for a week and almost died.

Jesse thought, now this is helpful and turned to the ring, "We don't have much time. What else can you tell me about Kumba?" The Stone replied, "Kumba must have the power of the stone to reconnect with his snake self in the bird realm. If Kumba obtains all his powers, along with the Rubella charm, then you will never be able to stop him"

"But I must save Emma!"

"Hard choice Jesse. Save her and possibly doom the world, or let Emma die and by doing so save the world"

"What if there's a third choice?" Jesse replied, "Kumba knows only of the 19th century. Nothing about today's technologies. That is another weakness. How can we use that against him?" "Think, Jesse. Think."

"Tell me how does the spell work? The one Kumba would use if he acquired the ring." The Stone explained, "He would have to light the eternal flame in a place of magic, which would be the ruins in your grandpa's land, next to the park." "The old Indian ruins?"

The Stone continued, "Then Kumba would have to place the ring in those flames. The flames would then burst telling him the spell is working." "Can you tell me a chant or spell which would simulate this same reaction?" Jesse asked.

"That could be done, but the risk would be high. What would you do Jesse? This is your biggest challenge and your greatest foe. What are you willing to sacrifice to save the world?"

"There has got to be another way," Jesse remarked, "I must save her. It doesn't matter what I have to do or must do. If I can't save her, then I don't want to be your warrior of Wonder. I must find a way!" Jesse took off on his bike to town to find an electronics store and purchased the items he needed to make his plan work. He came back home, locked the door to his room, and went to work. "What are you doing?" The Stone asked. "You will see," Jesse replied.

Jesse conceived his idea and told the ring of what he had planned, if he couldn't give Kumba the stone's power, then he wouldn't. The Stone was amazed with Jesse's creativity.

"Wow! That is very smart, Jesse, it's brilliant in fact, especially since Kumba only asked for the ring." "Right? I will give Kumba the Ring!"

"This is very risky, but could work," the stone replied.

"It has to!" Jesse expressed hopefully, "Yes, modern technology against an ancient voodoo wizard."

Berry knocked on Jesse's door. "Jesse, I want to help too?" "Okay Berry, I need you to go to bed and to sleep."

"I am not going to sleep with all this going on. Besides, Emma is my friend too and I want to help fight that evil man!"

"Okay," Jesse relented, "Listen closely. You can help, but you must do as I ask. You need to stay here. This is an important job and only you can do it." Berry listened intently, "I need you to enter the bird world as Berry and wake Blue up. Tell her what is happening and that Jesse needs her help. Can you do that?" "Yes. Yes, I can," Berry replied.

"Good girl, you must leave the window opened and have Blue come here to the house and collect the Stone and bring it to me at the old ruins!" "You're leaving the stone here with me?" Berry asked. "Yes and it is very important that you to do as I say." "Okay." Berry stated.

Berry went straight to bed and tried her best to fall asleep fast. In bed, she muttered,

"Don't worry Jesse. I will bring Blue's army and meet you at the park."

CHAPTER 33

The True Test of Wonder!

It was just before midnight when Jesse arrived at the forest and stood outside the ruins. Kumba was chanting towards the skies and preparing a spell to allow him to once again embody his snake self with the power of the Demon King and Morgana's Rubella charm. Thus, making him the most powerful wizard in the human realm. Emma was tied up and stood motionless as Kurly and Harry held her arms. Her face cold and still with her eyes glassy staring blankly, not blinking. Kumba shouted, "Did you bring the ring!?"

"Let her go first. I have the ring. I will toss it to you on the ground."

Jesse walked into the circle. He covered the ring with his hand and whispered to it to make it appear as if he was speaking to the Stone. Jesse had replaced the stone with a blue LED light he purchased from the store and placed it in the ring where the wonder stone was once held. "Do you take me for a fool?" Kumba boasted. Jesse's heart sank, thinking Kumba was on to his trick. "The ring must be handed to me freely, or given to me in a trade." Kumba reminded him. Jesse sighed in ease and said, "Fine, it's not worth my girlfriend's life, but you remove the curse you placed on her first," Jesse demanded.

Kumba held his charm above her head and chanted a few words. Suddenly Emma starts moving again, shaking her head to regain her senses. She could see Jesse approaching with the ring. "Jesse, don't give him the ring! You can't!" She yelled. The two young men quickly covered her mouth as Jesse moved further inside the circle. "That's close enough boy," Kumba said. He walked up to Jesse looked him in the eyes and held out his hand for the ring. Slowly Jesse pushed the button on the LED light as he removed the ring from his finger. The ring then cast out a bright blue light. "Please let this work," Jesse prayed.

Kumba's eyes lit up thinking the power would soon be his. Jesse dropped the ring into the evil wizard's hand. As Kumba gazed into its Flashing light he ordered them to release the girl! They tossed Emma to the ground, and Jesse rushed to her side. "Jesse, why did you give him the ring? I may have been trapped in this body, but I could still hear Kumba's speaking. He plans to kill all of us even if you hand him the ring!" Emma cried hysterically. Jesse whispered to Emma while untying her hands. "I didn't really give him the ring. Now run into the woods and hide! Quick!"

"I'll get help," Emma replied.

Kumba held the ring up high toward the sky as the LED lights flashed and began chanting his spell. Then he threw the ring into the purple flame. Jesse quickly cast a spell upon the fire just as the Stone had instructed him to do. A purple flame burst into the night sky. Kumba laughed maniacally believing the spell was working. A hard gust of wind blew beating hard against the trees. Jesse watched Kumba rise up, off the ground as swirling winds of red mist rose him up on a pedestal of red and purple flames. Kumba spread out his arms chanting to the Demon King to help magnified all these combined powers. The Rubella's red light was activated. It glowed shooting out a brilliant ruby light as if Kumba's chest was on fire.

Kumba once again shouted a spell and not just any spell. A mind controlling zombie spell, his specialty. By using his crow energy this spell allowed him to control any person who breaths the red mist. Much like the spell he used in New Orleans many years before, but even more powerful. Kumba seemed unstoppable! "Oh, the power!" Kumba shouts, "I now hold the power of the Ring of Wonder. I can feel it coursing through me!" He raised both hands towards the fire releasing red lightning from his fingertips into the glowing purple flames.

"Finally!" He laughed once more, "Now I have no need of you Jesse, I will have fun devouring you and your family, I think they would make good slaves, don't you? What a fool you are to hand me this power!" Kumba continued to chant over the fiery purple flames, while the Rubella charm's brilliant light blazed outward. Kumba's snake-half appeared in a mist over the flames and he greeted it, "Hello old friend, soon we will be together as one." Everyone watched as the two bodies began merging together as one, the man and the snake. In the crackling fire Kumba's face grew bigger and his gold-capped teeth were growing longer becoming enormous golden fangs. Kumba's giant serpent self- emerged has emerged.

Jesse clasped his hands together and chanted to form an opening between this world and the bird realm. The portal is opened, but nothing is flying through. Where are they? He thought. Jesse continued chanting. Kumba was growing larger every second. He was now taller than a school bus and twice as long. Harry looked over at Kurly and shouted, "Let's run for it, Kurly!" "We can't leave Moe here. That giant snake is going to eat him!" Harry shouted frantically. "So, you want to be eaten also?" Just then Kumba roared loudly which frightened Kurly.

Kurly knew Harry was right and quietly motioned Harry to make a run for the car, "Let's go Harry. We didn't sign up for this!" They got into the limo and on the way, they tried to convince both Shiver and Moe to come, but both simply stood where they were not flinching. Kurly waving bye to Moe as they drove off, watching the battle continue in the rear-view mirror. They didn't drive far when they saw the streets were full of people, all walking toward the park. The streets were full and stopped cars were blocking the exits. Kurly spoke out the window; "Where's everyone going?" But no answers. Harry came to a stop.

The two watched as the red mist rained over the town. "Look Harry, a red fog?"

Both wondering what these red clouds meant. "Turn around Harry, go down Walnut Street."

"Sure thing, but let's keep the windows up, I don't want to breath in any of that red fog."

They could see the people in the mist were starting to act different. They turned down Walnut Street, but it was also blocked, so they tried another road, but they could tell there was no way of leaving town. Kumba has used his crow powers to isolate their town and stop anyone from leaving, or going for help.

"The people all around us are just like Moe and Shiver, they are zombies." Kurly shouted. No matter how they tried, they couldn't get away without running people over through the growing crowd.

"Let's head back to the park." Kurly shouted. "Are you mad? Are you forgetting what's at the park?"

They sat and watched the zombie people surround the limo. "Look Harry, we cannot get out of town and if we got to be a part of this madness I would just as soon be with Moe."

"I agree with that, but you know if we go back, we may not make it out alive." Harry said softly. "So," Kurly stated, "Maybe we can do some good. If not, we can turn ourselves over to the sheriff and be safe in a cell."

"Let's do this!"

Harry and Kurly high five's each other and shouted in unison, "Were coming Moe!"

"Drive it like you stole it, Harry!"

Harry stepped on the gas, they were flying. "If we got to go Harry, it's been a privilege being your friend." Harry looked at Kurly and said, "same here bro, at least we will all be together even if it is for the last time."

Soon hundreds of people starting showing up at the park. They had seen the lights shooting up into the air like fireworks and were curious to come. Sheriff Piper pulled out a megaphone and said, "This is not a safe place to be. Everyone leaves and go home!" Many started walking off, but you could see the blank faces of the others were like zombies coming down the street. Soon the whole town would be there. Half of them are Zombies, and the rest are just spectators.

Berry had finally fallen asleep and woke straight up as her bird self, in the nest. "Wake up, Blue! Jesse is in trouble and needs our help!" She chirped. Blue rose from her slumber questioning what needed to be done. "Jesse needs your army now. He is fighting against Kumba," Berry urged. Blue told Willy to send off carried pigeons in all directions to spread the word, so they can gather their army. Soon all the birds that promised their allegiance to Blue, came quickly. Berry announced "Everyone, I need your help. Kumba is currently fighting the Wonder. We must stop him at all cost!"

Berry informed Captain Striker and his team of what was happening in the human world. His eyes lit up and proposed, "Could this be the fight of the Legend, which everyone speaks of?" "I am not sure, but we need to act fast," Blue said, "The barrier has been opened and the battle is already underway."

As the battle raged on, Kumba's golden fangs grew longer and sharper, flickering against the moonlight as venom dripped off the tips. "Ah, come and see what I have become!"

he cried out. Jesse looked at the portal opening, but there is still no sign of Blue's army. He darted toward the forest. Kumba saw Jesse and immediately chased him. "I'm coming for you, boy!"

Jesse hid behind a tree as the giant snake ripped through, knocking down the smaller trees like blades of grass along in his path. Kumba stopped and remained still for a moment listening for the slightest noise. "You will not escape me!" he warned.

The mighty snake had to weigh close to a tone ramming his way through the trees calling for Jesse, "Where are you bluebird man? Come out and face me, and I will let your family live." Jesse became nervous. Where are you, Berry?" he wondered while thinking of ways to stall the snake. Jesse came out from behind the tree, and looked up at the snake. He asked, "Kumba! Why seek the power of the Ring?" Kumba's head stood tall as he inched closer to Jesse.

"So, I can have everything I ever wished for and rule the world!"

"That's right," Jesse shouted back, "You have enough powers already to become a millionaire. You could manipulate anything. You could be a magician like David Copperfield. He's rich and has whatever he wishes." Kumba stopped in his tracks and said, "Who is this, David Copperfield?" Now that Jesse has captured his attention he continued, "That's right you haven't stopped running after that ring for so long, you forgot to ask yourself what you can accomplish without it." "Enough!" Kumba shouted, insulted that Jesse spoke to him

in such a manner. He gave Jesse a hypnotic evil stare. Jesse turned his head instantly being careful not to glimpse into Kumba's eyes. "So, you wish to rule the world?"

"With the ring I can!" Kumba hissed. Jesse yelled out, "Have you stopped to see if anything might have changed a tiny bit in this world in the last century?" "No, I don't want to rule the world, but I could! I would create followers, become Supreme ruler, gather a huge army and control the world as I wish! My own power has returned and merged with the snake.

The magic flames are lit up and no amount of water can put them out! I am unstoppable" Kumba exclaimed.

Jesse looked up once more. He could see the eagles from the zoo flying along with Striker and Blue in the lead. They came rushing through the portal, Yea! Jesse thought as they watched the many birds pouring through the opening, then dive down attacking the giant snake's head, but with little results. Blue flew in with them shouting, "I have it, Jesse!" Then tossed the stone into Jesse's hands. "Unstoppable? Well, not exactly," Jesse shouted, holding the stone up so Kumba could see, "I just gave you the ring like you asked, but the power was never about the ring. It was the stone in the ring!" Kumba went into deep thought saying, "Never about the ring?" He then realized he had been tricked! Still, he never wavered.

"I still have my own power plus the demon's power, and with the power of the Rubella charm, I will easily defeat you as I did your predecessor, Asher! He may have trapped me, but I killed him and I will kill you too! And since we did make a trade for your girlfriend, all I have to do is simply take the stone off your dead corpse!"

The giant snake then leaped toward Jesse to attack. His mighty body shaking the ground. Jesse jumped to one side telling the snake; "Lord Asher trapped you, I will too!"

"Yes, he did, but it cost him his life and it will cost your life as well!"

"You think so snake?" Jesse chanted and gave the birds the signal. Kumba raised his head toward the sky. He saw hundreds of birds descend overhead and even more pouring out from the circle of light.

"What is all this? You cannot stop me. As long as the purple flame burns, I am indestructible!"

Jesse answered, "Could you explain to me what would happen if you cast your spell without the ring's magic?" Kumba knew what this means, this means the spell will not hold and backfire, causing him to separate once more. "No, you cannot do this to me," he shrieked. He had to get that stone, or everything would be for nothing.

Berry flew up close to Jesse cheering, "I have brought the army!" Then she dropped a big bag of cat hair into Jesse's hands saying, "And here's a present from the Professor. The hair from a shaved Stank." Jesse smiled and told her, "Thanks Berry. Go home now. You have done your part."

Berry instead went to help the other birds attack Kumba. "No, Berry!" Jesse shouted, "Get away from him!" Kumba pulled his head back and hissed, "Ah, the sister." He quickly snapped swallowing the bluebird whole. Jesse and Blue were stunned.

"What now boy? Your sister tasted so sweet! Maybe I will eat your girlfriend next? Maybe I cannot eat you Wonder boy, but your loved ones, oh yes, the loved ones, they will make such a delightful snack."

Kumba sped off looking for Emma and other precious creatures he could feast upon. Sheriff Piper and her deputies moved to the edge of the ruins and watched in awe of the giant terrifying snake. "Sheriff?" one of the deputies asked, "Should I call animal control?" The Sheriff looked at him, "I don't think animal control would be prepared to capture anything like this." She held her hand up motioning for her deputies to wait, trying to figure out what they should do.

Harry and Kurly were unable to see as the red fog surrounding the town had become thicker. They came barreling through the parking lot at over sixty miles an hour, before they realized where they were, by then it was too late. "Aaahhhh," both screamed, Kurly shouting, "Hold on!" Everyone watched the gangsters come barrowing in through the park knocking down the guard rail and shooting up an incline. They hit the ground hard twisting to one side, and sliding across the grass almost turning over.

Kurly looked over at Harry and said; "OH man, I thought we were going to die before we had a chance to get out there and die later with Moe?" Harry looked at Kurly and chuckled, "Moe was right about your brain capacity, you know that?" Kurly put his hand on Harry's shoulder and replied "Thanks man, I love you too."

Moe saw Sheriff Piper and suggested "Come on, let's turn ourselves in bro." Harry and Kurly held up their hands shouting, "We surrender Sheriff, take us to a nice safe jail cell please?" Shaking her head sheriff Piper ordered the two to get down behind a tree. Watching from behind a tree along with the deputies Kurly stated, "We can't help Moe now. It's every man for himself!"

Kumba continued speaking his incantations up toward the sky trying hard to complete the ritual. By then the trees were filled with birds. Kumba turned to Jesse, "What are you doing? What is all this?" "What do you mean?" Jesse replied, "Is the big bad Kumba snake starting to get a little scared? They are just birds." He motioned to Blue, and the birds began to attack Kumba once again, very fiercely. "How are you doing this?" Kumba cried out. Jesse looked at Kumba and said, "You have been after this ring for a century, yet you never understood that the ring can never serve you!" Kumba fired into the sky scattering the birds in all directions. "This will not stop me!" he laughed.

Jesse formed a fireball and blasted at the snake. Kumba turned to him saying, "All I have to do is kill you and take the stone, and my spell will still work! Then I can rule this world!" Jesse shot another fireball toward Kumba's direction. The snake ducked and was about to fire back when Blue flew in front of Jesse in an attempt to block the fiery blast. Jesse jumped up grabbing little Blue in his hands causing him to drop the stone on the ground. The stone bounced off a rock and landed near Kumba. Laughing as he fired back at Jesse, "Ah! The Stone of Wonder, laying at my feet! You have lost boy!" Jesse was hit again by another fireball, and laid on the ground as the monster snake slithered forward to finish him off. Jesse rose slowly scanning the surroundings for the stone. Kumba moved quickly between Jesse and the Wonder stone and stared into Jesse's eye mocking him, "I now have my power and you dear Wonder boy are no match for me!"

"Rubella," Jesse called out, "The Wonder is sorry for sending you away with Kumba, but he had no choice at the time. Please forgive him and help us defeat this horrible man. The stone doesn't want you to be sent away again." He wasn't sure if the Rubella understood, but her light shut down. If she can think and is aware then she knows if Kumba loses she may get stuck in the nothing realm once again.

He reared back to strike Jesse and end the battle. Jesse held up the bag of cat hair and tossed it on the big snake's head while chanting a spell. The big snake inhaled the hair and started sneezing not knowing what hit him. A large crowd was now standing at the park watching the battle. Some were turned into Zombies, others were not, but they came anyway just to watch. Emma could be heard taunting the snake from a distance, "Hey, meathead!" "Ah-Choo, well if it isn't my next meal!" The King snake replied, sneezing constantly. Emma saw the stone on the ground and ran over to grab it. Kumba flung his tail knocking her on the ground. He licked his lips and said, "Another delicate morsel to fill my stomach. How nice of you to stick around, sweet, tasty

Emma!" "Leave her alone!" Jesse demanded. "Or what?" the snake laughed, his head swollen from the cat fur.

Jesse called for the birds, and they began attacking the snake once more. Something hit Kumba's head. He looked around and could barely see all the white drops splatting like rain all around him.

At first, he thought it was snow until a big splat hit him in the face.

"Bird poop? How will this stop me?"

Kumba thought Jesse was utterly foolish. Sheriff Piper went over and lifted Emma up out of harm's way and checked on her, "Are you okay?" Emma looked around for the stone, which was still lying on the ground. "I must get that stone! Can you distract the beast?" she pleaded. Sheriff Piper instructed her men to open fire at Kumba, but this had little effect on the beast. He swung his tail around hard throwing the officers off into the forest. Emma quickly went after the stone while the eagles grabbed at Kumba's head trying to keep him distracted. Kumba looked over at Jesse.

"All I have to do is destroy you, and this fight will be over!"

He slithered up ready to strike Jesse. Emma saw this as a chance to grab the stone. Out of the corner of his eye Kumba saw Emma pick up the stone. He quickly whipped his tail trying to knock her to the ground once more.

"Watch and learn young wizard as I take your heart!" Kumba looked at Jesse and sneezed, "I told you, Ah-Choo!

I will destroy all that you hold dear!" "No!" Jesse shouted as he could see Kumba's tail rise high into the air, and as

Emma looked up at Kumba with frightened eyes the huge tail slammed down hard. Smashing the ground where Emma had once stood. The crowd shouted in Awe, shocked to see Emma pounded so fiercely by such a large reptile. The ground shook. Jesse was so filled with rage as the snake taunted him, "Let's look and see what is left of your sweetheart." Kumba raised his tail up expecting to see a lifeless body. Jesse was horrified, thinking Emma was dead, but to his surprise? Emma stood up gloating, "Hah! I didn't feel a thing, you awful snake! The stone protected me, Quick Jesse catch!" She threw the stone over to him.

Kumba's eyes followed its trajectory and fired a blast at Jesse. Blue seeing this flew up, caught the stone, but took the full blast. Falling into Jesse's hands he cupped the little bird to protect her as he was thrown backwards from Kumba's next blast. The stone absorbed most of the blast, and sent it hurling back towards the giant snake. Jesse clapped his hands, and a colorful dome of light encircled both him and Blue. Then the ball of light surrounding Jesse exploded with a powerful force that knocked everyone in the park backwards and onto the ground. Even the birds were shaken.

Emma used the distraction to take cover behind a tree. Beside her was Sheriff Piper who whispered in disbelief, "What in the world is happening?"

"I'll explain later – if we live that is."

Emma's comment sent a chill down the Sheriff's back.

A luminous ball of blue light engulfed Jesse. Blinding the snake and all who watched. Jesse rose slowly up in the air, and as the light dimmed down an image of a massive ten-foot eagle with a bright blue glow and magnificent blue feathers stood clear in the night sky.

Kurly motioned to Harry to look, "I don't believe what I am seeing. Jesse has become a giant eagle?" Sheriff Piper and her deputies could only watch in amazement. It was the legend from the bird world! All the birds were mesmerized. The ten foot tall Blue Eagle stood glowing up in the sky. He turned his head towards Emma, winked at her, and gave out a loud shriek.

"Let's get it on snake!"

The watching crowd cheered at Jesse's comment. Kumba took a swipe at the large eagle (which is now both Blue and Jesse). He tried to sink his venom-laden fangs into the Eagle's heart. Jesse shielded himself using the Eagles giant talons, and squeezed them hard against Kumba's head. In return the evil wizard shot flames at the Eagle, halting the attack.

The Blue Eagle flew above the snake's head while Kumba headed for Emma. Jesse rushed to Emma and the officers to protect them as the snake snapped his mighty jaws in an attempt to strike anyone nearby.

The Eagle grabbed Kumba by his tail and dragged him backwards away from Emma and the deputies. Then swung the snake's body around and into the air hitting the snakes head against a big oak tree. As Kumba rose slowly in dizziness he shot a blast out of his mouth to the oncoming birds. This caused many of them to fall, which infuriated Jesse.

Kumba struck at the eagle once more barely missing him.

Jesse took flight using his powerful claws to grab Kumba by his enormous golden fang, while the other foot tightly held the top of the snake's head. His massive wings flapped as he mightily lifted the snake off the ground. Chanting, "Let's speed this up, shall we?" as he turned the snake's head to the side. More birds attacked ripping the Rubella Charm off the big snake's head, which fell to the ground and was quickly grabbed by Captain Striker. Kumba knew without Morgana's charm it would be hard for him to equal the Wonder's authority even with the Demon Kings added power.

To escape the Giants Eagle's grip Kumba must muster all his remaining strength for one final blast against it. As Jesse held him tighter Kumba hissed and opened his mouth. Out of it came a river of flames shooting straight out trying to roast the Big Blue Eagle.

Jesse Held the snake tighter and positioned his head toward the sky. Redirecting the flames upward away from himself, and any humans who may be in the line of fire. The crowd cheered again seeing the flames shooting out from the giant snake, like a light show. Kumba couldn't move, and for once again fear could be seen in his eyes.

Jesse along with the Wonder stone and the bluebird Wonder warrior came together and cast a mighty spell onto Kumba. He started shrinking, slowly transforming back into the dark voodoo wizard he was. He wiggled violently trying to free himself from the eagle's grip. Kumba finally shook free and began to fall. Then in mid-air something grabbed him by his robe. It was the mighty Blue Eagle. He dangled him high above the ground in the powerful talons. Jesse then dropped Kumba to the ground near the purple embers of the fire.

Jesse was no longer the great blue eagle, but the new Emissary of Wonder. Glistening against the night sky Jesse again transformed and could be seen draped in the dark indigo robe which from the inside poured a glimmer of blue light shining like diamonds. This was the robe of the last Wonder, Lord Asher. Out from the robe little Blue came flying swiftly out. "Wow, nice robe," Blue comments. "Maybe just a little outdated though," he smirks. "If you don't like the robe then you can choose your own outfit later." The Stone replies.

Jesse's face glowed, absorbing the power shinning from the stone's robe. Once again, the frightened wizard tried to escape his fate, twisting and screaming in pain, "No! This cannot be! I was so close." Purple flames began to consume the wizard. Shredding him apart and splitting once more his snake half from his human self. The flame grew smaller and smaller with Kumba's agonized screams ringing across the night air as he was ripped in two. Jesse held up his hand and called for the ring which had held the powerful Wonder stone. Flying up from the purple ashes, shooting like a rocket back into Jesse's hand.

Now Kumba was split into his two former selves. Jesse turned toward the snake and shouted, "Back to your prison!" Placing the king snake over the purple embers. Kumba snake half shrank and twisted into a purple glow. Swirling around till the snake disappeared into the flames, then vanished from site as the snake was transported back into the bird realm. Kumba became furious and tried to cast a spell on Jesse, who merely stood there smiling.

"What is happening? Why are you not turning into a frog?"

Jesse then turned to Kumba and laughed, "A frog? Is that your best plan, great voodoo king? Turn me into a frog?" He shook his head. Then a Celtic spell came from the Stone. They watched a ghastly figure pour out from Kumba's body. Extracting the Demon King from Kumba causing him to scream in despair, "No, don't leave me, you hate the Wonder as much as I do!" "Maybe so, Kumba King, I am a demon after all, I hate everyone!" Jesse confronted the Demon King. Holding him up frozen in place the Demon King spoke, "Wonder Stone, I see we meet again."

"Well, if it isn't the demon prince Ethereal, joining forces against me once again. This is twice now you have done this!"

"King actually, no longer just the prince. At your service Lord Wonder." Ethereal says bowing before the stone, "Have mercy great stone of wonder, I did aid you during my father's attacks on you centuries ago." The stone thought for a minute as Kumba watched on and said, "That is twice you have joined against me Demon King, I would be foolish to let you go."

"Have mercy light of wonder, let me go please and I swear I will never join sides against you, never again."

"Then be gone Ethereal, king of the demon realm and keep to your realm forever hidden from my site. For you now have two strikes against you!"

Ethereal faded to mist with a strange look upon his face unsure what was meant by The Stone's last comment. The Stone remarked, "I do not think Ethereal understands baseball."

"You think we better explain it to him, so he does understand?" Jesse questioned.

"And miss the fun. He will be in contemplation for centuries, always afraid of what two strikes mean."

"So, keep them confused is what you're saying?"

"Of course, you are learning. Now back to you Mr. King. You no longer have your magic, your Demon King, or your charm. As far as your magic you lost it when you performed the ritual without the stone. I had cast a spell which separated your two selves between the realms allowing the stone to absorb your magic. You are as normal as everyone else, but I see you're still a snake of a person."

Realizing he was outsmarted, Kumba pulled out a dagger and lunged toward Jesse, screaming, "I will kill you boy!" Jesse held the stone up and stood still as Kumba thrust the dagger against his body. Again and again, he drove it against Jesse's flesh, but it never seemed to go through.

"Sorry Kumba, that's the cosmic realm barrier I now possess. You cannot hurt me I am now the full Wonder warrior!"

Sheriff Piper stood up looking over the battle. She shouted at her deputies, "All right, let's get down there men."

CHAPTER 34

The True Test of Wonder!

The police were still unable to believe what they had witnessed, were placing handcuffs on Kumba and as they led him away. The crowd again cheered loudly, Jesse hoped nobody would recognize him during all this, but he could only hope.

Kumba sneezed constantly, his eyes swollen from allergies. When he passed by Jesse he cowered, afraid of what will become of him. It made Jesse feel triumphant.

"About time somebody taught that evil man something about fear, especially because he was so cruel and mean and with so many innocent victims."

The Wonder Warrior placed Blue on his shoulder and walked up to where Kumba had his alter. He whispered to the stone "You were right. The ring itself was indestructible. It was left undamaged by the flames." Kumba began laughing maniacally.

He then turned toward Jesse and said. "You should have killed me, Jesse. I will be back for you. I am part of this world too and I will get my power back and as for you bluebird, my other half will finish you!"

The officers yelled at him, "Move it! "While dragging him away, he continued to laugh in an evil unsettling manner.

"Just so you know that little bluebird is now part of this realm and also the bird realm. Do you honestly think you'll have any chance of escape now?

"Without your powers you are just a human behind bars. Now let that sink in."

"You may have taken my power for now, but I have been here before and know how to get them back!"

"Not if the king snake Kumba is captured, just like you. And I'm making sure of it," Jessie answered. "No!" Kumba shouted, "That would split my essence in half, permanently separated by the realms. I will become mortal, grow old, and die.

Don't do this to me boy!" "Consider it done," Jesse quipped.

As the cops shoved Kumba's head inside the car, Piper was shouting for the crowd to disperse, Kumba knew that his fate may have changed forever. Making a final swipe at Jesse while laughing, hoping to leave him in agony.

"Your sister tastes good. Have you forgotten I swallowed her?"

"Yes, but you were combined with the snake." The Stone continued; "Once you separated, there is a chance so did Berry, from your snake's belly." "Is that right, then where is she now?" Kumba grinned." My snake half will imprison her and eat her sooner or later, so she is as good as gone!"

"Oh, I wouldn't worry about her. She's at home sound asleep," Jesse replied calmly.

"May she never wake up?" Kumba yelled out.

"In your dreams!" Jesse rebutted, very worried about his sister. Emma ran up to Jesse locking him in her arms. "Are you okay?" she asked.

Jesse was in deep thought of his sister's capture. "Kumba has Berry!" he uttered.

"What do you mean? Kumba, as in that man in the police car?" "Not that Kumba. His snake self has her in the other realm, where she is a bluebird. My sister's body is still home asleep in bed, but if the snake kills Berry the bluebird, then my sister may never wake up."

Emma looks deep into Jesse's eyes, "Then go home and sleep and rescue her Jesse!"

The Stone spoke, "Your sister lives, but as a prisoner of the snake king, which is no longer your fight Jesse."

"No longer my fight, what are you talking about?" Jesse argued. "You were training this bird, not for yourself, but for her to become the warrior in her own realm. Since you cannot be in all one thousand realms at once training her is part of the Wonder's agenda.

Your very essence is now part of this bluebird.

Blue must defeat the snake on her own. That is the true test of Wonder."

"You defeated Kumba with your intelligence and your heart. This little bluebird must be the hero of her own realm, which you as the Wonder trained her for. How well has yet to be determined.

You have done your part. Now your test, the actual test,

was to help the bluebird become the warrior of her realm. All you can do now is watch and hope you trained her well enough to save your sister."

"So, my part in my training is the ability to train others?" "Yes, my dear Jesse."

"What if I became the giant eagle? Keeping that form for myself, so I can help my sister?"

"If you keep the form of the eagle, you cannot be the emissary. You will be like Lord Asher. Giving up the full power of the stone, as he did when he kept the gorilla form so he could continue fighting. You must trust in the little bird! The little bird Blue must defeat the snake on her own. That is your true test of the Emissary. If this bluebird fails as the Wonder warrior of her realm, then there is no victory. Even if you have already defeated Kumba in this realm." Jesse heaved a deep breath finally seeing the bigger picture. He then turns to Blue on his shoulder, "My sister's life is now in your hands Blue. I am counting on you."

"Have faith," Blue assured him, "I have an army now and we will do everything in our power to defeat that evil snake. Remember your sister is my brother, and I will save them both."

Off the little bluebird flew into the portal, and all the birds immediately followed. Jesse slumped down by the ruins with Emma. Looking up at the moon feeling anxious as he heaved a deep breath, "I still cannot believe what happened tonight. It's like I'm just in a fantasy world and this is all a dream."

Emma nodded in agreement as they both gazed at the strange purple embers glowing from the fire pit.

Once at home, Jesse found his sister laying on top of his bed. He pulled the covers over her, climbed next to her, and kissed her on the cheek. He whispered softly, "I am so sorry for getting you into this mess, Berry. I will get you back, I promise. I will make sure that you will always be safe from now on. Goodnight Berry." Jesse put his arm around berry and held her tight.

Against the morning sun Blue pecked on the window of Jesse's room. Jesse got up to let the bluebird inside.

"Good morning, Jesse. Just here to let you know that we already have a plan. We'll get that snake, and free your sister.""Thank you Blue." "My pleasure." Blue answered.

CHAPTER 35

Domain of the Snake King:

At breakfast Jesse sat at the table looking at the blueberry muffins his mom had just made. "Isn't Berry coming down?" Mom asked. "Don't wake her mom, she says she wants to sleep in," Mom simply shrugged her shoulders, "Must be tired from yesterday."

Blue became well-known across the land as a hero to all, known for her bravery and justice. She rid the land of those who would mistreat and abuse others. Everywhere she went she had an army of friends, birds, and bugs behind her. All night Blue and her army prepared their plan. Studying every loophole and possible scenario to make sure it works to a tee. She said to Clifford, "We need you and two of your friends to act as bait and get King Kumba to chase you into our trap. Can you do this?" Clifford was reluctant, but agreed knowing it is the right thing to do.

In the early morning the sun peeked through leaves and sparkled against the dew-soaked grass, the air was everything except sunlit at the rendezvous point.

"You mean you are going to let that snake capture you? Are you not afraid he will just eat you right then and there?"

Captain Striker asked Blue. "He might, but I believe I can handle it," Blue responded without batting an eyelash. King Kumba was resting on the grass when he heard Blue calling his name, "King Kumba! Come out and play!"

"You really are foolish aren't you, mettlesome bluebird?" "I came here to trade myself for your prisoner." A crow flew to Kumba and whispered, "That bluebird is the child of the commander, sister of that fat bluebird you recently obtained."

"Ah yes, I know, I've been expecting her. That pesky dogooder."

"So, you are here to trade yourself for your brother. Here's a more interesting suggestion: What if I just have a public execution of your brother right now, or should I say your sister?"

Blue remained calm as Kumba shouted to his guards, "Bring out the fat bluebird!" "Whatever you say, I am okay with it. Just release my brother." After contemplating for some time, Kumba agreed, "Deal. But you will submit to my rule and stay in this realm for as long as I am here, and I tell you I have been here for over a hundred years. I have many more hundreds to go."

"Deal," Blue replied, without flinching. "Blue, No!" Berry screamed.

"Quiet!" Kumba yelled at Berry before turning back to Blue, "First you must bow before me and swear fealty to me as your king!" Blue nodded then approached Kumba. Out of nowhere she exclaimed, "Kumba, the darkness is coming!" Kumba laughed, "You fool! I am the darkness! It was I who kidnapped those meddlesome bird soldiers! It was I who placed a spell on Shiver so he'd do the work for me! Even these rats do my bidding. That's how strong my magic is. In this realm, I am the power! Now, bow or I will eat your brother right in front of you!" Blue began to bow her head down making Kumba even more boastful of himself.

"Do you want to know a secret? I hold more power in this realm and if I die here all my power will go to the human realm. I know a spell in which I will no longer be rejected by that Wonder Stone! If Kumba the wizard dies I will have his knowledge, and I can perform the ritual without him and without your stupid ring!"

Blue simply listened and allowed the snake to blab. "May I ask something? Would you know of my father?"

"Hah! Of course. He's my favorite prisoner. Sometimes I have lunch with him and it's funny to have him plead for me to let him go." the snake laughed, "It is so precious hearing him cry as I ate his friends!"

"And just what will you do? Think you can save him? You're no match for me!"

Then the king's sake held Berry up by the tail, close to his face as if to swallow him. "Stop! What is it you want from me?" Blue asked.

"You know what I want!"

"You know I don't have the ring in this reality. How can I give it to you here? Besides your human-voodoo self has been stripped of his magic in the human realm. The ring will no longer work for you, no matter what magic you possess."

"No!" King Kumba cried in frustration, "This is your doing, isn't it? You pesky little bluebird!"

"Well, King, is it a deal or not?"

"Fine." Kumba ordered the rats to release Berry. He flew far from the snake's reach while shouting back, "You are a bad snake!" Kumba motioned to one of his rat guards to take Blue and lock her up in a pen. Blue found most of the missing birds in the same cage. "I am looking for the Commander. Has anybody seen him?" She hollered. A large and handsome bluebird waded through the crowd and spoke, "I am the Commander. Who are you?"

"I am your daughter, and we are here to rescue you." "Blue?" "Yes dad. That's what Mom calls me. She says it was you who wanted that name. She misses you. We all do and I will get you out of here."

The two embraces, crying on each other's shoulders. Grateful to have found each other. Blue told her father. "I am here to get you out father!"

"How are you planning to accomplish this Blue? I have been here for months with no way out. Do you have a plan to kill the snake?"

"No dad. If the king snake dies Kumba the human will have the power of both worlds. But if we trap the snake in this realm, we will imprison them both"

"But how do we do that?" The commander asked. "I have a plan," Blue said, beckoning everyone to come close, "Here's what we will do."

Eagles from the zoo along with the rest of Blue's army

arrived and began to attack King Kumba. Clifford knew this was the signal Blue mentioned. He went up to the cage and called for Blue.

"Dad, these are my friends. They are here to help us."

Hundreds of mice took the rat jail guards by surprise as they dashed toward them. The guards were frightened as the mice tied them up. The warden voluntarily gave the keys to Clifford and said, "I never agree with what Kumba does. We're just here because we're afraid, escape if you can?" Blue told her father to take the birds up to the skies where Captain Striker was waiting, "He will inform you what you need to do."

"What about you, Blue?"

"I have something I must do. Don't worry about me, dad. I have an army? This is why I am here. I need to do this."

Kumba was furious seeing his imprisoned birds flying free in the skies. He let out an angry hiss and called for the guards. A loud whistle blasted through the air from the Professor's kazoo, and hundreds of birds descended upon the dastardly snake once again. Kumba stuck his head up high fighting the bird attack from all directions, while trying to keep an eye on where the sound was coming. He had never heard a noise like this before. The only thing he could see was Clifford and two other mice mocking him and waving red banners at him, as if the mice were matadors and the snake was some bull. The silly mice turned around and shook their butts at him inviting him to chase them. Clifford whispered to Blue who was hiding in the Bushes, "Blue, are you sure this is a good idea?"

"You're doing great Clifford. Just follow the plan and wait till he comes after you. Then head for the trap."

The mice shouted louder at the snake, as he got madder and madder. Finally reaching his limit he shot out with lightning speed heading straight for the three little mice. Clifford was filled with fright. "Jumping jeepers! I cannot believe I volunteered for this!" he cried. The other two mice jumped and sped off while saying, "I don't want to do this anymore!" Blue yelled at them from a distance, "Just focus on the plan. If you mess up you won't get a chance to escape him!"

King Kumba remembered how Clifford helped Blue in putting that terrible hot rabbit in his mouth, "I'm going to get you for that, little mouse!" Even though he was frightened Clifford remained focused and stuck his tongue out at the oncoming snake.

"You aren't that tough, you overgrown worm!"

His two other friends shouted at Clifford, "Are you crazy?" King Kumba thought this was his chance to show all those around him what happens to those who stand against him. He slithered even faster in a furious rage after the three mice, while birds relentlessly swooped down pecking on his head to keep him distracted. The nervous mice began panicking and bumped into each other, before finally scurrying down the path. They stayed a safe distance ahead of the big snake, constantly looking behind them as their hearts pound. Kumba laughed,

"That's fine little mouse. I like to chase my food before I eat."

The mice, though hesitant, stopped once in a while along the path just long enough to keep Kumba in their line of sight. They stopped at the entrance of the trap which appeared like any plain old rabbit hole. Clifford held on to the arm of one of the mice who tried to run away.

"Be brave. We must wait for the big snake to see us run into the hole, or the plan won't work. Here he comes." The three mice stood and waited, Kumba came down the path, seeing the three gave out an evil stare, using his magic to freeze his victims. "Now move!" Clifford shouted. As Clifford took off, his friend Hinny was immobilized, he stood frozen as King Kumba moved near.

"Hinny run!" Clifford shouts. It was too late, Kumba picked Hinny up, laughing at the silly mice. "I told you I would eat you, throwing the mouse up into the air, opening his mouth as Hinny came back down. The mouse still frozen, his eyes were in terror, as he stared down the throat of the snake, soon to be eaten by the large reptile. Clifford was aghast, Blue took off trying to save the little mouse, but he was too late. Captain striker came swooping in, grabbing the mouse, just before he reached Kumba's mouth, infuriating Kumba. "Alright, that's enough." Kumba shouted seeing Clifford down the path still taunting him. Twisting his tail to springboard ahead, Kumba stared at the mouse which taunts him, both getting into position to run. Kumba raced forward towards the two mice.

Clifford avoiding eye contact held his position, till he couldn't stand still any longer. They quickly ran down and jumped into the hole. "Here I come little mice. Your friend escaped, but you won't."

King Kumba said as he headed straight for the trap. Clifford and his friend ducked under a trap door and into a side hole, then covered it behind them. The mice held very quiet and still as the snake rumbled past them only inches away, their eyes closed, holding their breath, and their hands over each other's mouth.

Kumba went straight into the hole, which was equipped with an old laundry bag that the professor collected from the dump. From outside Blue shouted, "Now!" Willy and his squadron of pigeons pulled tight on the strings closing Kumba tightly inside the bag. Up the bag went with Kumba squiggling and shouting mean words. He tried to summon his power to grow into a larger snake, but soon realized he couldn't.

"What's happening? Where is my magic?"

"I told you. You're no longer a snake with powerful magic. We have captured your human half and taken the power from both of you. You are now just a normal snake," Blue explained.

"You cannot stop me, you pip-squeak!"

Kumba kept resisting growing tired after a few minutes and simply became silent.

Blue flew back to the farmhouse and pecked on the window to share the good news with Jesse. Berry had woken up and heard the pecking and thanked blue for her rescue.

"What? You took down Kumba, that big scary snake,

without becoming a giant eagle? I thought you would be showing off that big muscular eagle body."

"Nah. Didn't need to. Kumba didn't even remember his part in the human realm fight. Besides, all the birds watched me take down the giant snake, so I thought I would make taking down King Kumba a community effort to bring the realm together."

"You're so smart and wise for your size," Jesse said. "You were the perfect choice to be a Wonder. I see why the stone chose you."

"Well Jesse, I better go now. Thank you for training me and for all that you've done."

"Same here. Thank you for saving Berry. I will miss you little bluebird."

"Little bluebird?" Blue mocked; just then Blue transformed herself into the giant blue eagle. "Thought it'd be fun to take this body on a long flight and show Kumba his new home. So long!"

Blue picked up the bag housing Kumba and took off with it into the skies. "Kumba, I think I am going to enjoy being in this warrior's body," Blue taunted him.

"Let me out of this bag, you blue twat. I am King Kumba, and I order you to release me now!"

"That's hilarious," Blue said, "By the way, I have some friends I want you to meet. I think you're going to love Tiny." "Not if I become too heavy for even you to carry," Kumba mumbles as he cast a spell inside the bag, but nothing happens, "Darn it! What have you done to me?"

"It's your own doing Kumba. You have no one to blame but yourself."

Kumba continuing to threaten Blue, "It doesn't matter where you take me. My magic in the other realm is too powerful. He will regain his magic and I will be right back here in the grasslands. I will make sure to eat everyone you have made friends with!"

"True," said Blue, "If you had any magic left, which you don't." A few hours into the flight Blue began mimicking an airplane pilot, "Hope you enjoyed flying Blue Airlines."

"We will be arriving at our destination shortly. Please exit to the right." Blue dropped the bag right in the middle of a thick rain forest in South America.

As the bag dropped mid-air, Blue shouted, "I hope you'll have a good time with your new friends! They are expecting you." "I am the King! I rule everywhere I go, and I will rule here too! I will eat your friends!" Kumba's voice sounded muffled inside the bag.

"I'm afraid this is the last time we will see each other, King Snake Kumba."

Down the snake fell splashing into a creek. The bag loosened and out came Kumba. He wondered while scanning the surroundings, "Where am I?" He slithered to a boulder in the river and raised his head up to show dominance.

"I am King! Is there anyone who would dare challenge me?"

He saw several pairs of hungry eyes, then the heads they belong to, and then the opening mouths of some crocodiles emerging from the surrounding waters. One of the crocodiles

said, "Boy, you look like a tender morsel." Another pleaded, "Let me eat him please!" From behind Kumba the water rose like a tidal wave revealing a massive anaconda. It was one of the biggest in all of the jungle. Kumba was busy boasting to the crocodiles that he did not notice the giant snake, rise up behind him. The crocodiles began to laugh. "What's so funny?" said Kumba, insulted.

"So, you want to be King, eh?"

Kumba angrily shouted, "That's what I said. Didn't you hear me you imbecile?"

The water behind him splashed and splashed as the anaconda drew closer. He slowly turned around seeing what he thought was a huge tree trunk. He glanced from bottom to top, and saw how large the giant snake was. The snake was five times as tall as the now average sized Kumba, and was as thick as a tree trunk. If Kumba could grow, then he would be more than a match for this snake, but in his present normal state he is as helpless as the mice he used to chase.

"King, huh? So, you wish to challenge me for my throne!"

Frightened, Kumba took off to the direction of the crocodiles in a panic. The reptiles chased after him ready to take him down. He crawled up the shore when a big chunk of flesh landed on him. Pinning him to the ground. "Where you going, little king? Is our little king scared?" the anaconda mocked him. Kumba was too proud to live as a prisoner, so he pleaded, "Eat me! End this!" The anaconda laughed, "Oh, we're not going to eat you. I promised a friend of ours not to eat you – so maybe we'll just play with you. For a while anyway. Name's Tiny, by the way, King Tiny." "Then what?" Kumba asked while trying to escape. Tiny placed his tail down on Kumba once more, restraining him.

"What's the hurry king of the grasslands? You will find many creatures here who would love to play with you."

Tiny bent over and whispered softly to Kumba, "We are going to become very close friends, little king. You are in my jungle now and if you wish to stay alive then I wouldn't 'Wonder' off!" Tiny roared in laughter. "That darn bird! He trapped me here, and without my power. I am nothing," Kumba pondered as he slept under Tiny's watch that night. As Kumba stared out into the darkness of the amazon's thick forest, he noticed his tail glowing, just for a split-second, and a sudden but brief surge of energy overcame him.

"My magic is returning! I am not doomed to remain here!"

He smiled as he went to sleep still wearing that devilish grin. He now knew that someday he could return to the realm of humans.

CHAPTER 36

Visitors from Beyond

Jesse and Berry were playing world of Warcraft in Jesse's bedroom. The evening was drawing to an end and they were thinking their problems were over. Pew- pew, pew-pew. "Shoot them again Jesse." Berry shouted! "Time for bed Berry," Mom called out. "Okay Mom!" She sighed as she reached to give Jesse a good night kiss. Jesse waited then looked at Berry, she was not moving, frozen motionless with her lips puckered out like a statue in the park.

"What is happening?" He asked the Stone as the house started shaking and rumbling. A loud noise was heard outside. "No idea," The Stone replied. Jesse walks down the stairs to see everyone in the house was frozen in time. He continued walking out the front door, and saw a space craft landing in the yard. Out of the space craft came three rough looking aliens. Two with weapons and one staring hard and long at Jesse.

"Hello little human, you remember me?" The alien said as he pointed to his missing eye. "No, should I?"

"Let me return those memories which I stole from you. I want you to remember who I am and what I had promised, I would do to you. So the fear will overcome you and I may relish in your pain."

Angrily the alien zapped Jesse with the same device he did when Jesse was seven. Jesse held his head as all the memories came flooding back. He remembered everything that the alien had said and done to him.

"Now you remember! The Stone! Give it to us!" The alien continued, "You cannot do anything, you haven't had the Stone long enough to merge with its powers warrior, so give it here and we will be on our way."

"Yes, I remember you very clearly now. You are why I am always so scared. It was you who gave me those nightmares all my life and you are back now to fulfill your vengeance.

Isn't that why you're here?

I must say are all aliens as dumb as you?"

"What do you mean?" The alien spoke while giving Jesse a one-eyed stare.

"You gave me back my memories and released your hold on me! The fear which I have experienced my whole life is now gone and you thought for some reason that was a good idea!?

Come on then, you want this ring? Then come and take it from me! Do your worst!"

They charged at Jesse shooting their blasters, which could not faze him. Jesse was now the full Emissary and held the rings full power. His Dimensional barrier is fully operational, so he just stood there smiling. They couldn't touch him. Jesse held up the ring opening both hands. He lifted the aliens up in the air paralyzing them. He walks up close to his one-eyed nemesis and the being began to tremble. Jesse moved up even closer, coming eye to eye with the upside-down alien and said, "What is the name of the person who sent you here after the Stone. Who up there even knows about the stone?" The aliens stayed silent.

"AL-righty then Dufus! You don't mind if I call you Dufus?" Jesse said sarcastically making fun and intimidating the alien, "Since we were never properly introduced?

No of course you don't mind!"

Jesse then reached under and held the aliens head and told him, "Look where you're at? Hanging upside down by your ugly feet, Man don't you ever wash these ugly suckers? Now think on this very hard! Dufus! I am not that little boy anymore! I am the Emissary of the powerful Wonder Stone! I retain its full power and I am in the Stone's service. It demands you tell me who sent you or else?" The alien softly whispered a name hoping his companions didn't hear him say it.

"You will leave this planet and never return!" Jesse commanded!

One alien inside the ship started the craft up when he saw his companions being held upside down. The ship opened fire and several large blasts fired from the ship. The flames surrounded Jesse and destroyed grandpa's garden, blackening the area. Jesse twisted one hand up and grabbed hold of the ship. He turned its blasters up towards the sky as it continued firing into space. Jesse kept holding it in place using one hand and throwing the three aliens on board with a sway of his other hand.

Slamming and crushing the door of the ship Jesse then flew up grabbing one side of the craft pulling the ship up into outer space. Hurling it around and around like throwing a shot put in the Olympics. Jesse picked a spot where no stars could be seen and tossed the ship with great force deep into the dark obis. Jesse flew back down and ran into the house where the family was unfrozen and acting normal. Not twenty minutes had past when the night sky lit up, but this time nobody was in a frozen state. It was another space ship and it was landing in the yard.

Now what? Jesse thought; the whole family was standing on the porch watching this event. Berry was ecstatic, mom was in shock, and grandpa passed out all before the door of the ship even opened. Even the Stone had no clue as to what may step out.

Slowly the door came down, and one human looking being came out seemingly to make an announcement. He barely got the words something Lord out of his mouth, when a large being emerged quickly from the ship. It was roaring with laughter as it pushed the others aside shouting; "Where is he!?

Where you hiding!? Shine my friend, show yourself! Jesse's hand rose up and he watched as the stones radiance and grandeur illuminated, even Jesse body was aglow.

Swinging his hammer joyfully, it was the God Thor himself. Prince of Asgard and Lord over the Nine Realms. Smiling as he headed straight toward the shinning stone, as a child would running to greet their friend. Even though

Jesse had come to grips with his fear, watching such a being rushing toward him would make anyone a little nervous. Thor grabbed Jesse around his waist and spun him in circles finally heaving over and setting him back down.

"Greetings New Warrior of the Wonder Stone! Now where is Torstenveurr!?" A name in which Thor had given the Wonder stone during their first encounter many years before.

The Stone spoke up, "Jesse this is Thor. I met him a long time ago and he gave me a name which means Stone Warrior in the Asgardian language."

Jesse was puzzled, He could hear his family mumbling, saying Jesse is the what? They were now becoming aware of what Jesse was trying to keep secret.

"Now if you don't mind, I want to speak with Torstenveurr!"

Thor grabbed Jesse hand and pulled the ring up close and started speaking with it, "How are you, old friend? How long has it been? Oh, really that long, I never knew what happened to you after the Battle of Midgard. Yes, is that right? Yea they were a fierce bunch." Both could be heard as any friends catching up after years of absents. Still speaking and laughing while Jesse was just standing there holding up the ring. He began feeling a little less important than a chair as the two continued.

Thor then held up his hands and announced, "I concur a Knight hood is in order. From what you have told me about your new warrior I believe the following is justified." Thor looked at Jesse sizing the young boy up saying, "Torstenveurr has told me of your resent victory. In my life time, I have witnessed Torstenveurr power personally. Now Jesse Mason, take a knee!" Jesse reluctantly did as he was told.

As Thor was busy speaking The Stone spoke to Jesse, "This is a great honor, Jesse. I have never witnessed Thor Knighting another." Jesse looked down and said, "Why do I feel that Thor is only knighting me because of you?" Thor overhearing this comment, came closer and stated "You! Young warrior is very smart. You are partially correct in thinking this way. Torstenveurr is very dear to me as you are dear to him but the honor I bestow, is also my honor to do so. Torstenveurr has shown me your testing young one." Thor laughed and continued, "I knighted you because you are deserving of that title, but it is also true that Asgard may yet need your services someday, so some of my motives are for the safety of my nine Realms!"

"Now Jesse Mason," Thor touched his hammer to each of Jesse's shoulders then announced, "Repeat these words and take heed to their meaning. For this is a great honor I bestow onto you:

"I will defend the weak and the innocent, in all the nine realms!" "Well more than nine in your case Jesse." He continued. "I will fight for Justice and be valiant and courageous in all things!

I must always speak truth."

To this you must swear!" Jesse swore the oath.

"Stand Jesse Mason Knight of Asgard and of our Nine Realms. Now stand! Knight of Wonder! "Protector of the Mulitirealms! …..There, so now we are connected. My old friend and my new friend." Thor tilting his head towards Jesse, sort of asking if Jesse was his friend? "Oh, of course!" Jesse agreed.

"Excellent!" Thor shouted, "We should celebrate, a toast to the new Wonder! Do you by any chance have mead? I think you refer to it as beer? Could you produce me a mug full?" "Are your asking me to magically produce you a beer?" Jesse wondering if that was even something he could do. Shrugging his shoulders Jesse told Thor, "Sorry."

"No worries young lad, just checking."

Grampa heard this and grabbed a six pack from the refrigerator handing it to Thor.

Thor smiled and while rubbing Berry's little head he said, "You little one has some of The Stones power, I can feel it within you, child."

It was time for him to go. Thor paused, "Well my friends if we hurry and leave now, we could catch up to those Draconian aliens. In which direction did you throw them Jesse?" Thor laughed as Jesse pointing up towards the stars. He kept laughing as he walked back to his ship mumbling; "That boy actually tossed a spaceship deep into space! I would have given anything to watch those aliens from inside their ship. Bouncing off the walls as they were slung around, Ha, sounds hilarious. That's sure is a new one for me. I may have a need of that boy and that kind of power one day. If you ever need me Wonder warrior, just send me a text, I will come."

"Oh, so you have a phone number?" Jesse asked. Thor looking confused said; "A phone of course not. Why would

I need a phone?" Berry giggled at Thor's comment. Thor stood and said, "Very glad to have met you Jesse and your wonderful family," then tipped his hammer as one would tip a hat.

"Take care of Torstenveurr!"

"Why were they here and who were they?" Berry asked? Waving and smiling at the spaceship. "Are they space cops?" Berry asked

"I've never seen a purple guy before."

They watched as the ship disappear off into the night. "What a strange and unusual evening, huh Jesse?" Berry stated. "Yes, that was a strange experience," Jesse continued, "Depending of course on what a person would call strange, little sister, especially in this uncommonly strange life we now live in. Particularly all the strange things you and I have already seen in just two of the One Thousand realms from which I have yet to be called to defend." "Well, I call a Green person strange Jesse, no matter all the other things I have seen when I am with you and my friend Mr. Torstenveurr!" Berry laughed at the funny sounding name. Jesse shook his head sat down and realized his life was never going to be dull again. Not with all the evil in all these realms. At least he was thankful he didn't have to protect those other nine realms which he was thrust into before they left New York.

Jesse hopes they have enough super heroes to contain their own realms, as Jesse has a thousand of his own to protect. "Well maybe if they need me, with him being such a good friend to Torstenveurr, the Wonder Stone."

CHAPTER 37

The Magnified Spell:

Jesse woke the next morning finally starting to relax a little after such an adventurous journey in the bird realm. He was starting to understand, just what his role in this life will become. He no longer carried the fear which engulfed him in his youth. He opened the window and stretched out thinking, what can I do today? The Stone laughed saying, "Are you forgetting anything Jesse?" Jesse thought for a minute and said, "What would that be."

"The Sheriff, do you suppose she might have a few questions?" "Oh yes, the Sheriff, she will most likely have some questions over what happened in the park last night."

Laughing once again the Stone replied, "You think so, or is it normal in this realm to witness a giant snake with golden fangs, fighting a giant brilliant blue eagle?"

"That would be a no," Jesse mumbled, "Just how am I supposed to explain any of this to the Sheriff, any suggestions?"

"Jesse, this realm is the same as any of the realms. Your job is to help bring balance. Just as when you were that little bird sitting on the forest floor who didn't know what to do then either. Every adventure is the same in all the realms."

"Great speech!" Jesse joked, "So the plan is to just wing

it!" "Ha-ha," The Stone laughed, "I think you are starting to understand." Jesse rode his bike into town to assess the damage and speak with the sheriff. After all the aftermath, with the town in shambles, people afraid to leave their houses, because most heard the stories of giant snakes on the loose. He could see Emma looking out the window in his aunt's shop. He stopped in and asked her, "How are things?" "You're not going to believe this!" Emma continued, "The Sheriff let the limo driver out this morning but he scared the town folks so much wandering around, she had to pick him back up and call his family to come and get him.

How are you doing this morning Jesse?" "I'm okay so far. I still need to visit the sheriff. Do you think she wants to see me?" "Laughing," Emma says, "After last night, I have no doubt she will." "Okay, you want to come with me?" "Shaking her head, no saying, "My parents are freak out from the stories of last night, so I have to stay close to the house and besides I have to help your aunt at the store. Come by and see me later?"

Jesse walked into the sheriff's office, the man we had called Shiver was there being picked up by some family members. He was unaware of anything which happened since the time Kumba first met him on that highway.

Jesse asked the sheriff, "What was going to happen to him?" "I called his folks to come pick him up. All I could charge him for is defacing private property, when he painted your aunt's door of her shop.

I would rather see him out of town, than deal with this magic stuff in court."

"Sheriff, did you need to see me about anything?" Jesse held Immediately Sheriff Piper led Jesse into her office and closed the door. She set down in her chair and leaned back.

She then looked straight at Jesse and said; I have been sheriff for almost six years, deputy before then, in all my life I have never witnessed and will never forget, what happened last night. Actually, I would rather not know, but I am the sheriff and I need all the facts, so after saying that, let's get started."

Jesse swallowed hard, nervous in his seat saying, "I'm ready." "Okay Mister, now start talking."

"Sheriff, you wouldn't believe me if I told you."

"After everything my deputies and I had witnessed at the park, don't worry, I expect an unbelievable answer, so just start talking."

Jesse started at the beginning explaining the human side of the ordeal. "One realm at a time Jesse," the stone whispered to him. Any more than that will just make things even less believable."

"Did you say something?" Sheriff Piper asked; Jesse shook his head, still nervous in his seat. "Relax Jesse." The stone spoke, as Jesse held a hand over it, the sheriff looked around the room trying to locate the voice she heard.

"This Mr. Kumba is a wizard of dark magic, you say, right?" "Yes, that's right. He was after me for this ring, which is also magic in a way, of sorts. The battle at the park was a wizard's duel, which we defeated Mr. Kumba with the help of the Wonder stone. That's really about everything, Sheriff."

Sheriff Piper stood motionless. She looked at the ring, then back at Jesse staring into his eyes determine to find out the truth. "Let me get this straight, you want me to believe that ring has powers?" she questioned. "The stone actually," Jesse corrected.

"Okay the stone! It is the Wonder and you're the spokesperson, for that ring, which you have on your finger?"

"Okay smarty pants, then let's hear from the mighty magical Wonder ring, or stone!" Sheriff Piper demanded, not really expecting an answer.

"My pleasure sheriff Piper." Spoke the Stone "Everything which has happened in your town, is because of one's overwhelming desire to control the power in which I hold. Kumba came to this town in search of me." Sheriff Piper jumped back after hearing the Stone speak. She then took a hard look and said, "So you are saying that you and this ring are responsible for saving the town from a massacre of an enchanted nature? That everything can be explained with magic?

As far as I am concerned Jesse you don't know anything either. Just the same as the rest of the town? Okay Jesse you can go."

"That's it Sheriff, you don't need me to write out a statement or anything?"

"Even if you wrote it down Jesse, what could you accomplish exactly, nobody is going to believe any of this, especially a judge?"

"I understand," Jesse remarked, "But what about those three baseball fans, Kumba's henchmen?"

"I have them on multiple accounts of destruction of property, and we still have the assault on you Jesse. I will make sure that they spend a few years behind bars."

"Sheriff, is there any way to let these fellas off? Kurly did help us some. I believe they had little to say about most of what happened and were probably being mind-controlled by Kumba and I'm pretty sure, they will tell the judge this during trial."

Sheriff Piper looked at Jesse and asked, "After all the trouble these three caused to your family and this town you want me to set them free?"

"Well, yes sheriff, besides what do you think a jury would do when all this comes out? The portals, the fights and you know, the magic and all?"

"Yes, I have been thinking about that very thing."

Kurly could be seen looking through a small window of a door with his hound dog eyes and hands together as if praying. He was motioning for Jesse to please help them. He turned to his friends and said, "Jesse is out there, he will help us, because I helped him." "Jesse isn't going to help us after all we did, and what you mean you helped him!" Moe shouted getting angry. "Sure did," Kurly replied, "Remember we didn't win Kumba's battle, we lost and are at his mercy."

"Oh yea, that is correct!" Moe shouted, "Thanks for reminding me, now get back to that window and beg some more you imbeciles."

Jesse motioned to the three using two fingers that he would be watching them as Sheriff Piper opened the door and let the three go with a sever warning. They promised to be better citizens of the town as they fled from the station.

Jesse asked; "Sheriff, is everything under control now?" "Well, there is still the missing land lord, Mr. Singh." Oh yes, Kurly shouted to Jesse. I saw the landlord after Kumba changed him! He turned that man, our landlord into a frog, I watch him do it!" "Okay that's enough of that. You three just get out!" Sheriff told them as she shook her head mumbling, "That's all I need now is to be chasing frogs!"

"What about me sheriff?" Jesse asked, "Any charges?" "Are you kidding," Piper replied, "The deputies and I still cannot believe what we saw last night. I've never seen a giant snake and a giant blue eagle, evil wizards and openings in the sky. Didn't even know such things existed. I have no idea how to write up this report and we all know nobody will believe it if we do. The question I have for you Jesse. Is it over?" Deep down Jesse had no idea if it was over, but told the sheriff that he thought it was finally done and she should have no problems later on. But magic finds a way and even though the Wonder Stone wasn't created with magic, it still draws those who seek magic, like flies to sugar.

"Then I can assume my town is back to normal, and if that is the case how about we just don't mention any of this. I am not sure how to handle magic, and wizards, and realms, and portals. I am just a sheriff of a small town. What am I going to do if this kind of thing happens again? You Jesse Mason seem to be the only one who can combat these threats?"

"Not to worry sheriff. I am not going anywhere."

She looked at Jesse and nodded her head. Jesse told sheriff piper that he would check on the landlord's family and headed to the apartments where he was greeted by Mrs. Singh. The family was sitting at the breakfast table still wondering where he went.

On the table was a shoe box, and in the shoebox was a frog. "Hello", Jesse said and introduced himself.

"I know who you are Jesse Mason and I know you have some powers." Mrs. Singh announced, with the children watching. Jesse was nervous and asked, "How do you know me?" "Are you kidding the whole town watched you battle, you're a wizard."

Wow! Jesse thought, then asked, "I have come to help in the search for your husband, have you heard from him?"

"Yes, I think I have," she cried as she passed a shoe box across the table towards Jesse.

"Not sure why I think this, but that frog is my husband! Unless you tell me it's not?"

Jesse and the stone conversed trying to figure out how to handle this situation. First the stone said, "We need to check and see if this is your husband, Mam."

"Well, I hope you and your talking ring can help, I don't know what else to do. I know that's my husband, can you help us?"

Jesse asked Mrs. Singh if she would take the kids into the other room, so he can proceed.

"That's my husband and we are staying right here! Now get on with whatever it is you have to do."

"That frog is Mr. Singh," The stone replied. "Why is he still under the spell? Everyone else was released?" Jesse asked curiously.

"Kumba must have had him look at an object to cast this spell and Mr. Singh's glasses magnified the spell. Which explains why the glasses shrunk with the frog so to speak. And possibly why the spell is holding tight."

Jesse opened the box and there sat a big bull frog with glasses on, just croaking away.

"I believe this is your husband Mrs. Singh." "Can't you do something?"

"Yes, I believe so, just stay back and hold your kids please." Jesse picked the frog up and set it down on the table. Mrs. Singh handed Jesse a table cloth. What's this for?" Jesse asked.

"To cover him up. I don't suppose his clothes are going to magically come back with him, do you?"

"OH, right," Jesse continued, waving his hand over the frog. The glow from the stone was blinding as it turned from dark indigo ink color to a sparkling bright blue over Mr. Singh.

The Stone chanted, "Altruist-Menoplos- Sayorso" and the frog started growing.

"What is going on, Is the spell not working? He's not turning back to a human. He is just a frog getting bigger!"

"Not to worry" The Stone announced, "The spell stuck hard. It will take a few minutes."

The frog continued swelling up getting bigger. Then the frog attempted to hop away. "Grab it Jesse, he must remain still." The Stone shouted as the lights continued from the ring. Jesse threw the table cloth over the frog and grabbed on tight around the frogs back as it continued to grow. The children's eyes grew wide as mother held them back. They watched as Jesse climbed onto the table, trying to hold the now two- hundred-pound frog, which was trying hard to jump away.

The table started cracking from the weight of Jesse and the growing frog. As the table crashed to the floor the big frog started to hop. Jesse was struggling to hold it. The frog slipped out from the cover, hopped from the broken table and jumped into the living room with Jesse still holding on tightly to the cursed man's back.

The children broke free from their mother grasp and climbed on Jesse's back just to have a ride on the big frog, as he kept jumping around the room. "Mom, come on this is fun," the children laughed. "This is weird" Jesse shouted, "How much longer you think this is this going to take?" Jesse was actually glad the children were adding weight on the frogs back. He was afraid the frog might jump out the window with him and how would that look to the neighbors? Mrs. Singh was shaking and worried as she stood there with her arms out waiting for a miracle. Watching and worried as Jesse and the children wrestled the mighty frog. Trying to hold it still enough for the spell to reverse. Mrs. Singh helped place the covers back over the frog, as they held its legs.

After a few minutes a fog of blue mist seeped out from under the edges of the cover. The giant frog let out a very loud CROAK and an enormous giant BELCH. Suddenly the frog transformed back to his human state. Jesse stood back up and helped Mr. Singh to the sofa. He still looked a little green and didn't speak much. Just looked around in shock as I am sure anyone would. The kids didn't seem to mind. They were just glad to have their father back.

They didn't even seem to care when they noticed their father catching flies in the air from what seem to be a long frog's tongue occasionally zipping out. After all, they knew he had once been a frog. Jesse asked Mrs. Singh if she would keep all this just between them. He didn't want the whole town to know, but he was afraid he was already too late. Mrs. Singh reassured him that she would keep it quiet and thanked Jesse as he left and headed home.

Little did Jesse know that in the coming month of August he would have his first mission in a reptilian realm where the massive battle of the Dismal straits was already underway!

Then be visited by some Gnomes and a Fairy. They will take him to the Gnome realm to save them from starvation and being hunted down by enormous Centurion wolves, because their Wonder Warrior was being held captive by the Red Dragon and Jesse must go there to fight and free their Wonder warrior. But those are different stories from different realms for different times!

Well, this is "The End" of this Tale!

We really hope you enjoyed our adventures. Be sure to read the soon complete story and adventures of little Jesse Blue the warrior bird in the Cinematic Illusion -

Dream of Wonder!

Wizards and Witches also invade this small town in search for the Stone of Wonder. Battle ensues between the rival factions and it is up to Berry to take up the slack and fight.

All this coming soon in the next -

TALES OF WONDER: Vol.2

Jesse must find, capture and ride the Red Dragon

A Reptilian realm, before the great battle of
the Dismal Straights